A QUESTION OF TIME

BY STEVEN LAZAROFF

www.stevenlazaroff.com

Ordering Information:
Quantity sales. Special discounts are available on quantity purchases by corporations, associations, and others. For details, contact the publisher at the address above.
Orders by U.S. trade bookstores and wholesalers. Please contact the publisher at the address above or by email: slazaroff@rodgerlaz.com
Cover by: Natasha Suranyi

Printed in Canada

Publisher's Cataloguing-in-Publication data
Steven Lazaroff.
A Question of Time/ Steven Lazaroff.
p. cm.
ISBN 978-1-7752922-0-3
1. The main category of the book —Historical Fiction.

First Edition

14 13 12 11 10 / 10 9 8 7 6 5 4 3 2 1

The story, all names, characters, and incidents portrayed in this production are fictitious. No identification with actual persons (living or deceased), places, buildings, and products is intended or should be inferred.

Acknowledgements

There are many people are to thank for their support of this novel.

First and foremost, my wife, who at this very moment is sitting next to me, on our living room couch, doing some last-minute formatting and about to start work on the cover art. A true partner in this endeavor, if there ever was one. Love you Nat, and I'll be forever grateful for all your input, and work.

My beta readers, including but not limited to; Joe Macri, whom I spent a day with at a trade show and basically forced him to read the very early manuscript in between client appointments. Joe, thanks for your early support. Paul Nestorowich, who I believe should have been a lawyer, your attention to detail helped enormously. Finally, John R.J. Lynch, who was instrumental in my developmental editing and shepherding, without you, John, this would have never seen the light of day. To Richard Lynch and Sierra Mullins for your wonderful manuscript critique, thank you. To my dad, Terry Lazaroff, my steadfast supporter, and life coach. To Mark Rodger, your feedback and comments halfway through this project were encouraging. Finally to the people that helped me with the enormous amount of research, Louis-Michel Emmanuel Breguet, Current Vice President responsible for Breguet's patrimony and strategic development, He recently published "Breguet, Watchmaker Since 1775" I highly recommend it. http://bit.ly/2knDaqj

And to all the others, too numerous to name here, thank you.

CHAPTER 1

WHEN JONATHAN LAMBERT SETTLED INTO HIS FIRST-CLASS TGV SEAT, he was still nursing amusement over the foolishness of one of his colleagues. She had been railing on about the theory of multiverses and parallel existence all evening in the hotel bar after the conference. This universe, the woman had said, is only one of what could possibly be an infinite number. An infinite number that had previously existed in the past, had ceased to exist in the future, and now existed once more. This death and rebirth of multiple universes was something that had happened forever and would go on happening forever. Except – and here was the point at which Lambert had begun to laugh outright; the moment that was probably responsible for his overconsumption of alcohol last evening in the hotel bar – that there was no 'forever' because there was no time.

'What do you mean, no time?' He held up his wrist, brandishing his watch with the Breguet signature. 'Look! It's eight-thirty. In thirty minutes, it will be nine o'clock. If that isn't time, what is it?'

His colleague's patience amused him so much he laughed even more. Perhaps he indeed had had too much to drink – but really! 'Universes expand,' she said. 'That's what they do. This one is expanding and has been since the Big Bang, but it won't expand forever. As it runs out of energy, it will begin to shrink. The smaller it gets, the faster the shrinking will be until everything has been reduced to a black hole of unimaginably tiny size – tiny beyond our imagination and filled with energy that is also beyond our comprehension. And the same will be true of every other universe. And when that happens, time will not exist. And then, suddenly, it will be impossible to hold that amount of energy in so little space, and all of those universes will break out again in another Big Bang. And time will flow once more.'

Lambert put a stern expression on his face. He was good at that. But he was also good at mocking people, which is why his colleague looked nervous when Lambert said, 'So the Buddhists are onto something? We are doomed to relive our lives over and over again until we achieve nirvana?'

'I don't think that's quite the same thing, Jonathan.'

'No?' And Lambert strove to keep the serious expression in place, although a combination of alcohol and what he conceived as his colleague's foolishness threatened to make him erupt into laughter. 'What do you make of the sound the most sensitive astronomical instruments have just picked up? From before the Big Bang?'

CHAPTER 1

Oh, that look of sadness on her face as she realised he was simply not educable. He feared he would laugh so much that he would lose control of himself. 'No sound can be heard from before the Big Bang, Jonathan. It's impossible.'

'Oh, but Sylvia, it *has* been heard. So distant in time, it's almost impossible to make out what it is. It sounds like… It sounds like 'Oops.'' And he had laughed again, and this time really did think he was in danger of wetting himself.

'Really, Jonathan, they might laugh at that in some other universe…'

'They might? You mean, in these other universes, though we can't see them, they can hear us?'

'We don't know. We don't even know how the multiple universes are aligned. They could be entirely separate from ours. Or we could all intermesh but in different dimensions. It's possible that we are here in many universes, though we can detect only the one we know. Your subject is history. Imagine if different forces caused the same situation to evolve differently in other, parallel universes. There could be a universe interlocked with ours in which Constantine did not throw in his lot with the followers of Christ, and everyone worships Mithras. Another in which Islam was not held back at the eastern gates of Europe, in which case – it is Ramadan right now, is it not? – The whole Western world is fasting today during the hours of daylight. Another perhaps where one can travel into the past.'

'Sylvia. Stop. You are right; my subject is history. And I am glad that it is because I am asked to believe only what can be extracted from historical and archaeological records and I'm not expected to parrot New Age maunderings about things that can't be seen and can't be known. I live in a world of reality, not one of fantasy.'

'And you need to step over that border, Jonathan. You need to acknowledge how little about this world we really know. The answer is one I've already given you. We don't know. We just don't know.'

Experiencing a momentary jerk in inertia from the TGV, Lambert aroused himself from his recollection of the previous evening with the realisation that he was laughing so much that the other passengers in his immediate vicinity were watching him with concern. He wiped his eyes. He loved these train journeys. The train cars were comfortable, they were clean, they were usually on time, and fairly soon someone would come to his table and serve him a decent meal. Meanwhile, the Belgian countryside flashed by. Soon it would be France. Compared with some other European countries, and for historical reasons that Lambert would have been happy to list, France's countryside had a low population density and it was much nicer to travel at extremely high speed through a predominantly rural and agricultural countryside than through, say, the American Rust Belt or the industrial centres of the Ruhr.

Had he drunk too much last night? Should he have a glass or two of wine with his meal? Oh, he thought he probably would.

AS JONATHAN LAMBERT SAT IN HIS FIRST-CLASS CARRIAGE and reflected on the trick of relativity that made it seem that he was stationary and the countryside was racing past, the conductor in the cockpit at the head of the train checked his watch. The panel in front of him had a digital clock, but the conductor liked the backup of an independent source. A nineteen year veteran with Thalys, there since it began operating the Train à Grande Vitesse, his motto was, 'Trust. But verify.'

He'd been offered many opportunities for advancement throughout the years, but promotion meant leaving the cockpit, and he didn't want to do that. He enjoyed the solitude of the job and the great speed the train could produce. The controls were mostly automated, and only thirty minutes or so of the journey was spent monitoring the sensors; the rest of his time consisted of revising the track signals, making sure department heads were delivering the highest level of passenger service and that all systems operated inside acceptable parameters.

Thalys, an international high-speed train operator, ran several routes out of Belgium but this – Brussels to Paris – was their cash cow, the LGV-1 line, one of the French utility SNCF's safest routes and one of the most boring to operate. The conductor observed the same prosperous agrarian countryside speeding by as Jonathan Lambert, but where Lambert saw peace, the driver saw boredom. But that didn't trouble him. Boredom meant safety and safety was his primary concern.

This day was proceeding like any other. He checked the sensors and made a slight reduction in speed for the curve in the track just ahead. The light drizzle when they had left Brussels was now steady rain, and it looked as though cloud would be with them all the way to Paris, but that didn't trouble the conductor. He knew every bend in this track. He could be driving in thick fog and, as long as the train's electronic warning systems were working, the journey would go to plan.

The train had crossed the border into France when a light began to blink on the instrument panel. It was an unaccustomed warning, and the conductor cut back further on the speed as he looked ahead through the cockpit window. He could see nothing, but the light continued to flash. The train carried 232 passengers, and the conductor did not want them to fly out of their seats as a result of emergency braking from high speed. They were his responsibility. He throttled back even further.

And then he saw it. A shimmering curtain of blue light, barely visible across the entrance to a tunnel under an overpass. Seventeen years at the controls of high-speed trains had given him an excellent eye for calculating time, distance and speed, and he knew the moment he saw the curtain that he was approaching it too fast. The single word 'merde' escaped his lips. He didn't like swearing, even when there was no one to hear him. The typical day was proving not so typical after all. He executed the ordained emergency procedures and slapped on the emergency brakes.

A Question of Time

CHAPTER 2

AGENT LAURENT NADEAU, TWENTY-THREE YEARS with the Central Directorate of the Judicial Police and now an Inspector, had been the man on call when a signal came in from a railway cop with the French rail service, the SNCF. The railway cop had been first on the scene when the conductor reported the strange incident. Shortly after arriving on the scene, the SNCF agent decided he'd like the view of a third party. The DCPJ investigates serious crime in France and has a first-line interest in terrorism since the two are often linked. Agent Nadeau had both of those things in mind as his eye moved from train to clouds and back again. Not much will ruin an investigation as efficiently as rain.

Now Nadeau and the senior SNCF agent, having completed a circumnavigation of the halted train, approached the conductor. 'Has anyone been hurt?' was the conductor's first concern.

'Not as far as we can tell,' said the SNCF man. 'Terrorism?' the conductor sputtered in a low voice. 'That's why he's here.' replied the SNCF agent, nodding to Agent Nadeau.

Nadeau said, 'You stopped the train immediately after you had come through that tunnel?'

'I don't think so,' said the SNCF agent. 'This is where the train stopped, but at the speed it would have been going, the brakes must have been applied before it ever went into the tunnel.'

'Is that right?' Nadeau asked the conductor.

The conductor nodded.

Nadeau had his notebook in his hand. 'What is your name?'

'Lefebvre. Martin Lefebvre.'

'So tell me why you applied the brakes.'

The conductor was clearly rattled. Nadeau was a non-smoker, but he kept cigarettes about him for just this sort of moment. He offered the packet and Lefebvre took one. Nadeau lit it for him.

'Thank you. I don't usually... I stopped some years ago... But many days like today and I can see myself starting again.'

'The brakes?'

Lefebvre blew smoke down his nose. 'There was a curtain... A curtain of blue light... A blue curtain of light... At any rate, a curtain. It was right across the entrance to the tunnel.'

There was an awkward pause in the questioning as Nadeau, and the SCNF agent exchanged a glance. 'There's no sign of any curtain across the tunnel now,' said the SNCF agent.

'Well, it was there. I can tell you it was there because I didn't see it at first. Not with my eyes. The first I knew of any problem was when the emergency light came on in the cockpit. The sensor had picked something up. And only something that was physically there – something real – could have made that happen.'

Nadeau looked at his SNCF opposite number who said, 'If the warning light fired, it would be logged in the system. The train will have to be taken out of service for a thorough check. The most obvious explanation is a system failure. The warning light came on for no reason. There was no curtain.'

'No,' said Lefebvre. 'I saw it. After I saw the warning light, I saw the curtain. And it was still there when we reached the tunnel. We went straight through it.'

'No impact?'

'Nothing. We were only making about thirty kilometres an hour at that point, but I was braced for some kind of blow. It didn't happen. We passed through it like gossamer.'

'Thirty kilometres,' said Nadeau. 'You probably could have stopped inside the tunnel, then?'

'I could. But it's against orders. We are told to stop in a tunnel only if there is no alternative. And there was.'

'Safety regulations,' said the SNCF agent. 'The passengers are a great deal safer outside the tunnel than in. Have you ever tried to evacuate more than two hundred passengers from a train stranded in a tunnel?'

It was a rhetorical question, and Nadeau didn't bother with an answer. 'That's all for now. We may need to speak to you again.'

The SNCF man said, 'I've spoken to Thalys. They're sending a replacement train, and your passengers will transfer to it. They'd like you to ride on that train as a passenger. You're to report to HR when you arrive, and I think you'll find you'll be stood down on full pay until medical reports are in.'

'There's nothing the matter with me.'

'Don't worry about the medical – it's routine. You had a shock. It often isn't until later that the full weight of an event like this hits you.'

Lefebvre shook his head. 'Can I ride in the cockpit with the other conductor?'

'We'd rather you travelled in the passenger compartment. You can sit in first class. Have a nice meal. Relax. I don't think you understand yet what you've been through.'

VARIOUS STAFF MEMBERS OF SNCF AND THALYS HAD ARRIVED, some parking at a distance and walking across the fields to get there as quickly as possible. Nadeau said, 'Have your agents reviewed the passenger manifest?'

The SNCF man signalled to a subordinate, who came at a trot and seemed disturbed. 'Is everyone accounted for?'

The subordinate shook his head. 'We are a man short.'

Nadeau stepped forward, taking centre stage and making sure that everyone knew who was in charge. 'A man? A passenger?'

'We've roll-called everyone. Three times. There should be a passenger called Jonathan Lambert in one of the first-class carriages. He isn't here.'

'He wasn't thrown clear? Did you check the fields around here? Under the train?'

'We've checked everything. I'm telling you, Jonathan Lambert was on that train when it left Brussels, and he isn't on it now.'

'Maybe he had an urgent appointment. Perhaps he's walked away to get transport.'

'We checked every house and every farm within a mile of here. God knows, there aren't many. No one has seen him. We had the local police ring the local bus company, the region's lone taxi driver and station. Same result. He's vanished into thin air. It's like he was plucked from here into a parallel universe.'

Nadeau said, 'I don't believe in parallel universes, and I don't believe that people simply disappear.'

'No, sir.'

'Every agent here had better call home. I think we're going to be working into the night.'

CHAPTER 3

EVEN BEFORE LAMBERT OPENED HIS EYES, he was keenly aware of the fact that the constant lulling motion of the train was missing from beneath him. The scent of the cabin as well a mingling of perfumes and colognes from the passengers around him were also absent. It smelled more like sweat and dirt. Who on earth had forgotten to shower?

Lambert opened his eyes, his brow furrowing when he found himself lying facedown, his gaze instantly meeting with blue sky. He sat up, abruptly, the sudden movement alerting him to the painful kink in his neck. He winced, his hand shooting up to massage it. However, one look around, and he forgot all about the kink.

'What on earth.....?'

It wasn't like 'We're not in Kansas anymore.' Nothing like that. Not just that he didn't have a Tin Man or a moth-eaten lion with him. Was it a lion? He didn't know. His parents had never taken him to see the movie and, being unmarried and childless, he'd had no occasion to see it with children, but in any case that wasn't how it was. In the movie, they'd set out on a great adventure. This didn't feel like an adventure. This felt like the worst kind of bad dream.

The hedgerow was broken by a tree, and Lambert huddled beneath it. He didn't try to fool himself with the thought that this was taking shelter against the sun. The sun *was* strong, but that was a side issue. Although he didn't understand how it could possibly be so sunny and clear when a few moments ago he'd been on a train travelling through heavy rain. But the reason he was sheltering was that he didn't want to be seen and he didn't want to be seen because he didn't know where the hell he was and therefore didn't know who it was that might see him. Would they be hostile? Friendly? Was that a chance worth taking?

He was conscious of the silence. And even as he had that thought, he realised that it wasn't silent. There was plenty of sounds. Birdsong. Cattle, and not far away. And was that the sound of a wheel? It was. Not a wheel with rubber tires on a metalled road, but the creaking of the wheel on a cart. An ancient wheel and an ancient cart by the sound of it. But the sounds that should have been present, weren't. No cars. No trucks. And no railway sounds. Which, as he looked around, was not surprising because there was no railway. And no metalled road, either because a road did run beside this hedge, but it wasn't any kind of road Lambert had ever seen before. It was beaten clay, and it was rutted.

CHAPTER 3

The cart was drawing closer, and Lambert was aware that he didn't want whoever was driving the cart to see him before he saw them and had the opportunity to assess the situation. As quietly as he could, he squeezed through the gap between tree and hedge. Away from the road. Out of sight of whoever was on that cart. And just in time, because now the cart was swinging into view.

Lambert stared at the driver. What was this? Had he somehow arrived in a historical theme park? He'd never seen a costume such as the individual on the cart was wearing, not in real life, but he could place it. He wasn't a historian for nothing. That guy was straight out of the late eighteenth century. Lambert faced a choice: stand up, greet the man, ask where he was. Or stay in hiding. He bottled it. He stayed where he was. The cart went by. Lambert watched till it had passed the next bend and was out of sight.

Think, he told himself. You're an academic. You have a fine brain. There's an explanation for all this, and you can find it.

And then a dreadful thought came into his mind. The previous evening, he had ridiculed Sylvia's theories about parallel universes and, in particular, the idea that it might be possible in a universe adjacent to our own to travel into the past.

An instant migraine began spreading through Lambert's skull, wrapping like dreadful fingers around his forehead. There was no way... And yet, what other explanation was there?

§§§

'LET ME GET THIS STRAIGHT,' SAID NADEAU. 'The passenger count and the ticket count match.'

'That's right,' said the SNCF agent.

Nadeau massaged his temples with two fingers, squinting his eyes shut and moving the phone away from his mouth so that the agent wouldn't hear his sigh. After a long day after which he'd finally laid down on his bed with a beer, this was not the news he wanted to hear. 'So the number of passengers we have is the number the ticket sales say we should have. We are not short of anyone.'

'So it would seem.'

'But...?'

'But we have matched passengers' personal belongings against passengers. That was simple enough; we just got every passenger to take from the train their own baggage and other belongings. And we have a briefcase and an umbrella for one extra passenger. There's one briefcase that is not accounted for. And one umbrella.'

'The obvious assumption would be that one passenger did not want to identify that briefcase as his or her own. Presumably because of what it contains.' Nadeau tucked his phone between his shoulder, and his ear opened up his laptop, which was never far from his side and always ready to be used.

'But it doesn't contain anything that would arouse suspicion. There are papers from a conference in Brussels yesterday. A hotel bill, and a Canadian passport.'

'A stowaway?'

'That was my original thought, but then I wondered why a stowaway would choose to sit in first class.'

'If there's a passport, there's a person to whom it was issued. Unless it's a forgery, of course.'

'The passport is valid. It was issued to a Jonathan Lambert. What's more, it contains some interesting stuff.'

Nadeau's brow furrowed. 'Like what?'

'I think you should wait to hear it from the guys in the mobile forensics truck. Can you be here bright and early tomorrow?' the agent asked.

'Sure, okay.' Nadeau wasn't exactly thrilled by the prospect of waiting. If this news had only come a few hours earlier, he wouldn't have to spend a whole night speculating. There was no way to keep himself from trying to develop his own theories.

'I'll see you bright and early then,' the agent said.

Once the call was cut off, Nadeau took a long pull on his beer, the enjoyment of it sorely diminished by the waiting game he now played. His personal cell phone buzzed beside him, and he swiped it up, half-heartedly. He exhaled when he saw who the text message was from. Eloise. She was a woman he'd met a few months earlier on one of the rare nights he chose to go out instead of staying at home to continue working. Before becoming a detective he'd had quite the social life, but absorption with his work had changed that over time.

It wasn't as if he didn't like flirting with a woman every once and a while, and he did miss the female attention he used to get, but there just didn't seem to be time for that kind of frivolity in his schedule anymore. The days when he and his buddies from college would go out every weekend and Nadeau would use his charms to bust open the heart of every girl he met were long gone. From time-to-time one of his chums would send him a snarky message saying that all the girls missed him out on the town and that he should stop working every once in a while.

When had he become such a workaholic? He thought to himself. He hardly knew.

Still, the moment Nadeau ventured out for the first time in a long time; Eloise spotted him quickly and set her sights on him. It hadn't been hard to return to his old lines and flirting tactics, and without batting an eye, he and the woman had engaged in some small talk, shared a few drinks and exchanged numbers before the night's end. Nadeau didn't have time for a serious relationship and certainly didn't want the pressure of having to keep one woman consistently happy amidst the chaos of his schedule, so he always found it a bit unnerving when Eloise reached out. She was very persistent considering Nadeau gave next to no effort in return. Her interest in him appeared genuine, which was concerning for a forever-bachelor, only interested in the short-term, low commitment types of interactions. It was so much easier to be absorbed with work than to juggled the emotional requirements of a relationship.

Hi, stranger! What are you up to? Haven't heard from you in a while the text message read.

Nadeau exhaled. Eloise never seemed mad that he gave her nothing to work with and didn't ask to meet up with her. He was sure that if she got even the slightest taste of the level to which he was committed to his job, she'd lose interest in a heartbeat. However, he hadn't bothered to explain it to her, so the occasional conversations continued.

Everything's fine. How's it going, cutie?

Though Nadeau by no means wished to pursue any sort of lasting interest in the woman, he did remember well that Eloise was far from shabby. She had a curvaceous figure, huge blue eyes, and was a classic blonde. Just the type of girl who was good to mess around with but never thought past flirtation or lipstick shade.

Things are good.

The answer came almost instantly, making it clear that she was still as eager as ever about him.

I'm managing to keep busy - How's work going?

Fine.

What kind of a case are you working on right now? Or is it a secret mission? haha

Nadeau's brow lowered. This was the first time she'd pressed him about his job and, to be honest, he didn't know what to do with it. Since he didn't know, he decided to leave her on text-pause for now. Or maybe until the next time she decided to text him. Nadeau swept his computer up into his lap, draining the last of his beer. He had lots of theorising to do and didn't feel like explaining the case to an Eloise who would, more than likely find it all to be boring and way over her head. The kind of woman he attracted always did, which was why casual interests and eternal bachelorhood were by far his best option.

Now, it was time to return to the question 'How does a man manage to simply disappear without a trace?'

§§§

ONCE THEY WERE SEATED IN THE POLICE station's spare office space, the supervisor of the forensics team offered Nadeau and the SNCF agent coffee from a Nespresso machine. The SNCF agent declined, but Nadeau accepted gratefully. He'd been up late pondering the kinds of conclusions the forensics team might have come to and formulating theories of his own, but the resulting drowsiness was nothing a little caffeine wouldn't fix. Settling down with the cup in his hands, he turned his attention back to the investigation, 'Tell me about this passport.'

'It was properly issued in Canada, a completely valid passport,' the supervisor explained. 'What's more, it contains a valid entry stamp at Charles de Gaulle airport. Jonathan Lambert entered France some months ago in a perfectly normal way. But we've checked with the IPRB database, and the passport is invalid.'

Nadeau perked up. The International passport record bureau would have had a record of the issuance of this Canadian passport. Something was indeed odd about Monsieur Lambert.

'Here,' the agent said, flipping open the folder before him and fanning out the papers within. 'Lies our proof that Lambert truly did legitimately undergo the necessary formalities in order to cross the border and therefore is a real person.' The corner of his mouth lifted in an amused smirk. 'Not some sort of ghost passing through walls and disappearing from trains undetected.'

'Let me see the passport,' Nadeau requested. Handing the folder over, the technician and the SNCF agent watched him leaf through the pages. 'It seems to have valid entry and exit stamps out of Charles de Gaulle.' he agreed.

'The required verification at immigration would have detected an invalid passport,' Nadeau said, jumping right back into the task at hand. 'I wonder if the passport was cancelled after he entered France?'

'So it would seem, sir,' the supervisor said. 'There's something else. Three other things, in fact.'

'Tell me,' said Nadeau.

'The briefcase contained Monsieur Lambert's wallet as well as his passport is also an item of interest. Credit cards, some academic papers from the Université Paris-Sorbonne, a driver's licence, and a ticket stub in the name of Jonathan Lambert were all found within. It seems Mister Lambert works at the university as a professor of Economic History.'

'A ticket stub? You mean, for this train?'

'Yes. But I have checked the ticket against company records, and there is no record of that ticket ever having been issued.'

'Is it a forgery?'

'It doesn't seem so, sir. The ticket has been validated and stamped. You see?'

He held out the ticket. Nadeau, who was not wearing gloves, examined it while taking care not to touch it. 'So what do we have? A man was travelling on a Canadian passport that is no longer valid using a ticket that was validated and stamped but never issued.' He turned to the SNCF agent. 'I don't like it one little bit. I'm afraid we are going to have to assume responsibility for this investigation.'

The SNCF agent, who could not have received happier news, struggled not to smile.

Nadeau said, 'You said there were three things?'

'Yes, sir,' said the forensics investigator. 'We contacted the University to see if he was on leave. The university has no record of a professor Jonathan Lambert.'

'No record of him anymore or ever?'

'Didn't specify, sir. They seemed to have never heard of him.'

'He's the invisible man. Or the vanishing man, I'm not sure which. And the third thing?'

'We showed the picture in Mr Lambert's passport to the two passengers sitting closest to that seat. They both recognised him. He was definitely on the train.'

'Curiouser and curiouser. Did they say anything about him?'

'Yes, sir. They said he had been laughing immoderately just before the train stopped. One said they thought he might be a little touched in the head, and the other thought he might have been drunk.'

'It gets deeper. He was laughing immediately before the train made an emergency stop. That suggests to me that he was expecting the stop. That it was arranged for him and that he always intended to leave the train here. The question is: why? For what purpose? I suppose the train has been checked for bombs?'

'It has,' said the SNCF man, even happier than he had been that he was not to be saddled with this investigation.

'Right,' said Nadeau. 'Please box up all Monsieur Lambert's personal effects and send them to my office.' And he handed both men his card with his contact details and office address. 'Oh, the conference in Brussels. What was it about?'

'According to the papers left in his briefcase, It was to commemorate the anniversary of the Battle of Waterloo. We haven't had time yet to check whether a Jonathan Lambert attended.'

'And now you need not do so. You may leave that to my people and I.'

CHAPTER 4

THE CART HAD DISAPPEARED, even the sound of that creaking wheel vanishing at last. Lambert sat in the shade of the tree and set himself to get rid of the fear – fear that was surely illogical – by thinking through his situation. It's a simple matter of academic research, he told himself, and that's what you are good at. Your field is economic history, which could be why you were unsettled by the sight of someone you could identify as belonging to the past. You grew up in Quebec, and now you live in Paris where you are studying for a doctorate at the Sorbonne. You live in Paris. You've been at a conference, you drank more than might have been wise last night, and you were so keen to make a fool of your colleague Sylvia that you may well have made a fool of yourself instead.

Well, so what? Your ego is not so fragile that you will fret long about something like that. You were on your way home. You were in the first-class compartment of the TGV. And now you're here. And here is... Here is what? What is this place?

You've listed the facts; now infer the explanation. It should be a simple matter of deduction which, once again, is something you're good at. So. The explanation. What is it?

And here was the problem. There wasn't one. He did not remember leaving the train of his own free will, and he did not remember anyone removing him from it. And, in any case, how could there have been a train when there were no rails for it to run on?

Panic started in his breast again, and he knew he had to quell it. Checking the facts had got him nowhere; it was time to check the body. He felt his head. No sign of injury, though he did have a splitting headache. And the rest of him: there were no indications anywhere that he'd taken any kind of physical knock. What time was it? He checked his watch, the only thing his parents had left him apart from a good education and was astonished to find that it had stopped. It was self-winding, so his normal physical movements should have kept it going, and it had a power reserve of at least thirty hours before it needed to be wound. How long had he been in this field? How long since he'd left the train? Or had the watch been broken?

When he wound it up, it started immediately. It wasn't damaged, and the conclusion was inescapable: he had lain somewhere for nearly a day and a half at the very least without moving. But where? Here? Or somewhere else? And had he been moved? If so, by whom? An awful lot of questions and a serious shortage of answers. He gingerly stood up straight, stretching his muscles, doing his best to remain hidden within the shrubbery though the road appeared deserted.

'Hey! You there!'

Lambert instinctively ducked, looking around him for the source of the voice. Once he'd turned full circle, he saw the man who'd addressed him. He hadn't even heard him approach, but there he was, regarding Lambert with the utmost wariness.

His clothes and the fact that he carried a pitchfork over his shoulder made him easily identifiable as a farmer. He was as undernourished and badly dressed as the cart driver.

'Greetings monsieur....' Lambert started.

The man's eyes widened to the size of saucers as he took in Lambert's foreign appearance. 'Who are you?' He asked, gripping the pitchfork over his shoulder.

'I'm a....' Lambert groped desperately for the right words. However, it was pretty difficult to explain such modern attire. To these people, he probably looked as if he'd just fallen from outer space. He wasn't able to come up with anything fast enough and paid for it.

In a heartbeat, the farmer swung his pitchfork forward, aiming it right at Lambert, widening his stance as if ready to plunge the fork right through the visiting man's middle at any given moment.

Lambert raised his hands. 'Please. Please calm down,' he tried.

'Do not be telling me to calm down. Who are you?'

'My name is Jonathan - you have nothing to fear from me.'

The farmer snorted, shifting his weight from foot to foot, nervously. Lambert realised that he'd never had a person be sincerely frightened of him before and he didn't like it. It made him feel like some sort of exotic animal. If he were honest though, to this man, he must not look far off.

'If you'll just let me explain...' Lambert took a cautious step toward the man, receiving a few threatening jabs in his direction with the pitchfork.

'Wow, okay.' Deciding it was time to try another tactic, he took a huge step backwards. 'Listen. I'm not going to hurt you. I'm not some alien....'

This explanation only caused the lines of confusion and fear on the man's face to deepen.

You're screwing this up royally, Lambert thought. 'I'm not some crazy person, I'm just.... Out of place. You see, I'm not from around here.'

'Yes, I gathered that,' the farmer said, raising the pitchfork to eye level.

'It's a little hard to explain, and you probably won't believe me even if I tell you....'

'If you give me a good enough reason why you're dressed like that, I'll let you go.'

CHAPTER 4

'Let me go? So, what are you going to do? Hold me captive? Impale me?'

The farmer wasn't amused at all by these suggestions and so his stance became even more tense, his eyes squinting in anger.

'Okay, okay, I'll tell you,' Lambert said. He was seriously starting to believe that this unassuming farmer had what it took to run him through. He wracked his memory, trying to think about whether or not the man would even be served a sentence for such an act. Considering he looked like he came from another world (which wasn't far off), impaling him would probably be considered self-defence or even his civic duty. Still, there was no changing the fact that a weapon featuring particularly sharp and rusty forks was pointed at him, so he had to try.

'I've come here from a very different.....' Time would be too drastic of a word. Using it might send the man charging at him without further ado. 'Place. I'm not sure how I got here, but I feel as odd about this whole ordeal as you.'

Lambert's insides jumped with anxiety as he watched the farmer's reaction to this answer play across his face.

'A sorcerer.....' the farmer hissed, his voice hushed in fear. 'Surely for such an event to happen without your control, leaving you with no memory of the process, magic must be involved....'

'No!' Lambert exclaimed, a bit too loudly. The volume startled the farmer who was alright on high alert, and he jumped, pressing the pitchfork toward Lambert once again.

Damn you, Lambert thought. You've only dug yourself into a deeper hole now.

Impaling a sorcerer really would be considered a public service. Lambert had the sick feeling that his short time in this historical period might be quickly coming to a close. The only impact he would make would be as a supposed sorcerer, most likely buried in an unmarked grave. It wasn't exactly how he'd expected to die.

'Look, I don't have any weapons,' Lambert said, thinking back on how people got out of these kinds of sticky situations in crime shows and such. 'You can even check my pockets. I don't have any source of magic on me....' He wasn't sure what a 'source of magic' would look like, but his words appeared to appease the skittish farmer somewhat.

The man was speaking French, which meant Lambert could not be too very far from home. What he needed was a phone so that he could call friends to pick him up. And it *was* French the man was speaking, although Lambert could not recall hearing that accent before. The strange thing about it was the stress on the word Monsieur. It wasn't pronounced as it usually is, as a mere acknowledgement of the presence of an adult male – it had a ring about it. The way it had begun as a greeting to a person of higher station. If this was a psychological experiment or a theme park, whoever organised it was carrying realism to great lengths. On the farmer's head was a small hat with a wide brim. Outside the pants that he wore tucked into ancient, dilapidated boots he wore a large, billowing shirt like a smock. Under the smock was another, tighter shirt, barely able to contain the overwhelming stench of body odour. Pinned to the side of his hat was a symbol that Lambert knew he should find familiar – an oval pin of white ribbons.

'May I ask where I am?' Lambert said, feeling that the fact that the farmer was markedly more relaxed now was a green light to get a few questions out of the way.

'This is the parish of Pontoise in the Île-de-France, Monsieur.'

'Hmmm, okay,' Lambert said. That meant little to him, but it was confirmation that he was in France. 'Forgive me, Monsieur, but those white ribbons in your hat. What do they signify? I'm sure I've seen them somewhere before.'

Now the farmer looked completely amazed. He took the hat from his head and looked at it. 'These ribbons? Why they say, I am a supporter of the new King. *Vive le Roi!*

Now they were getting somewhere. This man was about to divulge something that would give Lambert a clue as to where and when this performance purported to take place. 'Ah, yes,' he said, entering into the spirit of the thing. 'And which king is it?' Even as he asked the question, a thought came into his mind. That collection of ribbons in a circle was a cockade. Of course, he knew the Tricolore cockade of blue, white and red ribbons worn by the heroes of the French Revolution, but a white cockade predated the revolution. White cockades were worn by those who supported the Bourbon dynasty of the *ancien regime*. The farmer was going to present himself as supporting a king who had been dead a great many years.

And so it was because the farmer, who now looked very nervous indeed, replied, 'Louis-Auguste. King of France and Navarre. Who else could I be referring to?'

Lambert stared at him for a moment or two in silence. This was an act. It had to be an act. Didn't it? Because, if it wasn't... He said, 'What day is it?'

'It is Wednesday, Monsieur.'

'And the date. What is the date?'

'Monsieur, I do not understand the question. The day is Wednesday. The king died yesterday. I wear these ribbons in support of our new king. May he live a long and merciful life. I do not know what the date is. I do not understand what you mean.'

'Monsieur. What is the year?'

The farmer stared at him for some time without answering. He took another step back. And then he said, 'Monsieur, it is 1774. How can you not know this? Where have you come from?'

Lambert was possessed by a dreadful sinking feeling. Was this a joke? It felt less and less like one. If he was in the Île-de-France near the town of Pontoise, then where were the buildings? Where was the noise? Why was everything so quiet? Pontoise was no more than twenty kilometres from Paris. There should be roads, motorway, traffic. Aircraft, for that matter, and he looked up to observe what, really, he had already known: that there were no vapour trails in the sky. And where were the power lines? All he could see was an endless horizon of gentle hills in one direction and a small collection of low-lying buildings in another. However, one thing was for sure: it looked as if he'd be spending a little time here.

'I really must find something to wear that will make me less conspicuous,' Lambert mused to himself, though the farmer listened in. 'I suppose I could find such a thing in town?'

The farmer only nodded mutely. Lambert wondered if he thought speaking would cause the strange man before him to become less tame— exhibit the powers of sorcery he thought he possessed.

'Perhaps you would consider walking with me partway so that I might look less threatening to others?'

The farmer shook his head, vigorously. 'I can't be doing that, monsieur. It would be too.... Too....'

Dangerous? Suspicious? Yeah, walking around with a person who apparently appeared readily identifiable as a witch would be rather risky.

'Well, nevermind then,' Lambert said. 'I would ask one favour though?'

The farmer looked appalled at being asked for a favour after this encounter, but he nodded for Lambert to continue.

'I would appreciate it if you wouldn't tell anyone else about this? I promise, I won't do any harm, and I intend to blend in just fine. I'll get some recognisable clothes and.... Won't cause any trouble. Do we have a deal?'

The farmer hesitated for a moment before offering another nod. 'Well,' he said, jolting, seemingly having forgotten that he was still pointing his 'weapon' at Lambert. He lifted it quickly to his shoulder, reaching up with an agitated movement to straighten his hat. 'I'll be moving along. Good day.' The farmer turned to leave, sending a few suspicious glances over his shoulder as he made his way down the road.

Lambert could only watch the farmer go and hope that he wouldn't sound an alarm, sending whatever kind of police force was available to incarcerate him and burn him for being a witch.

He was seized by a growing conviction, however ludicrous it might be, that this was no joke and no experiment. It really was 1774. How he could survive here, he had no idea. His passport and his wallet must still be on the train in his briefcase because they certainly weren't with him. How was he to tell people who he was? And how was he to live? Even if he had had his wallet with him, you couldn't use credit cards in 1774, and the only money in the wallet was euros. No one here would know what a euro was. Besides, he could be quite certain that they could not be exchanged for anything of value. Like a meal and a bed for the night, to mention only two things he was going to need in a relatively short time.

As he considered his predicament, one thing became clear. There could be no more hiding. Unless he wanted to starve to death under the stars, he had to engage with the populace. He didn't want to, because he was afraid, but of this, he was quite certain: that he had no choice. Besides, he needed to find some suitable clothes. That is, if he could do that without being accused of sorcery.... He'd have to take his chances for the moment. Things would certainly be easier once he didn't look so out of place.

He began to walk in the direction of the low-lying buildings.

§§§

As HE DREW CLOSER TO THE BUILDINGS, he became aware of a group of small children playing on the side of the road under the supervision of a young woman. She was too young, surely, to be their mother. Perhaps an older sister? Young woman and children alike were all dressed in the same style as the farmer. Their clothing was threadbare and hung loosely from their skinny frames. What was even more striking was that most of the children were barefoot and their feet showed definite signs of weathering, as if they had never worn shoes throughout their young lives.

As he drew level with the children, he saw the way they looked at him. Full of doubt. You couldn't teach small children to act that way – their suspicion of him was genuine. He didn't care who might have set up a psychology experiment like this; even if it had been in the hands of Disney World themselves, they could not have mounted this level of authenticity.

Any hope that he was still, really, in the 21st-century disappeared. The young woman curtsied. Her face was a picture of uncertainty, but clearly, she saw before her someone of superior status in a time when superior status gave people power over you. And look at her. No earbuds. No earrings and no jewellery. Hair, hidden under a bonnet. This was no modern teenager. The children had stopped in their play to watch him, their fascination obvious.

Just before the buildings, he came to a small sign on which the word *Villiers* was written in a flowery script. The sign was crude and weathered and nothing like those that announced a hamlet in modern France. He looked back down the road. There were no other signs. No speed limits, no reflectors, nothing to warn drivers of the dirt road's limits. In the shade, tethered to a post, a horse was drinking from a wooden trough. Not a single motor vehicle in sight. No street lights. No concrete and no asphalt. Only dust and grimy wooden buildings without a touch of colour or decoration. Every step that took him closer to the buildings took him also deeper into despair. 1774. What was he doing here? How could it be possible?

If it really was 1774 and the king really was dead, then the king who had died was Louis XV and the new King the farmer celebrated was Louis XVI. That, to the historian in him, meant that this was the 12th of May.

Had some power of which he had no knowledge or understanding decided to teach him a lesson? If so, who was that power? What was the purpose of the lesson? And would he, when this was over, be able to find his way back to 2018 and the Sorbonne?

Lambert mentally shook himself, refusing to buy into his own speculations. He was not ready to give up hope that his colleagues had played a complicated practical joke on him, but that hope could not be squared with the reality reported by his senses. And especially the lack of noise. There was the sound of the wind, the sounds of birdsong, animals and subdued human speech, but the sounds of 2018 were absent.

A Question of Time

THERE WERE NO WORDS ON THE BUILDINGS WHEN HE REACHED THEM – only symbols representing the trade carried on there. What few people he saw radiated suspicion when they looked at him. Every step he took said that the farmer had been speaking the truth.

There weren't many people, but there were some. Heads down and turned away, there was a resentful air to their murmured greetings. Of course, they could be professional actors playing a part – but he only had to look at them to know they weren't. He had begun to hyperventilate. He didn't have panic attacks, had never had them, but he was having one now. Was it a surprise? Not to him. What sort of person would it take to handle this experience calmly? Someone without fear. Someone without imagination. Someone stupid – and no one had ever called him that. He needed to get himself in order.

In the centre of the little hamlet was situated a small pond, an area of rough grass and a single tree. Under the tree was a crude wooden bench. He couldn't imagine that anyone had ever had a greater need to sit on that bench to compose themselves, and so that is what he did. He sat quite still, focusing on what was inside himself and not the terrifying 'out there'. He concentrated on steadying his breathing. It didn't help that people were walking by him and that his mere presence in the hamlet was clearly part of the reason for their being there. Of course, he stood out. His clothes were nothing like the ones worn by the people around him.

The hamlet was a chaotic arrangement of buildings dropped down haphazardly on both sides of the main street. Clearly, there had been no town planning when this place had come into being. He could see no order to the construction and the materials used were overwhelmingly made of wood, with just the occasional stone building added in. No hint of anything modern. Stone walls, uneven wooden planks, no street lamps, no fire hydrants, nothing that even hinted at modern living. At one point further down the road, the sound of bellows and smoke rising from a massive chimney said that this was a blacksmith's place of work.

He could make out the spire of a small church. What he could also make out was a growing interest on the part of the people passing by and that they were doing less passing by and more standing still in twos and threes staring at him. Talking to each other. That the talk was about him was without question. If they approached him, challenged him, what was he going to say? What if they decided to rob him? Or worse? He was a knowledgeable enough historian to know that crimes of violence and murder were more frequent in the France of Louis XVI than they were in twenty-first-century Montreal.

His breathing was a little calmer now. It was time to get up and be on his way.

It was with a sense of relief that he saw that no-one attempted to block his way. Relief, too, when he passed the blacksmith's forge and saw that the men inside ignored him. They were engrossed in their work, holding superheated metal in enormous tongs and striking it on an anvil. There was nothing complicated about the things they seemed to be making – small agricultural implements for the most part.

The place he was making for was the church. He couldn't imagine 18th-century clergy taking part in a hoax. If anyone in the church were playing a part, it would be obvious. By the same token, if he found someone there who appeared to be genuine, he would know what in fact he did know but was determined to ignore for as long as possible.

And, of course, the church had a graveyard. He could end this charade, if a charade it were, by finding one gravestone. A gravestone with a date later than 1774.

He spent ten minutes or so walking the grounds, reading each grave marker carefully. The grounds were poorly manicured, overridden with weeds and small stones. Each minute made his situation more definite. Not only was there not a single grave with a date later than 1774, but there was also what appeared to be a very fresh grave and the year chiselled into the marker was 1774. The size of the grave said it was that of a child; the years marked on it said that the child had been only four years old.

He was utterly demoralised. He made no attempt even to enter the church and speak to the curé because he had accepted that there was no point.

And then it occurred to him that, of course, the church must be empty. A priest in a place like this would be a person of authority – perhaps the only one. If the curé had been in the hamlet, people so puzzled and confused by Lambert's appearance among them would have rushed to bring the priest to see him. It would have been the nearest thing they had to getting a protective God to stand between Lambert and them.

He couldn't go on like this. What he had to do now was to find a way to blend in with the rest of the populace.

ON HIS WAY TO THE CHURCH, he had seen what looked like somewhere where clothes of some description were on offer. Maybe a tailor, maybe a cobbler. He had no money he could use here, but people in the France of the eighteenth century would be far more used to barter than anyone of his own time. He retraced his steps towards the shop and entered without knocking. Inside, the shop was cool and dark. There were no lights, but he could see well enough. And the middle-aged woman could see him. That was obvious from the suspicious way she looked at him. She said, 'Good day, Monsieur.' Once again, that strange way of pronouncing the word – like the farmer, it was as though she were splitting it in two and emphasising the last five letters. 'Sieur.' And he realised that it wasn't really him she was studying so intently – it was what he wore. Because now it was clear; this was a tailor's shop, and not a cobbler's. And yet, he could see boots as well as clothes, so it must serve both purposes. Presumably, a hamlet of this size could not support two clothing businesses. There were a few crude mannequins with shirts on them. A small workbench with strings and needles for threading. Nothing that even hinted at the modern era.

No plastic. No signs. Not even any pictures on the wall. Of course, someone whose job was to make clothes for the rural poor of 18th-century France would be mesmerised by what a well-dressed denizen of modern Paris wore. He sighed and told himself to show a little courage. 'I'd like to see some clothes.'

Before answering, she looked for some time at the clothes Lambert was wearing. After a moment she said, 'What is it you are looking for, Monsieur?'

Well? What *was* he looking for? He took a deep breath, despite the overpowering smell of sweat and bad breath in the shop. Then he described the clothes the farmer had been wearing. Throughout this exchange, the woman's eyes never left his. If she's acting, Lambert thought, what she's showing is *Doubt* from *Actor's Manual 101*. Then, still, without speaking, she disappeared into an alcove at the back of the shop. When she came out, she was carrying a small bundle of clothes. She held them out towards him in silence. When he took them, she pointed towards the alcove as if to say, 'You can change in there.'

He came out looking for all the world like an 18th-century French farmer – at least as far as his clothes were concerned. His face and his hands said something different, but there was nothing he could do about that. 'Everything seems fine,' he said. 'Madame. I would like to trade my own clothes for these. Not the shoes,' he added because he knew he had some serious walking to do, and he did not want to walk far in the boots of a two-hundred-year-old peasant. 'But everything else. Can we come to an arrangement?'

She picked up the clothes he had placed on the counter. A battle fought itself out on her face, and her mouth opened slightly, revealing several rotten front teeth. On the one hand, the trader's desire not to show any respect for the quality of what was on offer. On the other, astonishment as she handled cloth of a quality she had never felt in her life before. And then she came to a zipper, and she stared at Lambert, her face a picture of wonder. Lambert took the garment from her and moved the zip up and down, showing how it worked. However hard she tried, she could not conceal her admiration. 'Oh! Oh!' Her mind was made up. 'Monsieur. I will give you what you are wearing and twenty-four livres in exchange for your clothes.'

He had no idea what twenty-four livres would buy, but he would be glad to have any usable money at all in his pocket. He nodded. 'I accept.'

Back into her alcove, she went, and this time when she came out she handed Lambert a small leather pouch. He opened it and poured the coins it contained on the counter. The head-on each coin was one he was familiar with. Louis XV. Louis 'The Beloved' from the Royal house of Bourbon. He found that he was shaking. He counted the coins. 'Sixteen coins?'

'Yes, monsieur, the amount is correct.'

'But you offered me twenty-four livres.'

To the wide variety of emotions that had been on the woman's face since he entered the shop was now added the look of someone who thought she might be explaining to an idiot. 'Monsieur, each of those coins is one half of an Ecu. Each is worth one livre and a half. I think you are not from around here?'

'No, Madame, I am from Antwerp.' How quickly the lie came when it was needed. He smiled. 'That explains my odd clothes.'

Visibly relieved, the woman was happy to explain that the Ecu was a typical silver coin in the kingdom of France and was worth three livres. She went on to say that she, alas, was but a poor shopkeeper and so carried only the quarter Ecu and half Ecu coins, but the amount she was giving him was the one they had agreed.

This was to be a complicated method of calculating value for someone who all his life had known only the decimal currencies of the Canadian dollar and the euro. He tucked the explanation away in his mind. He had no doubt he would need it again. He returned the coins to the little pouch, but when he tried to put the pouch in a pocket, he realised that a pocket was something he didn't have. 'Here,' said the woman, and she gave him a simple rope to act as a crude belt. Then she tied the pouch to his waist and showed him how to tuck it inside his pants. 'Against bandits,' she whispered.

Another reminder that he was not to enjoy the standards of law and order that he was used to. Lambert was not a violent person, and he was keenly aware that, if attacked, he was unlikely to be able to defend himself effectively. But there was nothing for it; he must get on. Anxiety settled on him like a cloak. He said, 'Could you direct me towards Paris?'

The woman pointed in the general direction of the road outside. 'That way. It will take about four hours on foot.'

Lambert did not fail to notice that this time when she had spoken to him she had not added the word Monsieur. When he took off his own clothes, had he also put off the right to respect? He nodded his thanks to the woman and stepped out into the road.

A Question of Time

CHAPTER 5

INSPECTOR NADEAU HADN'T EXPECTED his investigation of Jonathan Lambert to be as smooth as silk, but he had anticipated that some general information about the man would be easy enough to get. And here he was, sitting in his office, having spent the better part of an hour being bounced from official to official, first at the Canadian embassy in Paris and then in the Immigration, and Refugee's offices. Now, he was on hold with the Citizenship Canada office in Ottawa. Nadeau exhaled, glancing irritably at the clock on the wall. He'd been waiting over fifteen minutes. It shouldn't take this long to answer a simple question.

'How inefficient can they—?' he muttered to himself, cutting his own words short when he heard the phone finally being picked up again on the other end.

'Agent Nadeau?' the official on the other end said, oblivious as to how deep Nadeau had been fuming while he waited.

Nadeau cleared his throat. 'Yes? What did you find?'

'Unfortunately, I found nothing, sir.'

'You mean, during all that time you were unable to....?'

'No, I searched in all the relevant databases and spoke to several people in my department. I can assure you there is no record of this man, Jonathan Lambert, with the passport number you provided anywhere.'

'That's impossible,' Nadeau said, clenching his fist, more than ready to resume his fuming. He'd had about enough of people telling him that no trace of Lambert could be found. If the man weren't real, there wouldn't be evidence of his existence, for God's sake.

'How can you have no record of this man? You issued him a passport!'

Being a government official himself, Nadeau knew the futility of losing his temper with the man assisting him, but enough was enough.

'I'm sorry, sir, but I'm afraid you'll have to check your information again. Are you certain you have your facts straight?'

Nadeau took a deep breath, working hard to calm himself down. One thing you had to say about Canadians: they were polite. God knew how the British would have reacted if he'd talked to them like that. Or, worse, the Germans. But this Citizenship Officer in Ottawa who had been assigned to help him deserved special accolades for the brand of patience he offered. Nadeau was at the end of his rope and ready to snap. Still, this man refused to raise his voice in return.

Even in his anger, Nadeau knew the truth: the official was being a saint and Nadeau was taking out his frustration on him when he had nothing to do with this dead end. The Citizenship Officer had given every impression of taking it seriously when Nadeau told him he was leading a missing person investigation concerning a Canadian citizen who had vanished on French soil. But they were getting nowhere. The information simply would not materialise.

'I'm sorry that we could not supply you with the information you were looking for today,' the officer said, his politeness failing to lapse for even a moment. 'I will certainly have our office give you a call if we find anything.'

'Thanks.' Nadeau responded, careful to insert kindness into his tone. It wouldn't undo his earlier exasperation, but he could try to end the conversation well in spite of his own frustration with the situation. 'Yes, I'd appreciate if you'd send along anything else you find. Thank you again for your time.'

Nadeau exhaled, scrubbing at his tired eyes before his gaze focused blearily on the items in front of him: Lambert's personal possessions which proved he was actually a living person. Or at least he used to be...He picked up the wallet. Nothing fancy, it was made of simple brown leather and well worn. It contained several hundred euros in denominations of ten and twenty. Not unexpected for a passenger on a business class ticket from Brussels. But what was he doing in Brussels? Thought Nadeau. Yes, yes, the conference – but was that the real reason? Or just a front, a cover for something Nadeau did not want to find but was charged with unearthing?

Maybe twenty years ago, the thought of a possible terrorist involvement would not have raised itself, but a lot of things had happened in twenty years. Most likely there was an entirely innocent explanation. Probably Lambert was even now walking around France in a state of amnesia. Nadeau briefly fantasised that someone would call soon and say they'd found a man who didn't know who he was but who appeared to match the details on the bulletin he had put out. Probably. But until that happened, Nadeau had no choice but to factor in the possibility that this man represented a real danger to France and its people.

What else was in this wallet? Credit cards. Receipts for meals and taxis in Brussels. A ghost would have no need to eat or find transportations (ghosts flew from place to place, didn't they?). An old photograph of two people, older than the picture in Lambert's passport but with clear facial similarities. Parents, probably, thought Nadeau. He put the picture to one side, planning to send a copy to some contacts he had in Montreal and ask them to make enquiries. Did anyone in Canada know these people? Did anyone know their son?

No doubt about it. If Jonathan Lambert's identity was faked, a great deal of sophistication, ingenuity and technology had gone into creating it. No one did that without good reason.

Always a man for detail, Nadeau updated the report on his laptop, separately noting the facts he had established, the questions he had put out into the world and the tentative theories he had begun to develop. He turned to Lambert's satchel, and it's documents. Pulling them out, he spread out the documents on his desk. What he was faced with appeared to be a collection of papers written by students at the Sorbonne engaged in a history course on economics. The name 'Professor Jonathan Lambert' appeared on all of the papers, either on the title page or in a covering letter. Nadeau entered into his laptop the name of every student who had submitted a paper. They would all have to be spoken to, either by Nadeau or by someone to whom he delegated the task.

What did they know about Lambert? Had he regularly turned up for seminars? Or were there unexplained absences? Did he seem to them to be the person he was supposed to be? Or had his behaviour ever raised suspicions? They'd have to be careful how they asked those questions – students at the Sorbonne could be very suspicious of authority, and they weren't known for their love of the police.

He would probably ask a female agent to conduct the interviews. He wouldn't say this to anyone, given the outrage any suggestion of sexism could trigger these days, but it was a fact that a woman was less likely to upset student sensitivities than some of the men they employed in this place. Really, you'd think he sent out agents armed with truncheons and rubber hoses to beat the truth out of people.

He turned his attention next to the folio of a Brussels area hotel. Four nights bed-and-breakfast and some room service had been charged to a Visa card. The number of the Visa card matched one of those in the brown leather wallet. Casually rotating the credit card between his fingers, deep in thought, he picked up the phone and dialled the hotel phone number at the top of the folio. After a moment, the call clicked through, 'May I speak to your manager on duty?' He was put through without comment.

After several rings, the phone at the other end abruptly picked up. 'Yes?' The man replying, sounded distracted.

'Hello. My name is Agent Nadeau. I am with the Central Directorate of the Judicial Police in Paris.' He listed his credentials, including his agent identification number and asked the manager to write them all down. 'I need to confirm some information on the folio I have found in a missing person investigation. Can I give you the folio number?'

'You can give me anything you like, Agent Nadeau, but you will understand that our hotel cannot confirm or deny any information about our guests without a written court order. I don't even know whether you are who you say you are.'

Nadeau sighed and gave the manager the phone number of the main switchboard together with his extension number. After instructing the manager to immediately call him back, he hung up. Tapping his fingers impatiently, he stared at his phone. A few moments later, his phone rang. The now-familiar voice of manager said, 'I'm sorry for the additional security steps. We have a fiduciary duty to protect our clients' personal information.'

There was nothing unusual these days about the gatekeepers of information being wary about sharing what they knew over the phone, and Nadeau kept his thoughts to himself, restricting himself to giving the folio number. 'I have a four-night stay at your hotel, including two-room service charges. It's in the name of a Jonathan Lambert and the folio was paid with a visa credit card.'

'Just a moment.' After a pause, the manager said, 'I'm sorry, Agent Nadeau, I can't find what you are looking for on this folio number. As far as I can see, that number was assigned to an American couple who stayed with us last week. They came in on a prepaid voucher from one of our booking engine partners.'

'Yes. I see. Could you possibly check whether there is a record of a Jonathan Lambert ever staying at your property?'

'I did that already. We have never received this man as a guest in this hotel.'

Nadeau thanked the manager and hung up. He ran his fingers through his hair. This was turning into the most frustrating enquiry he'd ever had. Who the hell was Jonathan Lambert? How had he managed to slip in, leaving actual traces behind him, yet essentially vanished from the memory of every person and computer system that should have remembered his presence?

Nadeau stood to his feet, desperately needing to leave the aggravating and inconclusive evidence behind for the rest of the night. He needed a drink. Bad.

§§§

BY THE TIME HE WAS ON HIS SECOND DRINK, Nadeau had to laugh at himself. He'd been a fool to think that alcohol would remove thoughts of Lambert's mysterious disappearance from his mind. Still willing to give it a fair shot, he lifted his glass, signalling to the bartender for another.

'Why couldn't you have just chosen a simple profession, Nadeau?' he muttered under his breath.

'You could have been a bus driver. Or a real estate man or something. That way you wouldn't have to chase disappearing travellers all the way to kingdom come. As if you have nothing better to do with your life....'

'Talking to yourself?'

Nadeau glanced toward the female voice only to be caught off guard. It was Eloise.

'Does this one on one conversation you're having mean that you need another actual person to talk to?' Eloise was dressed to the nines and already had a drink in her hand. She was obviously ready to go and, strange though it was, Nadeau felt rather receptive to the idea of some company.

'Sure.' Gesturing to the seat next to him, he invited her to join him.

Perhaps if a third drink didn't do the trick, a conversation with the girl he'd been putting off and had left on text pause only a couple of days earlier would do the trick. One could never tell for sure—anything was possible.

'Haven't seen you out in a while,' Eloise said. It was apparent that she wasn't holding Nadeau's aloofness against him, and the foggy agent was actually grateful for that.

'Yeah, I've been busy.'

'With work,' Eloise filled in, her eyes remaining on him as she took a sip of her wine. 'You never did tell me what kind of case you were working on.'

Nadeau managed a slight laugh. 'Oh, you mean whether or not it was 'Mission impossible', top-secret status?'

Eloise toyed with the straw in her glass, her brow wrinkling adorably. 'I was actually thinking more along the lines of 'Men in Black.'' She shrugged, offering a half-smile. 'But, you left me to wonder.'

Nadeau straightened his shoulders, realising for the first time that he was slouched over like a hunch back. The drinks must have done their job better than he'd thought. Or perhaps it was just now hitting him when he actually wished he was a little less foggy. As long as there was a pretty girl in front of him (planned or not), he didn't want to appear completely wasted.

'It's all rather dull, really,' he said. 'I'm sure a girl like you wouldn't be interested.'

Her brows rose, quizzically. 'A girl like me?' Her expression became mischevious as she leaned toward him. 'Tell me, do you really think you know what kind of girl I am? In my opinion, you haven't even taken the time to find out.'

Nadeau, reflecting momentarily on her aroma discernible from the closeness of her body couldn't argue with that. 'You're the kind of girl who I'm sure would rather talk about something more interesting than work.'

Her mouth quirked in amusement. 'Try me.'

Chapter 5

What the heck? Nadeau thought. I'm buzzed, yet the annoyance of the case still lingers. She'd demanded to know so why not tell her?

'How does a man just disappear?'

Eloise blinked before her look became ponderous.

'Disappear? You mean, like vanish into thin air?'

'Yes, precisely.

'Hmm, I like this case already.'

'Yeah, well, I don't.' Nadeau shook his head. 'The darn thing is just one dead end after another.'

'So, I'm guessing no one knows what happened to him?'

'You've got it.'

Eloise drew a heart in the condensation on her glass with one fingertip, thinking. 'There's always kidnapping.'

Nadeau shook his head. 'No way.'

'Why not?'

'Here's the thing,' Nadeau said, raising his hands in front of him as he tried to set the scene. 'A certain college professor takes a trip on the train. A kind of an emergency, or, more accurately, an emergency stop of the locomotive is required. From that moment on, Lambert ceases to exist.'

'Huh....'

'The thing is,' he went on. 'Not only did his physical person disappear, but so did every memory of him in the minds of others. All evidence of the digital and physical fingerprints he should have made on the world around him wiped clean. Gone.'

Nadeau downed the last of his third drink, clunking it back onto the table with more gusto than he intended. The action made his buzzed brain vibrate even more. 'I mean what did the guy do, evaporate?'

'That's one possibility,' Eloise said with a chuckle. 'Spontaneous evaporation of the subject and everything he ever did. I've wished I could make that happen to me before.'

'Really?' Nadeau wasn't sure what it was... The stress of the week, the almost constant solitude, just him and his work, or the alcohol, but the agent felt truly interested in Eloise's answer.

Eloise laughed, tossing her immaculately curled, blonde hair as she shifted on the barstool. 'When I was in college. One night I made a fool of myself at a party and said all sorts of things to this guy I had a huge crush on. I was so confident that I could drink as much as I wanted and still keep from doing anything stupid.'

'You were proven wrong.'

'Quite thoroughly. It didn't help that I had a friend try her best to convince me that there was no way I would be able to keep complete control of myself. I was sure that she was wrong and closed-minded to hearing her thoughts on the matter, though she had plenty of evidence to support her claim. So, I would have jumped at the chance to have myself, and the memory of me erased from the face of the earth. I'd also completely botched my debate speech earlier that day, so I already wanted to crawl into a hole and die. Watching my demise play out on video before my eyes was just the icing on the cake.'

'Someone caught it on video?' Nadeau asked, working hard not to laugh.

'Yep.' Eloise covered her face in self-pity. 'The friend who'd tried to convince me that I would only be able to handle drinking a certain amount caught the whole thing on her phone and showed it to me the next morning while I was suffering from the worst hangover I've had to date.'

Nadeau and Eloise shared a laugh over this before falling into companionable silence. It only lasted a few moments before Nadeau spoke.

'I guess sometimes we are put in our place by being forced to experience the existence of the things we try to deny are possible.'

Eloise nodded. She motioned with one hand. 'Hey. Maybe this Lambert had gotten too big for his britches and was being put in his place by the universe.'

Nadeau's brows rose. 'Maybe.'

'Maybe there was something in his past that caught up with him.' Eloise's eyes were alight now as she warmed to her subject. 'Maybe there was something he didn't want anyone to know about, so he found a way to make himself disappear.'

Nadeau was already shaking his head. 'None of the evidence indicates that there was anything for him to run from.'

'It doesn't really sound like the evidence has been that reliable, though. I mean, a lot of facts have seemingly evaporated, right?'

'You know, you make a good point...'

Eloise's chin raised in triumph. 'See? And you thought I'd be bored.'

'I stand corrected.' In truth, Nadeau had never attracted a girl like Eloise before, neither by mistake nor on purpose. But, now she was in front of him, and she was finally getting the wheels in his head turning again, which was a blessed relief after the roadblock he'd been battling with.

'Maybe you've got something there....' Nadeau sat back, rapping his knuckles on the counter. 'The past..... I'm not sure he was running away from anything, but I do wonder what forces might be related to his disappearance.' He was lost in thought for a moment.

When Nadeau looked back over at Eloise, it was to find her grinning.

'You find this funny?'

'No,' she laughed. 'I'm just glad that I finally got you to talk about your work. You're the hardest bachelor I've ever tried to crack open.'

Chapter 5

'Well,' Nadeau said, working to regain some of his previously solid front. 'I wouldn't say you've exactly cracked me open.'

Eloise's lids lowered as she studied him. 'I agree. I think there's still a great deal more work that I'd be happy to do in that area.'

Nadeau chuckled. He was glad he'd ventured out tonight. Eloise had helped clear his mind and maybe even his case, albeit just a little.

§§§

The road had become busier, with clusters of hamlets and larger villages more frequent as Lambert drew closer to Paris. His feet were aching from the uneven terrain of the dusty road. Pausing momentarily at the outskirts of a small hamlet, he pushed the pain out of his mind. He had walked further than a man more accustomed to cars, taxis and trains had any business to walk. He was also keenly aware of the waning light. Dusk was approaching, and he did not want to be on the road after dark. What he needed was an inn or an auberge where he could spend the night. Rumbling with hunger, his stomach wanted one of those things, too.

He spotted a larger building with stone walls on the ground floor and crude wooden planks on the second. The roof was well thatched. Outside the building was a sign displaying a smiling pig on a spit, an apple in its mouth. Some food at the very least, he thought, and every possibility of a bed for the night as well. He was nervous about entering, but his hunger was greater than his anxieties, so he walked up to the entrance and entered.

Inside the building, it was dark and cool. He stood in the doorway, letting his eyes adjust to the dark and his nose adjust to the cacophony of odours. What he saw was a large, open room with crude tables and stools. A few patrons were eating, and no one paid him much attention. Thank heavens he had changed his clothes.

'Yes? What do you want?' asked a man behind the main bar, presumably the innkeeper.

It was disrespectful, but at least it wasn't hostile. He said, 'I'd like to eat, and I'd like a room for the night.'

The innkeeper looked him up and down. Then he said, 'One livre for soup and bread and a room. There's an outhouse out back for your other needs.'

Lambert fished a half Ecu coin from his pouch and handed it over. The innkeeper walked over to the bar and laid ten small copper coins which, Lambert realised, were his change. He swept them into his hands and dropped them into his pouch. He had to believe that he was not being short-changed. Until he had a better understanding of the coinage, he didn't want to insult the man by counting his change in front of him. The innkeeper waved a hand towards the room. 'Sit wherever you want.'

There was a fireplace in the corner, and Lambert decided to sit near it. The day had not been cold, but it had been humid, and he wanted to feel the warmth of a fire.

A young woman dressed like the teenager he had seen earlier in the day put a wooden pitcher of water on the table. Her face was severely pockmarked from some long-ago affliction and gave him pause. She wore a bonnet, and her arms were completely covered by a simple white blouse. 'Will you be using your own spoon? Or do you need one from the kitchen?'

'I need a spoon, please.' Nervous though he was, he felt amusement at the idea that he might carry his own cutlery with him. He felt something else, too. Satisfaction. Here he was in 1774, and he was managing. He'd found somewhere to eat and somewhere to sleep, and he had not aroused suspicion. He was being accepted. What a story this would make when he found his way back to his own time!

The girl brought a dark hunk of bread on a simple ceramic plate. Nothing to spread on it, and no condiments – just a dry hunk of bread on a plate. A large wooden bowl of soup quickly followed. 'Bouillon de boeuf,' said the girl. Beef stew. It smelled delicious. Lambert had not realised just how hungry he was after walking all that way. And he would not be the only one. The farmer had said this was 1774, and that had been a time of great hunger among the ordinary people of France.

Louis XVI was on the throne, and the Revolution would not come to pass for another sixteen years. Taking solace from that thought, he turned his mind back to his study of France. There had been many reasons for the French Revolution, but the most important was class inequality. Too many poor people were working too hard for too little reward in order to support rich nobles and clergy.

The First Estate had been the ordained members of the Catholic Church from archbishops and bishops all the way down to parish priests, monks, Friars and nuns. They occupied a prestigious place in the social order. Belief in God, religion and the afterlife was deeply ingrained in the people and present in everyday life. The parish priest – the curé – baptised his flock, married them and buried them. He heard confessions and was in other ways, too, a central and integral figure in the lives of everyone. It was also the clergy who legitimised the King's divine right to rule.

Then you had the Second Estate, which contained the French nobility. Men and women with aristocratic titles, each of which conferred a different degree of nobility and established a person's rank in society. Court nobles were the closest to the King and had more prestige than nobles of the robe who got their usually inherited rank from the administrative or judicial position they held. Nobles of the robe did not have the right to call themselves Duc, Comte or Baron, but they had a great deal of influence.

The Nobles of the Sword were men from old families whose ancestors had fought for a King and been entitled in gratitude.

Finally after all that came the Third Estate, which was essentially, everyone else. They maintained the system through crushing taxes and various kinds of service they were obliged to deliver to the first two estates. Even here there was a pecking order with rich merchants and professional people holding a superior position to the simple peasant who worked on the land. It was a sobering thought for Lambert that his present position would put him squarely into the third estate with no useful skills and no influence. A man, in fact, who counted for nothing. He was going to have to think very carefully about how he conducted himself until he could find his way back to modern France.

Lambert had often thought, for purely professional reasons, about what could have been done to avoid the French Revolution. There hadn't, for example, been a revolution in England, even though their society was equally stratified and Lambert had always believed that there were two main reasons for this. One was that English people could raise their status.

It was known as 'raising yourself into the middling sort.' The rigid demarcations in France had not allowed this. And the second was that the government in England had taken more care to relieve the position of the peasant class so that they did not find themselves as completely crushed as their opposite numbers in France had been. The French poor had been invisible to those who might have helped them until it was far too late to prevent an explosion of discontent that would sweep the *ancient regime* away. Up to now, those thoughts had simply been an academic exercise. Now, in 1774, in France, they had a much deeper and more personal importance.

'All finished?' The maid's interruption dragged Lambert away from his thoughts.

'Yes. Thank you. It was good.'

'Is there anything else you want from the kitchen?'

'Would there be a pastry on offer?'

The maid laughed, and Lambert realised that he had committed a faux pas. Pastries were luxury items, and it might be some time before he could again enjoy one. The maid said, 'Let me show you to the room.'

He realised at that moment just how tired he was. He experienced a day of unfathomable events, overwhelming anxiety and a great deal of unaccustomed exercise followed by a good hot meal. The maid was right; it was time for sleep. He followed her upstairs to a simple room with a cot, a small wooden table, a stool and a bucket of water. There was an unlit candle on the table, and the maid showed him where he could light it if he needed light once the sun had gone down. Then she said, 'Is there anything else you require from me?'

Her eyes implored him. Her pockmarked face was flushed. Lambert was shocked to realise that she was offering herself, almost certainly out of desperation. He took from his pouch one of the copper coins the innkeeper had given him as his change and handed it to her. 'Thank you very much, Mademoiselle. You have been very kind and helpful, but tonight I wish to be alone.'

She demurely took the coin, thanked him and left the room, no doubt relieved not to be required to deliver an intimate service in exchange for the money.

And now Lambert was alone. His mind was tired. Everything he had seen, heard and smelt since he woke in that field had been alien to him. It had all taken its toll. He slumped onto the cot. He took out the copper coins and counted them again. Nine, after he had given the 10th to the maid. If half an Ecu was one and a half livres, and he had received ten sous in change, then half an Ecu must be worth about thirty sous. He would have to be careful with his money because he knew just how much help the state would provide to a penniless peasant. None whatsoever. That was one of the factors that had led to the Revolution. He was alone in this strange world, with no one to help him and no support system. He locked the latch on the door, took off his shoes and lay down on the cot. Still fully dressed, he fell quickly into a deep sleep.

HE WOKE WITH A START. SOMETHING HAD WOKEN HIM – some sound. But what? The answer came quickly. It was nature's alarm clocks – roosters – four or five of them so far as he could tell. Dawn must have broken. He looked around. He had been undisturbed throughout the night. Everything was in its place, his money pouch still at his waist, and he experienced relief as he put his shoes on once more and used the water from the bucket to wash off some of the grime from the previous day. He was conscious of a body smell he was not used to, but he found a certain solace in the knowledge that he would fit in better if he were as generally unwashed as the other people he was encountering. His teeth felt fuzzy, and breath stank from the previous night, he used a corner of his shirt to rub his teeth and rinsed out his mouth with some of the leftover water from his bucket. 'I'll have to get a toothbrush.' thought Lambert.

Descending the staircase from the rooms of the auberge, he spotted the maid from the previous evening, waiting on tables as well as the innkeeper, still behind the bar. He was offered a small piece of cheese and a small piece of bread and shown the door. This was not the kind of hospitality he was used to in European hotels, but he understood the sentiment. He was no longer a paying guest, and he had to make way for the next client who would come wandering in from the road.

HE HAD SPENT THE WHOLE OF THE PREVIOUS DAY in a state of anxiety, sometimes mild and sometimes overwhelming but always there. And now? He was surprised to find that what he felt now was closer to excitement. He set off on the way to Paris with a spring in his step. Paris. He would have an opportunity to see the city as it was before the revolution. How could any historian ask for more? He could drink in the atmosphere and see what the place looked like before Haussmann and his ilk changed it to be more like Paris of modern times.

The road as he approached the outskirts of the city was still unpaved and littered here and there with animal refuse. Keeping his shoes clean was a challenge, and he wondered about his earlier decision to hold onto them. This environment would bring about their rapid ruin.

But there were more important things to think about. The people he encountered on the road were haggard, often wearing nothing but threadbare rags that had been patched and patched again. Lambert couldn't help but notice the speed with which they moved. Everyone rushed about as if time was extremely valuable. Some of the better-dressed people, it was true, were less rushed and strolled about as if gawking at the sights and sounds of the chaos.

One thing he noticed was that they enjoyed the day and talked among themselves and for the most part ignored the poorer citizens, however much the poorer outnumbered them, as though they simply failed to see them. Men and women carried baskets of every kind of merchandise – bread, vegetables, wood and many other things that a big city would demand daily. He was struck by a large number of women carrying buckets of water.

The result, presumably, of the lack of indoor plumbing. And every space was occupied by men and women selling odds and ends in what to him seemed overwhelming chaos but, to the citizens of the day, was presumably the normal state of affairs.

He approached what he thought must be the Gate of St Denis and his eyes fell on the city as it had once been. St Denis was one of the oldest streets in Paris, there were, of course, no cars. A lot of people were walking about, far more than he had seen so far, and a few horse-drawn carts wound their way through the crowd. The buildings were smaller and lower than he was used to; they were made mostly of wood though some had stone foundations. Buildings more than three stories tall were the exception.

He spent most of the morning making his way along St-Denis, past sites he could barely recognise from his own era. It was remarkable how the city had changed. There was a cemetery next to the fountain of the innocents that he knew wasn't there in his era. The fountain itself, still a landmark in his era looked very different, having been moved and rebuilt several times after the late 1700s.

The smell of the area was overpowering. A small wall behind the fountain barely hid what was obviously a large outdoor cemetery. Stopping to purchase a small kerchief, and a bunch of dried flowers from a street vendor, he emulated much of the street population and pinned the dried flowers on his vest while keeping the kerchief close at hand to cover his nose and mouth throughout the worst of the stench. Resigned, he carried onwards towards his ultimate goal of reaching the Latin Quarter or fifth arrondissement, the quarter where he lived and worked before that fateful train journey. As he plodded on, avoiding the occasional fast carriage that barrelled through the streets without regards for the safety of the pedestrians, he was happy to see several familiar landmarks, mainly on one of the two islands of Paris, Ile de la Cité. As he walked across the island, he stopped in front of the Palais de la Cité and the famous prison of La Conciergerie. Taking a moment to drink it all in, he was continually amazed by the way the city had changed in two and a half centuries. He was witnessing the construction of buildings that in his own era were considered old.

At last, he came to the Sorbonne, his place of employment in the modern era, where it stood even at that time. It comforted him to think that he knew its halls and rooms, and he had a strong desire to explore it, but he knew what a mistake that would be. His appearance would forbid it. He looked like a common peasant, and a common peasant would never, at that time in French history, be allowed entrance to such a building.

Instead of exploring the Sorbonne, His thoughts turned to the present, and he decided that he had better take care of his immediate needs. He bought a cheap and quick lunch from a street vendor and asked if the man knew of any rooms to let in the neighbourhood. The vendor directed him to a building not far from the Hotel de Cluny. *Cluny.* The name brought back the memory of a museum of his own time, though today it was just a tower. Unsure exactly what it was being used for, he passed the tower and looked for the building described by the man who had sold him his lunch. Finally, he knocked at the door.

'Yes?' came a voice from inside.

'I'm here about a room for rent,' said Lambert, noticing how once again the honorific monsieur was absent in words, in tone and civility. It was clearly due to his appearance. Yesterday morning his clothes had caused him to be taken for a noble. Today they did not.

The door was unlocked and out came a middle-aged man, short and slightly balding, who examined Lambert from head to foot. 'What are you looking for?'

'A simple room for rent. I'm new to the city, and I don't know how long I'll be here.'

CHAPTER 5

'Ten livres a week, payable in advance every Sunday.'

Lambert knew he was in no position to negotiate, but said he'd like to see the room first. The man led him up two flights of stairs and down a very dark hallway to a room at the back. It was simply furnished with a small cot for a bed pushed against the far wall, a chair and a small table, a chest at the foot of the bed and a sort of wardrobe.

The man said, 'The rent includes daily delivery of water. You share the commode with the four other rooms on the floor. It's one of those doors we passed in the corridor. Now, listen. I don't know you, and you weren't introduced to me by anyone I know, but I'll take a chance on you. Give me any trouble at all, and you'll be on your way. I want only hard-working tenants, and I won't stand for requests for charity from the likes of you.'

Lambert nodded and was given a small copper key for the door to his room and a smaller key for the chest. In return, he handed over what he thought was ten livres. As far as he could tell, that was about half his remaining money. He needed to find a way to earn some more funds and fast.

'Thank you,' said the man, visibly relieved at Lambert's ability to pay. My name is Jacques, and my wife's name is Aurélie. You may see her from time to time cleaning the halls and common areas. She'll clean your room if you want her to, but that's an extra charge.'

Lambert thanked him again and asked if there were any job opportunities in the area. Jacques told him most employment that was available was on the right bank in the first arrondissement and not there in the fifth. He left Lambert alone with his thoughts in a room that was drab and impersonal and not at all what Lambert was used to. It was, though, at least for a short time, his own.

STEPPING OUT THE NEXT MORNING TO THE SIGHTS, THE SMELLS AND THE PEOPLE were almost overwhelming. Lambert's shoes were being ruined by all the animal refuse he kept stepping in, and his nerves were increasingly frayed by the amount of begging and human suffering he witnessed on the streets. He wouldn't have called himself particularly religious, but he did have a deep-seated conviction that people were entitled to receive respect and consideration, whatever their station in life and no-one should be allowed to starve. That was a view that he knew was common enough in twenty-first-century France, but it did not hold in the time of Louis XVI.

As an academic, grotesque inequality and appalling poverty were familiar to him as causes of a violent and bloody uprising, but still little more than headline notes for a lecture. As a peasant walking the streets of 1774 Paris, they were real and in his face. Again and again, he had the thought: why did no one do anything about it while there was still time? Was intervening to help the desperately poor really so unthinkable?

Wandering the city, He kept his eyes open for basic necessities he might require. Some extra clothes, something that he could adapt as a toothbrush and toothpaste. Clean rags to wash with. Essentially everything he felt he might need to survive while maintaining basic hygiene. As he walked about, he observed the people in their daily lives bustling here and there in a frenzy of apparent economic activity – an economic war that most of them were destined to lose. There did not seem to be many leisure pursuits. He took the time while wandering to reflect on the troubles ahead for the people of France. Devastating famines. Immense economic hardships. The state was deeply in debt, but that was something that ordinary people knew very little about.

It would not be true to say that the populace was still completely quiescent, for pamphleteers roamed the streets distributing provocative words to anyone who would accept the pamphlet – but very few did. The ones who had the most to gain couldn't read. Those who could read didn't seem to care. Each day, the news was filled with overheard discussions about complaints of price control on grain. It seemed the King's Minister of Finance, Monsieur Joseph Marie Terray, had introduced price controls on grain to make it easier for the common people to afford bread but the Law of Unintended Consequences had played its part once more, and the result of the price controls had been hoarding and profiteering on the black market. The people who had been intended to benefit from cheaper bread found instead that it was completely beyond their ability to afford. The atmosphere was tense.

Lambert, of course, knew all about Terray. The man was, by the French standards of the time, a radical financial reformer. He had put forward some really first-class ideas, or so Lambert considered them, but he had run up against the resistance of the nobility which, in the end, had inevitably influenced the King.

His successor, Anne Robert Turgot would carry the reform flame, and If this had been a lecture at the Sorbonne, Lambert would have said that it was a great pity because if the proposed reforms had taken root, they would have eased the French people's suffering. They would also have improved productivity because Turgot believed – and Lambert agreed with him – that too many lands owned by the nobility were left fallow. En chaume was the French expression. Putting more land into cultivation would have increased the availability of food and reduced its price, but it would also have reduced the nobility's hunting grounds and the land where they pursued leisure activities. The nobility had the ear of the king and people who were starving for want of bread did not.

Perhaps the hardest part of Lambert's walks around the city was the sight of so many small children begging for the means of survival. When a young girl of seven or eight years of age, dressed in what could generously be called rags, her feet bare and calloused from years of neglect, her hair knotted and unkempt, held out her hand, palm up, and said, 'Un sou, monsieur?'

It would have been so easy to drop a coin into the outstretched hand. The result, though, would simply have been that he would be mobbed by more begging children. He had little enough money as it was. He certainly didn't have enough to relieve the poverty of every child in danger of starvation.

Through all this, he couldn't get out of his thoughts the misery and death that the revolution would bring in its wake. Not just the great political and class purges. Not just the mass executions of the revolutionaries. That was bad enough, but it was dwarfed by the effect of the wars Napoleon would fight in the revolution's aftermath.

He shuddered at the thought. Military deaths were estimated at between two and a half million and three and a half million soldiers, but the number of civilians who died, mostly from famine and disease, was anywhere between 750,000 and 3 million. Terrifying numbers when you realised that the population of France at the time was less than ten million, and Spain, Portugal and England were all smaller, though, in the end, it would be the English and the Prussians who, together, delivered the coup de grace to Napoleon at Waterloo.

And so, probably inevitably, the thought came to him. You're an educated man, Lambert. These people around you don't know that, but you are. Given the explosion in knowledge in the nineteenth and twentieth centuries, you probably have more knowledge and information stored in your head than any person in France, however, educated and however high in the social scale. There is a disaster coming, you know it's coming, and you know why it's coming.

'So what are you going to do about it?' he murmured to himself under his breath.

You don't know whether you'll ever get back to your own time. You do know that if you're still in Paris in this era when the revolution arrives, your life will be in grave danger, just as everyone else's will be. So doing something to fend off revolution isn't just about altruism. It's about self-preservation.

And so preventing the revolution became his raison d'être. Something or somebody had arranged to transfer him here with all the knowledge he possessed. Was it conceivable that that had been done for no reason? The more he thought about it, the less prepared he was to answer that question with the word 'Yes.' There must be a reason he was here, and it must be to improve the lot of the people and nation of France.

As Lambert Settled into his small, rented room for the night, he found himself wishing for a few of the comforts of the modern world. Access to a hot shower on demand was at the top of his wishlist along with a brand of beer he recognised and a TV for watching the evening news. There wasn't a mirror in the room, so he wasn't able to look at his reflection, but he was sure that if he looked half as grimy as he felt he'd wish for a shower all the more. Getting a bath prepared was quite the project and had to be scheduled in advance. He turned to the washbasin to clean his hands and face. It was all he could do at the moment when it came to clearing his skin of the endless dirt and muck on the streets. He'd taken to leaving his footwear outside the door because of the odour the soles of his shoes had accrued. It was nearly impossible to rid them of the smell of animal urine and faeces, but at least he could wash his body, at least partially.

Once tolerably clean, Lambert settled down in bed. There was nothing he could do about his craving for a familiar beer or TV, so he took to thinking. There was a lot of time to do that in an era that offered little in the way of entertainment.

Lambert stared at the ceiling, his mind meandering back to his earlier stroll down the destitution-lined streets. If there truly was a bigger purpose for his transportation backward, surely the knowledge he possessed should be used to help the people of this less fortunate time. There was much he could offer to them in the way of practical comfort, cleanliness, efficiency, all things that he'd taken for granted in modern times. If he was to be here for any length of time, it was only right he should offer help in these areas.

Then there was the vastly more important aspect that he had the ability to offer insight on. Lambert was not a stupid man. Every time he reached this point in his musing, he told himself not to be so grandiose. Avoid the revolution? Save the people of France from the stupidity of the Estates? Him? How? He also knew the danger inherent in this line of thinking. He was a student of history, and you could not study history without being aware of the mayhem that had devastated the lives of so many humans as a result of a dream of nobility and glory on the part of one individual.

Enough, Lambert, he told himself, sitting up in bed, his own thoughts making him suddenly restless. Put it behind you. What he needed was a job that would sustain him during this time here, however long that could be, not a dream of grandeur. And he needed it fast. Fast as in 'now.'

He didn't have the kind of skills that were in demand among 18th-century employers. Okay; maybe he could start a business. But to start a business, you needed capital, and he had none.

He glanced at his watch, the Breguet he had inherited from his father. If his situation became sufficiently dire, he could sell it. He baulked at the thought. His father had been an avid horologist, and this Breguet had been the centrepiece of his collection. In the modern era, it would be worth well over twenty thousand euros. But now? In any case, the financial value of the thing was unimportant compared with its sentimental value. If it came to the point where it was; sell the watch or starve to death, he would probably bow to reality. But not otherwise.

Lambert tucked it safely away, thinking that this was for the best since wearing it would attract a great deal of suspicion and attention.

So what was he going to do?

And then the thought came to him that, whatever kind of job he got, he would probably find himself spending at least 40% of his earnings on food. So why not look at the food business for employment? It wasn't completely ridiculous. He had put himself through college working in several restaurants. He was fairly confident in his ability to prepare food for cooking. So where were the establishments that could use him? Resolving to pursue this course of action, he settles back down, at ease that a path lay in front of him.

Waking up the next morning, and without any semblance of a formal plan, he walked along the left bank of the Seine river. Crossing the Seine on the Pont Royale to the right bank, he inquired to passing people that would give him the time of day as to some of the better eating establishments were.

Eventually, he wound up at a food hall – something the French called a Table d'Hôte or host's table. Situated at 10 Rue des Bailleul on the corner of Rue Jean Tison, the location did not stir any modern memories.

The neighbourhood had changed too much from his own time.

Careful inquiries revealed that it was owned by a man called Roze de Chantoiseau. Situated inside the Hôtel Schomberg d'Aligre, it had a few things that appealed to Lambert: proximity to power, great visibility and lots of foot traffic. The hotel was a stone's throw from Perrault's Colonnade, the eastern-most face of the Louvre Palace.

He went in and asked for an opportunity to show his skill at chopping vegetables and preparing food. The kitchen manager looked him up and down, pondered a moment as if in reflexion and eventually gave him a knife and some vegetables to cut. Lambert, unsure as to exactly how the kitchen manager wanted the interview to start waited until he was told him to get on with it in a rather curt fashion. When he had done that to the kitchen manager's satisfaction, he was given some meat to de-bone. It was nothing he hadn't done before, and he did it to the manager's satisfaction, leaving on the bone not a single scrap of edible meat. The manager smiled and immediately offered a wage together with free food during the working day. Lambert gratefully accepted the offer. Working at Roze's hall would keep him from starving and allow him to advance his agenda.

And he'd be able to pay the next week's rent, which was just about to fall due.

CHAPTER 6

For Nadeau, too, it was the end of the first week since the 'incident.' In his case, it had been yet another week of dead ends and frustration. He closed his laptop and ran in his mind through everything that had happened.

The Canadians had been no help whatsoever. They had no record of ever having issued a passport to Jonathan Lambert. They had issued a passport with the same number but to a thirty-two-year-old woman from a small town in Quebec. He had checked the entry stamps with the Direction Centrale de la Police aux Frontières, and that was another dead end. As far as they were concerned, no Jonathan Lambert had entered France anywhere, and certainly not at Charles de Gaulle Airport on the date his entry stamp indicated.

Then there was his Visa credit card. The account did not exist. The number embossed on the card in Lambert's wallet was genuine all right, but the person who held that card was a French national living in Nîmes, and the card was issued by a French bank.

As for the Université-Sorbonne, they confirmed that every student's name on the term papers in Lambert's possession were the names of actual history students. But that lead went no further because not a single one of the students acknowledged having written the paper with his or her name on it. Some of them, upon close inspection, said that the paper was written in a style similar to theirs, but they still denied having written it. And did they have a History Professor called Jonathan Lambert from Canada? They did not.

Nadeau thought back to the dimly lit bar and the theory he and Eloise had begun to fabricate as he sat in a semi-intoxicated haze. Most likely, if he hadn't been slightly drunk, he never would have considered an idea as preposterous of some enigmatic link to the past. But, in light of the fact that he had literally nowhere to go when he pondered all other possibilities made thinking outside of the box not seem quite so ridiculous. At this point, he had to be at least a little open to a less-than-straight-forward explanation for all of this as the typical avenues offered him no answers whatsoever.

And now his reverie was interrupted. 'How goes it, Inspector Nadeau?' Nadeau did not need to look up to know that the question came from his direct superior and unit director.

'Sir, I am completely at a loss over the missing person, Jonathan Lambert.' He took care to modulate his tone; it did not pay to let the director know that you were becoming frustrated. He'd been known to take a case away and give it to someone else. 'For the sake of your sanity,' would be his explanation, but no one took it as anything other than a statement of no confidence.

'The train passenger?'

'Yes, sir. Dead ends whichever way you look. Our government, the Canadian government, the Sorbonne, the credit card companies, the hotel – not one of them has ever heard of him. He's a ghost.'

'A foreign agent, then? He'd have to be, to have that good a cover story and documentation of that quality.'

'You'd think so, sir, wouldn't you? And that has certainly been in my mind as the only logical explanation. But the level of the cover story is greater than anything I've ever seen. The guy had taxi receipts and lunch receipts paid for with a Visa card that doesn't exist. Who goes to that sort of length to create a cover story?'

'Well. Look on the bright side. No one was injured. There was no loss of property. And if the man is planning an atrocity in this country, we can't intervene because we don't know where he is.'

'No, sir. That's the problem with missing persons – you don't know where they are.'

The director eyed Nadeau coldly, as though suspecting that the man was making a joke at his expense.

Nadeau mentally kicked himself for letting his feelings show. 'Perhaps we'll get lucky, and it'll turn out to be London he's planning to blow up,' said the director, 'In any case, we have new cases coming in every day, and I need you to work on some other files for me. If there are no real leads on this guy, you'd better wind that investigation down.'

'Drop it?' Nadeau kicked himself again. He'd only said that because he knew the director would not want to be the person who'd dropped a case if it later turned out to be a terrorist atrocity.

'Did I say drop it? No, Nadeau, of course, you don't drop it. Just push it a little way down the priority list. Okay?'

Nadeau nodded, the idea causing him frustration and relief at the same time. He wanted this case solved now. After all of the agony it had inflicted upon him already, the idea of leaving it unsolved, hanging over his head was aggravating. However, perhaps it was good to turn his attention to something else for a time before his inadequacy in this situation reduced him to a complete wreck.

Speaking of turning his attention to other things, a few moments after his unit director left his office, his personal cell phone rang. It was Eloise.

'Hi Eloise. How goes it?'

'Fine. How are you?'

'Fine.'

CHAPTER 6

'Uh-ah.'

'What do you mean by that?' Nadeau could hear the smile in Eloise's voice even through the telephone.

'I haven't known you for that long, Nadeau, but you're a pretty rotten liar. Let me guess: You haven't eaten since breakfast, and you've been staring at your computer for the past, oh, four to five hours straight. Now, tell me I haven't hit it right on the head.'

'You haven't hit it right on the head,' Nadeau answered, spitefully even as guilt set in. He glanced at his watch and realised he had missed lunch and there was no denying that his eyes felt like sandpaper from looking at his laptop.

'Yeah, sure.' Eloise's tone made it clear that she was buying none of it.

'In truth, I've been told to put the case aside for a time. Or at least not give it so much of my energy,' Nadeau said.

'Good. Then it's time for you to get some proper nourishment. You're coming to dinner with me.'

Much as he hated to admit it, Nadeau's indifference toward Eloise had lessened a great deal since their encounter in the bar, and he was shocked to find that he even enjoyed her company. It was a rare phenomenon for a man who usually never saw a woman more than once.

Nadeau heard himself agreeing. He had the feeling that an intelligent conversation with an exciting woman would be just the thing.

§§§

DE ROZE'S HALL WAS A SIMPLE AFFAIR. People arrived at a set time and paid a set amount of money to be seated on a stool at one of many long tables in a communal hall. They were given a bowl of whatever the kitchen manager had chosen for the menu that day. It was a true table d'hôte, and if the patrons did not like that day's menu, they could simply go to another hall serving something else.

Lambert worked long and hard to impress his fellow workers. He set out to complete every task given him to the highest possible standard while taking no longer than he absolutely had to. The other kitchen workers liked the way his work made theirs easier, and he had the respect of the kitchen manager. When Lambert came up with ideas to speed the preparation of the bouillons and casseroles, he listened.

And through all this, Lambert thought about the process at work and how it could be improved. There were still in what he continued to think of as 'his' era places that operated in a very similar way. Go deep into rural France – the France that Parisians referred to as 'la France profonde' and for which they claimed to have immense respect as the true soul of France while mostly taking care not to go there – and you would find places where the locals went for lunch and sat down to eat whatever the *chef-patron* had decided should be on the menu that day. But there was also a huge variety of different kinds of restaurants and Lambert could not rid himself of the thought that bringing 'today's' restaurant ideas to 1774 France would be likely not only to meet with approval but also to boost profits.

He decided that he was going to suggest changes to the restaurant's owner, de Roze. He knew, though, that was not something he could do as simply as he might have done it in the 21st-century. His work was in what was known in 'his' time as a veg prep. That might not place him on the same, lowest, level of staff as the *plongeur* whose job it was to wash pots, pans, plates and cutlery, but he was not a great deal higher. This was a France that paid close attention to minute gradations in social levels. De Roze would not welcome an approach as any sort of equal. It might even get Lambert fired, and God knew there were plenty of people ready to take his place. When he arrived one morning and saw the owner sitting at a table at the back of the room counting receipts, he held his hat in his hand and approached diffidently to ask whether the man had a moment he could spare.

'Sit down,' barked de Roze, and went on looking at his receipts. Lambert took a seat, knowing that even being invited to do so was a positive step. It implied at least some level of regard. He waited for de Roze to finish what he was doing.

The man looked up. 'Out with it. I pay you to work, not to sit and watch me counting receipts.'

Lambert began by thanking him for his employment. 'Monsieur,' he said. 'I have an idea for your establishment that I believe might please your customers.' He had wanted to say 'our establishment' and 'our customers' but that might have been seen as unacceptably presumptuous.

De Roze looked at him. 'Go on.'

'Every day, some customers enter the hall, learn what we are serving and leave.'

'That's right. What do you expect? Our choice for that day's menu is not what they are looking for.'

'Yes, Monsieur. Exactly. People have different tastes, and you lose them to other halls. If they like it there, they may not come back here.'

He had the man's attention. No one likes to lose business to the competition. 'So what are you suggesting?'

'What if you offered choices? A menu on a card, from which, if they did not like one item, they could choose another?'

'On a card? Sounds preposterous to me. How could we make that work?'

Lambert described the innovations he had been thinking about. Changing the preparation of food to simplify the offer of a multiple-choice menu. Breaking up the large tables to smaller tables where customers could enjoy at least a modicum of privacy. Perhaps put a candle on every table to extend the hours of service and, turn over the table twice in an evening. Taking a deep breath, he suggested that de Roze might even like to think about investing in linen for the tables. 'If you make the experience of dining a little fancier, you might attract a more affluent clientele. People who have more money, which they can share with you, Monsieur.'

There was no change in de Roze's expression to suggest what he thought about Lambert's suggestions to convert his business model to an 'a-la-carte' one, but Lambert knew that he had been listening closely. He sat deep in thought for a while. Then he said, 'No one else is doing anything like that.'

'No, Monsieur. You would be the first. A completely new market. Every other hall, every other eating place would look second rate compared with this.'

De Roze nodded. 'I will think about what you have suggested. It seems innovative, yet simple. And now, perhaps you'd like to go to the kitchen and do what I'm paying you for.'

'Thank you, Monsieur.' As Lambert walked away, de Roze called after him in a voice loud enough for the whole staff to hear. 'Whether I follow your ideas or not, Lambert, I'm very happy with your performance. Keep up the good work. And the good ideas.'

§§§

A FEW DAYS WENT BY, AND THEN DE ROZE asked Lambert to implement the changes he had proposed. He was given a budget for the changes and told to break apart the tables and refit them as he had described. The kitchen manager was not entirely delighted with Lambert's new status and occasionally questioned these innovations, but all could see that the changes Lambert was making would save time and effort. Lambert went on suggesting ideas, like putting up a menu board with multiple choices. At first, all of the dishes were simple, but as the staff got used to the new system, they became more complex and varied. Lambert was at pains to make it seem that the ideas had come from the kitchen team rather than from him alone. Twenty-first century HR management in an autocratic century environment – but it worked.

And so did the innovations. Lambert knew that that was the most important factor. More customers were coming to the restaurant, they were coming more often, and they were spending more money. However hard Lambert worked to make it clear that this was a team operation, the person who mattered was de Roze, and de Roze knew who was at the root of his improved prosperity.

Meanwhile, Turgot, the King's newly minted finance minister, started to press his reforms and his reforms continued to have results other than the ones intended. It became increasingly difficult to source some of the basic necessities for the menu that Lambert wanted to have in place, and he found himself limiting the menu to compensate for the lack of basic provisions.

When Lambert had first woken in the field, he'd been able to remember nothing about his journey backwards in time. He knew he had been travelling on a TGV. He knew where he'd been, he knew why he'd been there, he knew where he was going. And then, with an apparent loss of time that he recognised only because his watch had stopped, he had been in a field by a road that knew nothing of railways and nothing of motor traffic. And that was all he could remember.

Not much more had returned to him in the weeks following, but there was one new memory. A blue light. A blue curtain or screen of some kind. He had a clear recollection of passing through something blue immediately before he was dumped into oblivion. But what it was, he had no idea.

He even begged approval from de Roze to take two days off work and, leaving on Sunday morning and returning late Monday evening, he travelled back to the road where he had first found himself. He was searching for a blue curtain, but he searched in vain. And yet, he was certain that he had seen it and equally certain that it held the key to his translation back to 1774.

All through that summer, he spent long days working at the restaurant to pay his rent and in the evenings he visited public reading rooms. If any of the other readers wondered how it came to pass that someone who was clearly one of the Third Estate's more lowly members was able to read a newspaper, no one ever mentioned it. What he was searching for was any mention of a blue light. There was nothing. If anyone else had seen a blue curtain, they either hadn't mentioned it, or news of it had been suppressed.

He did read about other things, though. There were a number of reading rooms that carried French newspapers and one or two who also had the papers from London a few days after publication. The English papers carried stories of North America which, as a Canadian, he read with fascination. The news of events unfolding in the Americas was not only detailed but also accurate. What was in the French papers, on the other hand, was mostly propaganda sponsored by the state. There was, for example, very little reporting of the difficulties faced by the French people as a result of food shortages and widespread corruption. Lambert knew from his previous life, and from conversations whispered between people who trusted each other, that flour shortage riots had been a constant feature of 1774 France. If they were mentioned at all in the French papers, it was as a minor rebellion by agents of foreign powers that had been put down accordingly. It was reported that the government had imprisoned several rioters, and Lambert knew that that had been intended to set an example, but the damage had been done. People were now more at ease to demonstrate openly against the regime. The King and his courtiers might see that as a troublesome development; Lambert knew that it would turn out to be far more than that.

England, too, had its clique around its king, but the English newspapers were prepared to discuss events in a way that was impossible for any French editor. The people of Boston had thrown their tea party that previous December and in June the British Parliament had blockaded the port of Boston as a form of retaliation. If they had had any sense, which Lambert believed they had not, they would have known that this would cause resentment in everyone in Boston and not only in those who espoused ideas of revolution. The same, of course, was true in France but, while an English newspaper might say so, no French journalist could summon either the courage or the freedom to follow them. It amused Lambert to wonder whether, if he had been moved to 1774 Boston instead of France, he might have attempted to stop the American revolution. Almost certainly not, he thought – because whatever level of freedom was available in the modern world had stemmed from that event.

Pragmatism – that was the thing. In the province of his own birth, Quebec, the English King granted very special concessions. French landowners retained their rights under the French Civil Code. The huge majority of the population was both Roman Catholic and of French descent and the King had granted them generous concessions in order to placate them so that he could focus his attention on problems developing further south. He wanted to avoid a French rebellion in British North America while his redcoats struggled to overcome Washington's revolutionaries.

For Lambert, this ability to hear at first hand as they unfolded people talking about events that he had only been able to read about was a fascinating reward for a historian. As he walked home each evening from the reading rooms, where he had recorded in his diary the events that were happening together with notes from his academic memory of when the next events were expected, he began to formulate a plan. It was a rough plan, and he would have to work very hard to achieve the milestones, but he knew something needed to be done. This was a time of great social tension in France, and it would only get worse.

§§§

NADEAU HAD BEEN WORKING ON A PROPERTY CRIME. He'd completed the report, ticking the boxes necessary to close the case and refer it to the Juge d'Instruction, who would decide whether it should be brought to court. It was a satisfying feeling to close a case, and even more satisfying to know that he was ahead of his workload. He turned his attention to the brown banker's box under his desk. This was where the documents from the Jonathan Lambert case were stored, and Nadeau made a point of working on it from time to time and updating his report to say that he had done so. If Lambert surfaced somewhere as a terrorist, and the whole thing became a political hot potato, Nadeau did not want to find himself in a position where the Director could hang him out to dry. He had been told to push it down the list of priorities, but not to drop it. And that was exactly what he was doing.

He had contacted the provincial police force of Quebec and, in the usual Canadian spirit of cooperation, they had happily run the full family name and turned up a colossal number of Lamberts.

It was a popular name. The Lamberts were one of the oldest and most significant families of greater Europe and now of the Americas and Australia. 'He might as well have been called Smith,' muttered Nadeau.

Distracted by this line of thought, he started researching historical records of the family name and learned that the Lamberts had come to England with William the Conqueror and fought at the Battle of Hastings. Before that, they had owned land in

Normandy where they originally arrived as Viking Raiders around 940 AD. The earliest Lambert Nadeau had been able to get back to had been the first Count of Mons. Nadeau noted from one website the rumour that the Lambert line could be traced all the way back to Mark Anthony by way of Boadicea. 'And, no doubt, Old King Cole and an uncountable bunch of Kings of Europe,' he thought.

Well, what was the point of looking at the roots of the name? It could not, after all, be Lambert's real name. The only explanation for this man had to be that he had been the agent of a foreign power.

Not just any foreign power but one with the money and resources to craft a cover story so thorough that it would deter anyone from investigating it at length. Nadeau had seen enough movies to be able to imagine the government apparatus capable of fleshing out the back story for the thirty-something white male whose face stared back at Nadeau from his Canadian passport. It wasn't, though, only the amount of work that had gone into the creation of the non-existent Jonathan Lambert that bothered him. Any agent for whom a foreign power was prepared to spend that amount of time and money had to be engaged in a nefarious project of great impact and importance. No, Director, you're not going to dump this on me if it all turns to ratshit. And he updated the report on his laptop with his latest searches and thoughts before tossing the passport back into the box and returning his attention to his current workload.

CHAPTER 7

IT WAS THE FIRST WEEK OF SEPTEMBER 1774, and the changes in the restaurant had been in force for three months. Towards the end of a particularly busy day, de Roze asked Lambert to stay after the last service and join him at a table in the back of the restaurant.

'You have performed very well throughout the summer. Don't think it has gone unnoticed.'

Lambert had not known what to expect, but it had not been praise. 'Thank you, Monsieur. I have enjoyed the challenge.'

De Roze pushed his chair back and slid his right hand over his belly, something he did when he was relaxed and feeling content. 'I have an arrangement I'd like to propose that I think would benefit both of us.'

'Yes, Monsieur?'

'I'm thinking of opening another... Not another Hall... Another restaurant. Somewhere on Île Saint-Louis.'

Lambert liked the sound of that. It was an affluent part of the city which he knew well both from his explorations in modern Paris and in the Paris of this era

'I think that's the place where we could have a great opportunity to use the concepts and changes you have brought in. Perhaps we can even improve on the level of service, to attract more affluent customers. I've found a suitable location. My concern is not to lose what we've achieved here. So what I'm suggesting is that I promote you to be general manager of this restaurant. Instead of a salary, you would have one-quarter of all the profits. After expenses, of course.'

It was a generous offer. He'd only been employed by de Roze for about four months, and the man was putting a great deal of faith and trust in him.

'My son will keep the books and ensure that we go on being profitable.'

The son was a fair-minded boy, and Lambert did not believe he would be swayed by greed to reduce Lambert's share. 'Thank you, Monsieur. It's a very fair offer. Of course, I accept it.'

'A fair offer? You think so? Perhaps so, but the opportunity is one you have earned with a lot of hard work and some very good ideas. And you can stop calling me Monsieur. From now on, it's Mathurin. All right?'

CHAPTER 7

Inviting him onto a first name basis reinforced Lambert's sense of an elevation in status. He felt a degree of satisfaction.

'I would be pleased to do all I can to get your new restaurant up and running, Mathurin,' Lambert said, reaching out to shake his boss' hand.

De Roze gave him a firm handshake. 'Then we are agreed. I'm certainly glad you came in and asked for that job.'

'As am I.'

De Roze grinned. 'We'll talk more soon. As for now, we have customers to attend to.'

Lambert agreed, following De Roze out of the room, though his mind was still full with anticipation about the upcoming project. He couldn't wait to get started.

§§§

LAMBERT LAY AWAKE, LISTENING TO THE RUCKUS going on outside his window. The two men had been at their hollering for nearly half an hour. He sat up rubbing a hand over his face. The truth was, even if they were to cease their drunken arguing, it wasn't as if he was ready for sleep. His thoughts on the plans he and de Roze had been putting in motion for the new restaurant were on his mind 24 hours a day and practically 7 days a week. The progress they'd already achieved was great, but every detail continued to weigh on Lambert's mind. With all of the knowledge he'd brought back with him from modern times, he felt a particular responsibility not to let anything that would help things to run smoother slip his mind.

Lambert stood, knowing he wasn't going to be able to get back to sleep and took a walk to the window, looking out at the brawl that had now graduated to a fist-fight. Neither man was sober enough to do any real damage as the swings both men took were so far from hitting the target that it was doubtful there would be a real winner.

Lambert watched for a few more moments before walking back to his bed, absently reaching into the drawer where he kept his watch. He placed it on his wrist, missing it's constant and familiar weight. He laid back, holding it up to study the face. There were moments when he found himself missing the comforts and routine of his old life. But, the fulfilment that came from imparting all of the information that was only available to him due to his experience with modern times was not something he wished to trade. He had a purpose to fulfil here, he could feel it and had already seen it! There was still so much that he could do to help de Roze and even the city at large. Not wanting to rush things, he'd been holding back on some of the more radical menu ideas and innovations for the restaurant until a suitable time arrived. That suitable time, he reflected, was now upon him. It was time to dive into the purpose he was still discovering with full force.

THE FOLLOWING DAY, Lambert found himself seating a customer he had not seen before. Well dressed, clean-shaven, the man was clearly a bourgeois. He wore a fine coat and a small gold chain leading to one of his coat pockets was almost certain to be attached to a pocket watch.

'Good Day, Monsieur. We have several choices on our menu today. They are all displayed on the board over there, but shall I go over them with you?'

This was a practice he had adopted in case a customer should be illiterate. Lambert thought this man could almost certainly read, but you never knew and it was not wise to take outward appearances for granted. The customer, however, needed no assistance in reading the menu. 'I'll have the lamb stew and root vegetables, along with a glass of red wine from Bordeaux.'

Adding a choice of wine, and the place it came from had been a recent innovation. The restaurant had always served wine, but Lambert had moved in the direction of a wine list with several different choices where prices varied according to the quality of what was offered.

The intention had been to extract an extra sou of revenue here and there, and it had been immensely successful. De Roze had been surprised that people placed so much value in the ability to choose their wine but to Lambert, who had been accustomed to wine lists since he had first been old enough to drink alcohol, it was an obvious way to add a layer of sophistication to the service and to mark them out even further from other eating places.

In the early days, he would have said 'from the competition,' but right now he didn't think they really had any competitors.

'Very well, monsieur.' Lambert took the order to the kitchen and returned with a glass of wine while the dish was being prepared. He was about to walk away from the table when the man stopped him.

'Wait a moment! What is that on your wrist?'

'What?' Lambert asked. His heart dropped into his stomach when he realised that he was wearing the watch. He'd forgotten to take it off the night before after being caught up in musings of his old life. As a daily shower wasn't an option, he'd had no reason to take it off that morning.

'It's merely an item of jewellery I find attractive,' he said, working hard to sound nonchalant.

'Jewelry? It's a timepiece, isn't it?'

Improvising quickly, Lambert apologised to the customer saying that he was needed in the kitchen. Hurrying there, he felt a sense of danger about this customer and delegated a member of staff to look after the man for the rest of his meal. Sometime later, the employee approached Lambert. 'He wants to see you.'

Covering his anxiety as best he could, Lambert went back to the table.

'I want to talk to you about that timepiece,' said the man. 'If you don't agree to meet me, I shall lodge a complaint with the court.'

Anxiety had been replaced by something stronger. 'The court? For what purpose?'

'Meet me at the mathematics hall at Collège Mazarin tomorrow evening at half-past eight. If anyone tries to prevent you from entering, tell them you have an appointment with me.'

'But, Monsieur, you have still not explained why you want to meet me?'

'That is simple enough. I want you to explain how it comes about that you have on your wrist a timepiece on the face of which is my name and my signature. My name is Abraham-Louis Breguet. You can tell anyone who attempts to block your way at the University that you are there to see me.'

The two men stared at each other in silence. In the case of Breguet, the silence carried obvious overtones of threat. For Lambert, it was shocking. Then Breguet stood up, paid his bill and left.

LAMBERT ARRIVED AT THE MATHEMATICS HALL of Collège Mazarin early, not wanting to offend Monsieur Breguet or keep him waiting any longer than necessary. He had given careful thought to the impending encounter, trying to find an explanation that the clockmaker would find satisfactory. He had failed. For all that, and in spite of the worry that he could not help feeling, it felt good to be back in the University. Walking the hallways, he felt a sense of familiarity, almost as though he had returned to his own era. Had he indeed been in his own time, he would have googled Breguet to prepare himself with knowledge of the man and his background. As it was, he had to settle for the little he could remember. Breguet was, he knew, connected in some way to the nobility, but he was not certain of exactly how. He did know that over time, Breguet would frequent the court and be called upon to make watches both for high-powered figures of the *ancien regime* and, later, for members of Napoleon's court and entourage. If he failed to handle him carefully, the man could become a serious problem.

On the other hand, this meeting might also be the seed of an opportunity to increase his influence and make inroads into the task of changing French society. There was a delicate balance to be struck.

He entered the mathematics hall unchallenged. Evidently, the time of day allowed for a more relaxed attention to college security. Breguet was seated at a table, reading from a rather large book.

'Good evening Monsieur Breguet.'

'Ah, Monsieur Lambert.' Breguet closed his book, which Lambert now saw was about mathematics. 'You brought the timepiece?'

'Yes, Monsieur.' Lambert took the watch from his wrist and handed it to Breguet.

Breguet turned the watch over in his hand. He seemed astonished by the sophisticated technology it represented. 'How did you come to have this?

'It's an inheritance from my father.' So far, so true, but Lambert had no idea what direction the conversation might take.

'It's a very fine timepiece. I've never seen one so thin. I like the way it's attached to a strap to be worn on the wrist instead of in your pocket. Very convenient for the wearer.' He went on examining the watch. 'What I am most curious to know is how my name and signature happened to be on the face when I had nothing to do with its manufacture?'

Lambert was resolved to bluff. The truth was something he could resort to only when there was no alternative. 'I have no idea how my father came to own it. As I said, it was an inheritance. I was born and raised in Quebec. Perhaps you have family there in a similar profession, and my father bought this timepiece from them?' As he said it, he could see the disbelief on Breguet's face. Doubt that he would get away with this story intensified.

Breguet said, 'If this timepiece had another name on its face, perhaps. Or even if it was signed in another way. But this is the exact manner that I use of styling my signature, and the spelling is precisely the way I spell my name. Do you see the flair at the beginning of the letter B, and at the end of the letter T? That's how I sign. No, Monsieur Lambert, I'm afraid I don't think you are telling me the truth. Must I force it from you with another threat of denunciation? '

The situation was impossible. However it ended, whatever risk he ran, Lambert decided he had no choice but to come clean. Speaking very softly, he said, 'Monsieur Breguet. What I am about to explain you will find almost impossible to believe, but it is the truth. I ask you to keep an open mind until I am finished.' He went on to explain that he had been born in Montreal in Quebec in 1975.

Two whole centuries into the future. He watched Breguet's face carefully as he spoke, but the man scarcely reacted at all as Lambert explained how people lived in his era, how they worked, and how they spent their leisure time. He told him about the many innovations between now and then. He explained that people carried in their pockets computers attached to a web from which they could obtain information on almost any subject under the sun. He talked about automobiles, transportation, rockets that took men into outer space and eventually the moon, and aircraft. He described all of these innovations with such coherence and accuracy and delivered his description so quickly that Breguet must have realised the man speaking to him was either telling the truth or was a raving lunatic. 'The last thing I remember, I was travelling at more than three hundred kilometres per hour on a train. Then I woke up on a dusty road north of Paris.'

'Kilometres?'

And Lambert remembered that the metric system would not be introduced until Napoleon's time and tried to explain that it was a unit of distance that combined with time to give a measure of speed.

Breguet then wanted to know what a train was. As he went through his explanations, Lambert could see the conflict in Breguet's face.

It felt so good to confide in someone and share his story. It was several months since he had arrived here, and in all that time, he had had no opportunity to tell anyone the truth. He resolved to convince Breguet that the truth was what it was. Then came a flash of inspiration. 'Monsieur Breguet. Advances in the medical field in my era are remarkable. Take, for example, the practice of dentistry.' He went on to describe cavities in teeth which he knew was something Breguet would be familiar with, and then he described how a modern dentist would drill out the cavity and replace it with a filling made from a polymer or a resin. It was clear that Breguet was wondering where this conversation was going. 'Monsieur Breguet,' said Lambert. 'Look at my back teeth.' And he opened his mouth wide under the light falling from a small lamp.

Breguet peered inside. 'Remarkable. I have only seen teeth in that condition in small children.'

'Look more closely, Monsieur.'

And Breguet did, And he saw the fillings close to the back, neatly contoured to the teeth as it painted on. 'I see. The advances you describe are unimaginable. They speak of magic and sorcery or sophistication of science that I could never fathom. And yet, you have shown me two things to lend credibility to your story. Your teeth and your timepiece.'

'Yes,' said Lambert. 'It may please you to know that your house is very famous in my time. Your name is associated with luxury and prestige. Not many people can afford to own a timepiece with your name on it. Your descendants have done very well. It was fortunate for them that you did not lose your head to the guillotine.'

'Lose my head? To the what?'

Breguet looked shaken – shocked, in fact – and Lambert realised once again how easy it was to overstep the mark. Not for the first time since he had arrived in this era, he took a deep breath before plunging in. 'Monsieur Breguet. I sometimes wonder just how aware the better off people in this country are about the grain famines?'

'Grain famines? Well, I know things aren't always as good for everyone as they might be, but famines? That's pitching it a bit high, isn't it? I hope you're not one of those foreign agents we keep being warned about.'

'Monsieur. People in this country are starving. And by people in this country, I mean the majority. It seems to me that the biggest problem is that they are simply invisible to people who could make a difference. People like you, Monsieur. No,' he held up his hand as Breguet was about to speak, 'I really would like you to hear me out. Don't listen to me as a social commentator or a rebel – hear me as someone who has come back from the future and is able to tell you what the future looks like in France unless something is done. And by the future, I mean the very near future. Within your lifetime, Monsieur.' And he went on to describe how the people suffered under price reforms and speculation and aristocratic greed. How the protests would grow louder and more frequent. How a sentence from Marie Antoinette would enter the annals of history, imperishable for all time: 'If there is no bread, why don't they eat brioche?' How the protests would become an uprising that would lead to the overthrow of the King. And then the Terror, and the use of the guillotine to bring to an end the power and influence of the nobility and clergy. And all the time he talked about these things, he watched Breguet's face and saw the growing horror there. Quietly, he ended, 'You survive, Monsieur. But only just.'

Breguet's face was white. He seemed in the grip of fearful emotion. 'Please,' he whispered, 'leave me. Go. And do not return.'

Lambert hesitated. Was leaving the right thing to do? But then, what choice did he have? He picked up his watch, attached it to his wrist and turned towards the door. Once there, he took a last look at Breguet. The man was in a state of shock, sitting at the table in silent contemplation.

Lambert left him there.

IT WAS ABOUT A WEEK SINCE LAMBERT'S MEETING with Breguet in the mathematics hall, and he had not yet been denounced as a madman, a practitioner of divination or a devotee of some other black art. He had begun to relax. Knowing the extent of superstition among the people of this era and their belief in sorcery and witchcraft, Lambert knew what could happen if a person of authority accused you of having some sort of supernatural power. His anxiety, high at the beginning of the week, had begun to recede. What he focused on was improving the restaurant.

Every day, he walked from his rented room in the fifth arrondissement to his restaurant in the first. Every day, the walk reminded him of the constant threat of revolution. Single mothers starved on the street, begging for scraps of food or money.

Handicapped men crawled about or swung on their crutches telling anyone who would listen that they were veterans, they'd fought for France, and they deserved a place in society. The things he saw almost overwhelmed Lambert, who was not used to the sight of such grinding poverty. Raised in Canada and later living in modern-day France, he was used to a well-developed social safety net put in place to help the poor.

Well, thinking about it only went so far, and it certainly did no good. He had to start somewhere. And there was food at the end of every day that was going to be thrown out. Leftovers. Overripe vegetables set aside from the evening meals. Bread that was two days old. And so he instituted in 1774 France the soup kitchens of 1930s North America. The bread, the vegetables, the leftover soups and stews were stored and brought out the next day to be served free of charge to the itinerant and the poor of the quarter. He coached his staff to be polite and courteous to poor people arriving at the door. Eventually, they came to an understanding. The poor would eat a midday meal at no charge. In return, they agreed not to trouble Lambert's customers by begging in the evening anywhere near the restaurant.

It worked well. Lambert won the affection of the neighbourhood poor and, instead of facing a gamut of beggars, was greeted politely as he walked to and from his home. He felt safer now, walking backwards and forwards, knowing that he had friends on the street who were grateful for his generosity.

His clientele changed, and he found that he was getting more repeat business. He trained the staff to turn over tables more quickly with offers of 'early bird' dinners and late suppers at lower rates than dinners served during the main hours of operation.

French society tended to eat late, but some people always ate early, and he was succeeding in capturing both markets. Something else he succeeded in was attracting more members of the bourgeoisie. They talked to him as he seated them and from time to time, he was invited to a salon. Eventually, he decided to accept an invitation that came from the wife of one of his wine vendors.

But what happened at a salon? He didn't know, so he consulted with de Roze who told him to expect poetry recitals, talk about the arts, and discussions of politics and philosophy. De Roze warned him, at least for his first few salons, to keep political thoughts to himself so that the first impression he gave the bourgeoisie would not be controversial. And then he said, 'And I hope you're not thinking of going there dressed like that.'

If he'd thought about it, Lambert would have realised that he had taken several upward steps through society's strata and it was time to update his wardrobe. He went to see a tailor and ordered an outfit in preparation for the salon.

§§§

PHILIPPE BOLDUC, LAMBERT'S WINE VENDOR, lived in a part of Paris that was well to do but not overtly wealthy. The exterior of the townhouse was modest and unremarkable. It seemed to Lambert when he arrived for the salon that the man was making an effort not to seem too rich.

He entered the courtyard in a carriage he had hired for the evening. The servant who had been assigned front door duties took his hat and cane and led him through a large vestibule and main hall. A winding marble staircase with a polished dark wood bannister led up and off to the second floor. The walls, elaborately stuccoed and trimmed with gold leaf hosted some paintings depicting idyllic vineyards and farms. Against the walls stood small tables bearing richly appointed vases and statuettes. A few upholstered mahogany chairs stood in the entrance and at the base of the winding staircase was a large pendulum clock. Whatever efforts his host might be making to conceal the fact, it was evident that the wine business was booming.

The house valet led him upstairs and politely asked him his name. 'Lambert. Jonathan Lambert.' He knew the French had an interest in first as well as last names. Everything in this society was judged, from the type of carriage you rode in, the area of the city you lived in, to the clothes you wore – and names were also important. What your parents gave you as your given name and what your surname was conveyed a great deal of information.

The valet opened the double doors and called out, 'It is my pleasure to announce the arrival of Monsieur Jonathan Lambert!'

He walked in, self-conscious and self-aware. There were about thirty people in the large room standing in groups of three and four spread out among musical instruments, tables, statues and divans. The buzz of conversation dropped for a moment as people stopped talking to each other to look at Lambert. He nodded a greeting to one or two people he recognised from among his clientele, and the air of animated discussion resumed. 'Monsieur Lambert.' Someone was calling him from behind. He turned to see a young man, neatly dressed and with a powdered wig who looked like the kind of young man who grew up surrounded by wealth. 'May it please you, I shall introduce myself. I am Jérôme Pétion de Villeneuve.'

A noble. His name ended with the nobility participle in front of his nom de terre, or 'name of the land.' He was from Villeneuve. France had a number of Villeneuves, a name which merely meant 'new town' though new could mean any time in the last eight hundred years, and so it was not immediately clear to Lambert where exactly in France the young man came from.

'I am pleased to make your acquaintance, Monsieur,' said Lambert, bowing a little and touching the front lock of his hair as was the convention.

'It is a good group tonight. Madame Bolduc has assembled philosophers and poets to provide our intellectuals with stimulation. Who knows? We may even witness a good debate on ways French society can be improved.'

He waited, clearly hoping for some reaction, but Lambert had been warned by Roze to keep his politics close to his chest and simply nodded.

'I understand,' said de Villeneuve, 'that you have set up a distribution of food to the poor? That is a fine example to set in our city. More people need to see the poor as a challenge to be addressed and not simply a scourge to be ignored. Is there some theological influence that generated this interest in you?'

It was true that the clergy was usually responsible for distributing food to the poor when they ever got round to it, and so it was not unreasonable for this young man to wonder whether Lambert was influenced in his actions by the church's teachings. 'No,' said Lambert. 'I simply tired of the poor begging from my clients as they came and went from my establishment. I feed the poor, and they make life easier for my customers by staying away in the evening. I already have the staff and the facilities, and the food we serve them would otherwise have gone to waste and so it costs us very little.'

'I understand, Monsieur Lambert. But, believe me, your actions have not gone unnoticed. Your reputation grows, and that brings opportunity as well as challenges. There may be people who wish to take advantage of a successful businessman like you.' He gave Lambert the easy grin of a man who had never known want. 'That is why I introduced myself to you. For, you see, I am a lawyer, and I hope soon to be an advocate.'

Now Lambert understood. A young man wanting to make his mark and seeking out successful men by trolling salons. In effect, cold calling. He suppressed a smile. Ambulance chasers were the same everywhere and in every time.

'Your reaction suggests that you appreciate my introduction, Monsieur Lambert?'

'Of course. One never knows when one might need legal counsel.'

Villeneuve handed Lambert a card on which was printed his name and an address, and Lambert chastised himself inwardly for failing to have had his own cards printed.

The handing out of cards as a means of introduction had begun during the reign of Louis XIV. It began as a polite way of requesting a meeting and applied to women as well as men.

The etiquette around the calling card was handed down from the French court and the rules for its use were both sophisticated and rigid. He must get some. 'I'm sorry,' he said. 'I don't have a card myself. My establishment is on Saint Honoré. You will find it under the sign de Roze.'

'Ah, yes. I know it. De Roze. He is your partner? How is he? I have not seen him for some time.'

'He is well. He is working on the construction of a second restaurant along the same lines as the establishment I run.'

'Well, Monsieur Lambert, if ever I can be of assistance, please don't hesitate to call on me. You have my office address; if I am absent, please leave word with my secretary.'

'Thank you, Monsieur. I shall certainly not forget you.'

At that point, Madame Bolduc announced the beginning of a poetry recital and Lambert settled down with a glass of wine and some canapés to listen to the poet. A young woman caught his eye. Petite and demure, she was in the company of an older woman made up in the colours and fashions of the era.

They talked quietly to another couple throughout the recital. The young woman wore an air of boredom. She looked for a moment in Lambert's direction; when their eyes met, she turned quickly away with a faint nervous smile.

Lambert nodded in the general direction of the matron sitting beside the young woman and said, 'Monsieur Pétion, do you know who that woman is?'

'I do. She is the widow of the Galimard family. Perfumiers and glove makers. From Grasse, I believe.'

'And that is her daughter?'

Pétion gave Lambert a smile that was at once knowing but also friendly and understanding. 'That is her daughter, though I cannot for the moment, remember her name. If you like, I can introduce you?'

'I would like that,' said Lambert. He knew that he could not simply walk up to a group and introduce himself. Certainly not a group in which ladies were present. This society had customs and traditions that must be followed, and they included one that said you must be introduced to someone new by someone who had been introduced to them in the past.

When the recital ended, animated conversation broke out once more among the guests. Pétion took Lambert by the elbow and walked across to the foursome. 'Good evening. May I introduce Jonathan Lambert? Young Lambert is a successful man of business, partner to de Roze in the establishment at l'hôtel Schomberg d'Aligre.'

Introductions were made, and small talk followed, but Lambert was totally tongue-tied by the presence of the young woman. He had caught her name in the introductions – Mademoiselle Amélie Galimard – and quickly forgot everyone else's. He was hopelessly smitten. Pétion began a conversation with the three adults, manoeuvring Lambert towards a separate discussion.

Amélie said, 'I have heard about your establishment, Monsieur Lambert.'

'Please, Mademoiselle. Call me Jonathan.'

She averted her eyes. 'That would not be appropriate, Monsieur Lambert. We have just been introduced, and we do not know each other.'

Ah, the conventions of the era. In his foolishness, he had put her in a difficult position. He must change the subject. 'I understand your family is in the perfume business?'

'It is. And we also manufacture gloves.'

In the France of the time, even the better-off members of society were by no means sweet-smelling. Water was feared in the belief that it carried disease and people preferred to stay away from it as much as possible. Lambert was reminded of that fact every day in his interactions with staff and customers. It was this, and the need to cover the smell of gloves, that led to the widespread use of perfume in France. One of the first things to be done with the leather that was to be turned into gloves was to bathe it in urine in order to soften it. After that, aromatic oils were applied for further softening and to reduce the smell of the urine, but for the most part, the damage was done, and at least a faint whiff (and often far from faint) remained. Grasse was a town in the south of France often associated with the production and use of these aromatic oils. Amélie told Lambert with an air of pride that Grasse was home to some of the world's finest glove makers, and the manufacture of scents to apply to leather had evolved into the production of others to be worn on the body.

She held up her gloved hand to Lambert. Not knowing what was expected, he brought it to his nose, taking in the pleasant scent.

'Did you enjoy it?' she asked.

Lambert would have liked to deny to himself the stirring he was feeling. 'It is wonderful,' he said.

She leaned closer to him. 'I wear it all over my body.'

To the evident relief of Amélie's mother, Villeneuve interrupted at this point. 'Monsieur Lambert. Allow me to introduce you to other guests.'

They bid adieu to the little group and walked away. 'That seemed to go well,' said Villeneuve.

'I must see her again. I have to.'

'I'll see what I can do. In the meantime, you need to meet these people over here.'

The social ice being broken, several other people approached Lambert and made their introductions. It seemed the principal purpose of the salon was to see and be seen, and Lambert knew that he must arrange immediately to have his own calling cards printed. He found the evening both instructing and useful – but what remained most powerfully in his mind was Amélie.

CHAPTER 8

LAMBERT WAS SUPERVISING A SERVICE AT the back of the restaurant when two men entered and were shown to a table. Although he was at the other end of the room, the hair rose on the back of his neck. He turned to see who had come in. Breguet. And not alone; the man with him was well dressed in a powdered wig and a haughty air. The last two months had seen an improvement in Lambert's ability to gauge the different strata of society, and he knew that this man – whoever he was – was noble.

The sumptuary laws had been introduced to France to limit conspicuous consumption on the part of the prosperous bourgeoisie. Allowing a bourgeois to appear to be as wealthy as, or wealthier than, the local nobility would undermine the noble's reputation as the powerful and legitimate ruler.

Only the nobility was allowed to use embroidery and to have gold or silver threads in their clothes. So what Lambert was looking at was Breguet, a man about whose attitude he could only guess, and a confirmed noble. The temptation to leave the restaurant was strong, but he knew he must resist it.

He stopped the waiter who was heading towards the table. 'I'll take this service.'

Walking up to the table, he smiled and greeted the two men. 'Monsieur Breguet. It's a pleasure to see you here again.'

'Monsieur Lambert.' Breguet's attitude seemed cordial and not at all hostile. Lambert might even have used the word amiable. 'How have you been?'

'Very well, Monsieur Breguet.'

'Antoine. May I introduce you to the proprietor of this establishment? Monsieur Jonathan Lambert. Jonathan, this is Monsieur Antoine Lavoisier.'

The name struck Lambert like a thunderbolt. He was stunned. Seated at one of his tables was the man known in his era as the father of modern chemistry. He was the author of several papers and one of the major scientists of the day. It was he who had recognised and named oxygen and hydrogen and helped establish the metric system.

Breguet said, 'Lambert here is responsible for the success of this establishment. Wait till you see the level of sophistication in the preparation of his dishes and the fine selections of wines and spirits from all over France. He is an unusually intelligent acquaintance of mine. We have had interesting discussions on the future of mankind. He has a sense of business, and he can see developments in technology that could benefit this nation.'

Lambert after a moment to recover from his initial shock turned to Lavoisier, 'Are you not an appointed member on the King's commission on gunpowder?'

Lavoisier looked at Breguet and then back at Lambert. 'No. I am not. But I find your question interesting. I am in the opening stages of discussing this very subject with the court. The Academy keeps me quite busy. Have you an interest in the subject?'

The Academy of Science in France was the leading scientific and technological institution of the day. Breguet had brought Lambert an amazing opportunity.

Was it intentional? It must be. 'Well,' said Lambert, 'I have wondered why the Academy has not been able to develop smokeless gunpowder. My understanding is that it has interesting qualities that can improve the explosion as well as reducing the amount of smoke and residue produced at the incendiary stage.'

Lavoisier sat back in his chair, a look of astonishment on his face.

Breguet beamed. 'You see, Antoine? He is everything I described. You must invite him to your laboratory and show him around.'

Lavoisier looked thoughtfully at Lambert and nodded. 'Tell me, Monsieur Lambert, what do you know of gunpowder? How did you come to imagine that it might be smokeless? Have you been a military man?'

'No, Monsieur Lavoisier. I simply have a recollection of reading about the possibility. I forget the title or the author.'

'Can you demonstrate how it can be applied?'

Don't give yourself away, Lambert thought. And, whatever you do, don't sound arrogant. 'I think I might be able to, Monsieur.'

He must take care. Lavoisier was no small-time noble. He was connected to the court and the King's administration in so many ways. During the revolution, his connections would lead inevitably to a meeting with the guillotine.

Lavoisier said, 'Come to my laboratory tomorrow at eleven. You'll find the entrance between the Church of the Celestials and the dock of the mall on rue du Petit-Musc, not far from Saint Germain.'

These instructions were handed out as though Lambert would have no difficulty in remembering them, but Lambert had grown up with computer-generated maps and then with smartphones that used GPS. He hadn't been in the habit of paying close attention to directions when they were given, preferring to receive a text and click on a link to find his way. Saint Germain, he thought. It was on the left bank, he knew that, but here it was being referred to as being also on the right bank. The man must mean Boulevard Henri IV. That was where the museum of the arsenal was situated. He said, 'Thank you for the invitation. I'd be delighted to come, and I hope

Monsieur Breguet can also attend?' With any luck, Breguet would know how to get there.

Lavoisier said, 'Of course, Breguet, you must come too. Perhaps one of our experiments can help with those devices you are so fond of creating.'

The appointment settled, Lambert made some recommendations on dishes and wine, took their order, and instructed the kitchen to take particular care in the preparation of the dishes.

WHEN THE TWO MEN HAD FINISHED EATING, Lambert approached their table once more. 'Was everything to your satisfaction, gentlemen?'

Lavoisier looked briefly at Breguet. 'It was a wonderful meal and a great ambience. I thank you for your hospitality, Lambert.'

'We now offer a table reservation service, should you wish to have a tabled reserved for you and your guests at a particular time.'

'Lambert,' said Lavoisier, 'you continue to surprise me. Don't forget; eleven tomorrow morning. I'll be expecting you.' He stood and made his way to the door where the man Lambert employed as host handed him his coat, hat and walking stick.

Breguet smiled at Lambert as he picked up the bill. 'Nobles. They think the world owes them everything.'

Lambert returned the smile. 'You invited him. You could be sure he would take advantage. Give the bill to me, and I'll cancel it.'

Breguet made no objection to handing Lambert the tab, and Lambert stuffed it into a pocket. Lambert sat down. 'Now, tell me. Why did you come back? And why did you bring him?'

'Because I believe you. I took the time to reflect on everything you said, and I started looking at all the poor people on the streets. It was as though I was seeing them for the first time. And it's unsustainable. I can see how they will eventually break.'

'Thank you for believing in me. Did you say anything to Lavoisier?'

'I did not. Your secret is safe with me. I will not speak of it with anyone. So. What do we do next?'

'Next?' said Lambert. 'Next, we go tomorrow to see the laboratories of the Royal Arsenal.'

CHAPTER 9

LAMBERT STOOD BACK AS BREGUET POUNDED the golden knocker at the centre of one of the great wooden sets of double doors. Moments later, one of the doors swung inward, and a uniformed maréchaussée stood before them. It came as no surprise to Lambert that the door should be protected by an armed guard. This was the Royal Arsenal. If the King owned the building, it was only natural that it should be protected by a constable whose task in a city that was not under threat of war would, essentially, be to keep the peace.

'Messieurs, how can I help you?'

Breguet said, 'We have an appointment with Monsieur Lavoisier at eleven.' They had arrived early because Breguet felt that being punctual would make a good impression. There was also the fact that, as a watchmaker, it would not look good for him to turn up late.

'Yes, messieurs, he is expecting you. Please follow me.'

They entered a large courtyard surfaced in stone

surrounding buildings of various sizes. They walked past target dummies made of straw, two and four-wheeled wagons covered in tarpaulins, and finally past some small cannon. The courtyard had a very martial appearance. The maréchaussée turned towards one of the larger buildings and entered it via a small wooden door. Giving them a little time for their eyes to adjust to the dark, he brought them to what looked like a waiting-room or interview room. The only decoration was a Bourbon family crest carved in stone on one of the walls. This building was functional rather than decorative. The maréchaussée told them to wait while he told Lavoisier they were there. He was gone in a moment, leaving the two men alone in the room.

'Interesting place,' said Lambert.

'It's a military compound. They test explosives and work on munitions. Improving the King's weapons to win the next war.'

'Hmm. It didn't do much good in the last war. In my day, we call that the seven years' war. It bankrupted most of the nations of Europe.'

And then, after a moment, Lavoisier was there. 'Messieurs!' He seemed animated and excited. 'Welcome to the Royal Arsenal. Thank you for coming. Were you offered no refreshment? Or somewhere to sit? Those ignorant maréchaussées. Not the brightest. Simpletons who only know how to follow basic instructions. Let's put that right. Can I offer you both something to drink?'

'Thank you, no, I don't need anything,' said Lambert. Breguet nodded in agreement. Turning to the crest on the wall, Lambert said 'I was looking at the crest carved in the wall.'

'Ah, yes. Put there by a former resident of the Arsenal, Louis-Auguste de Bourbon, the illegitimate son of Louis XIV by one of his mistresses.'.

Lambert had a flash and said, 'The Cellamare Conspiracy.'

'You know of it?' asked Lavoisier. 'A nasty controversy. It arose after the death of Louis XIV and almost ended the royal line. We have to ask ourselves how long the Bourbon-Maine house can survive.' He looked closely at Lambert. 'For a man from the former colonies of Nouvelle France, you seem up on your history.'

'I had a strict aunt who schooled me mercilessly. She was a proud woman and very loyal to the Bourbon dynasty.' Once again, Lambert found that the lie came easily when it was needed.

'Yes. Well, now come with me to the laboratory and show me this idea of yours.' He led them down corridors, giving a brief history of the Arsenal which he ended by saying that the man who was presently commander did not spend enough time at the Arsenal even though he had an apartment in the compound.

They came to a small room containing workbenches. The walls were of stone and contained only two exits – the one they had come in by and another at the opposite end. Lavoisier gestured towards a workbench and looked at Lambert. 'Tell me, Monsieur Lambert, what do you need to show me this smokeless idea?'

Lambert had been preparing for this since the night before. It was basic chemistry taught to many high school students. He was glad he had chosen to study chemistry and not biology as most of his friends had done.

Biology was an easy credit. All it needed was to win favour with the school's biology teacher who was an avid curler. Take biology, join her curling team, you had a credit. It was that simple. He said, 'I need a generous quantity of sulphuric acid and the same of nitric acid. A good measure of cotton, a basin and a large bowl of water with some drying racks. I'll need a beaker to measure each liquid accurately and a glass stir stick. Also some clamps or pincers. And finally, some cloth to wipe down everything after the process.'

Lavoisier smiled. 'Good heavens, is that all?'

'Oh, and Monsieur Lavoisier, you may want to document the process on paper.'

Lavoisier summoned an assistant and asked for the needed materials to be brought to the workroom without delay. As they waited for them to arrive, Lambert laid out an elaborate lie. The process he was about to demonstrate, he said, was not his own. He had observed his uncle manufacture smokeless gunpowder, which he called guncotton, many times in his youth. What he used the cotton for was to clear fields for the plough. It had not occurred to him that there could be military applications. The land in New France, he said, had been wild and clearing it extremely difficult.

Lavoisier and Breguet both nodded, having heard stories of the huge trees that had to be cut down and the countless hours spent by colonists in removing trunks, roots and boulders from the land granted to them to plant to make the colony self-supporting.

The assistant returned with an assistant of his own, carefully carrying all the needed materials on a tray. They laid everything down on the workbench and stood back. Lambert looked at them, and Lavoisier snapped 'Out!' They left the room meekly to the three men.

Lambert began with a warning that the reaction could be volatile and that they should probably observe him from a distance. He picked up a cloth, folded it in a triangle and tied it across his face. Then he laid the cotton flat on the bottom of the basin. He measured two parts of sulphuric acid to one part nitric acid into a beaker and poured the now bubbling mixture all over the cotton, watching the mixture lose most of its volatility after being poured.

Wisps of smoke and bubbles rose from the mixture, and he used the glass rod to mix the cotton so that it was thoroughly soaked. He took the cotton out and laid it on a drying rack.

Then he used clamps to lay another measure of cotton into the vat of liquid, taking care not to get any on his hands. Again the process with the glass rod; again the cotton was spread on a drying rack.

All the while, Lavoisier watched intently and recorded the process in a notebook.

'It's done,' said Lambert. 'We need to let the cotton dry completely and undisturbed. Once it is dry, it needs to be washed in cold water, dried again completely, and the process repeated every two days for a total of seven more times.'

Lavoisier looked up from his notebook. 'That would take nearly two weeks. When will we see the product display the properties you promised?'

'In two weeks, Monsieur Lavoisier. Trust me. You will not be disappointed.'

Lavoisier repeated the instructions he had been given. Wash in cold water, allow to dry for two days, repeat seven times.

'Oh, and Monsieur Lavoisier, the cotton is extremely dangerous. Do not let your assistants handle it without proper protection and keep it away from open flames – that is most important.'

'I shall see that the room is locked except when the cotton is washed under my supervision.

Lambert reflected on what he had just done. He had shown two men how to produce nitrocellulose, otherwise known as gun cotton. It was not supposed to arrive on the scene for another hundred years. The first act in his mission to change the course of French history had been performed. Something flickered on the very edge of his vision. He looked up. There it was in the doorway – a thin curtain of blue light. It was there for only a second, and then it was gone, but Lambert felt as though his whole world had turned over. It was clear the other two had not seen the blue light, and it took an enormous effort on his part to say nothing.

'AS WE HAVE TO WAIT NEARLY TWO WEEKS,' said Lavoisier, 'would you gentlemen like to join me for lunch?'

'I certainly would,' said Breguet. 'I'm famished.'

Really, Lambert would have preferred to be on his own, thinking about that momentary sighting of the blue curtain and hoping it would return when no one was with him, but he could think of no reasonable way to avoid the invitation. 'That's very kind,' he said. 'I'd be delighted.'

Lavoisier led them to a much larger and taller building in the courtyard. 'These are the administrative offices, and the offices of the Maréchal.'

So, thought Lambert, a Marshal is in charge here. French marshals had a long history. It was typically a military distinction rather than a rank, and fairly common to see a Marshal as a steward of a branch of the military. 'Which Maréchal is currently serving?'

'Lewis Nicolas Victor. He is also the King's secretary of state for war. He's only just been made a Maréchal.'

The name meant nothing to Lambert. He knew the big names from French history of the era, but his historical knowledge was influenced far more by economics than by military matters.

Lavoisier went on, 'It also helped that he was the King's gentilhomme de la manche.'

A close personal friend of the King as he was growing up, then. He sensed a sharpness to Lavoisier's description of the man.

Modern historians accepted that the politics of that time favoured nepotism and royal connections over scientific and academic achievement.

They entered the administrative building and Lavoisier guided them to a room well-appointed with ceramics and sculptures, with tapestries and paintings on the walls. The centre of the room was dominated by a table of richly polished wood surrounded by upholstered chairs. Lavoisier took the seat at the head of the table and gestured that they should sit to the side. A steward entered the room and poured wine into goblets.

'A toast, gentlemen,' said Lavoisier, 'to our success with this experiment.' He raised his glass and both men bowed their heads in acknowledgement of the toast.

Food was brought in successive waves. Appetisers, sweetmeats, a rince bouche of lemon ice, and then the main course of fowl after which came succulent pastries. Lambert was impressed. If this was how nobles of the lower levels ate, one could only imagine what was on tables at court.

As course followed course, the discussion turned from the experiment to the bounty of the table. Lambert made his comment as light and unthreatening as possible when he remarked how varied the meal was and how at the same time it pained him to see the poorer members of society suffering starvation in the streets.

'Yes,' said Lavoisier. 'The poor are born to their station in life, and they must make the best of it, but it is sometimes difficult to watch how hard it can be. The peasants in the countryside at least have it better, because they produce the food and they ensure their larders are well stocked before they bring their product to market. Although it must be said, the current situation is... difficult.'

Lambert knew that the rural areas were not hurting as much as the poor in the city, but they were heavily taxed, and their productivity suffered as a result. The motivation to work hard was less powerful when the nobility and the clergy took most of what was produced. A peasant of the third estate paid several taxes. First came the property and income taxes known as the Taille. There were two parts to this tax: one on property and the revenue someone would earn throughout the course of the year, and the other on the total value of property possessed. This was an ancient tax, originally levied as what amounted to protection payments to a local lord.

Neither nobility nor clergy had to pay it; the nobility because they were the ones providing physical protection and the clergy because the protection they provided was spiritual. Everyone in the country paid a head tax directly to the Crown, which was fixed according to their rank in life, and after that came a direct tax on income. When times were hard for the monarchy, a second income tax would be levied, and that caused extreme resentment.

And, as if all that was not enough, there was a tax on salt and other taxes on tobacco, wine, liquor, textiles, wood, livestock, playing cards, hides, soap, paper and a host of other things. Not only was the list long, but it also varied by region, and it could be changed at any time with no discussion or negotiation. Why should the state negotiate? The people of the third estate were completely unimportant. Powerless. And, as Lavoisier had suggested, the general feeling was that this was what God intended and so nothing could be done about it.

And *then* they had to pay customs duty, known as the Traite when they moved between regions. Smuggling had become a huge business in France because there was money to be made simply out of the pricing difference involved in buying a product in one region and selling it in another.

And then came the final indignity: the tithe peasants had to pay to the church and the compulsory labour service they had to provide to the local nobility. You could not, after all, expect an aristocrat to plough his own land or harvest his own wheat – though heaven help any peasant foolish enough to try to divert some of the grain he harvested to relieve his own family's starvation.

It all amounted to a huge burden placed on the poor of society – a burden from which they could never hope to free themselves. Lambert himself had received visits from several tax officials to verify the finances of his establishment. Although he left the bookkeeping to Roze's son, he was keenly aware of the bite on his profits and understood some of the pain that was felt when it came to taxation.

Lavoisier said, 'I myself, purchased a share in the Ferme Générale when I was young, and this has allowed me the freedom to work on my scientific interests without financial worries.'

So you did, thought Lambert. And that purchase of a share in the private enterprise responsible for collecting taxes in the name of the King will ultimately be why you lose your head to the guillotine.

But that was not something he wanted to say out loud. Instead, he said, 'I'm curious to understand why there is no study of agricultural reform. If agricultural productivity improved in the countryside, the Crown would receive greater revenues and the people would not be having such a hard time.'

'Yes,' said Lavoisier. 'You are right. If our nobles were less concerned with perfumes and hunting and had to pay for the land they leave unworked, they might be more inclined to lease it to peasants who would work it properly.'

There was a great deal Lambert could have said at this point, because agricultural reform was at the heart of his own historical specialisation, but really they had made enough progress for one day with the guncotton production. But this was a matter that could not lie dormant forever.

The meal ended, and Lavoisier accompanied the men to the exit from the compound, thanking them both for their good company. The three men resolved on a follow-up appointment two weeks later to demonstrate the gun cotton in action. Lambert said, 'Please, Monsieur Lavoisier, ensure that open flame is kept away from the cotton. It is not a material that relishes inattention.'

'Have no fear, Monsieur Lambert. We will pay close attention to your instructions.'

CHAPTER 9

And with that, the great double doors closed behind them.

AS THEY WALKED AWAY FROM THE ARSENAL, what Lambert would really have liked would have been to try to generate the blue curtain once more. As he had no idea what had caused it to appear in the first place, that was not possible. All he could do was take comfort from the fact that he had seen it and that it had coincided with what just might turn out to be a re-channelling of French history. Perhaps if he was successful in producing another such turn? Well, time would tell. In the meantime, there was work to be done. He said, 'Abraham. I have a few ideas I'd like to share with you.' When he had first used Breguet's first name, he had wondered what the response would be, but it was clear that Breguet did not object.

Breguet said, 'Let's talk in this cafe.'

They took a seat at a table in the back, away from groups of angry men carrying on loud conversations about the reforms society needed.

Both men knew that wherever conversations of that sort took place, at least one of the men taking part would be an agent of the Interior Ministry. A secret policeman in modern parlance. They had no desire to be caught up in that sort of intrigue.

There had been cafes in Paris since the late 1600s. They were often the centres for social and cultural exchange, and they became convenient places to meet people, read newspapers, and catch up on gossip. They reflected the pulse of Paris. Recently, they had also become centres of insurrection.

The garçon appeared quickly, took their orders and disappeared after providing a small lamp for the table. Breguet said, 'What do you want to talk about?'

'Agriculture. Productivity. What France is doing wrong and how it could change. Because of my education, I think I have a good grasp of the problems – the challenges – society faces here to stave off the coming troubles. Farmers aren't producing enough. It's not just down to poor farming; taxes are too high, and there isn't enough land available.

Too many nobles let their land lie fallow because they simply don't need the income. They don't need the income because they are extremely rich and they pay little or nothing in the way of taxes. We can't easily change the tax regime because the King and his ministers wouldn't allow a reduction in tax receipts right now. Not when the Treasury is broke. The state is as poor as citizens on the street. The disastrous last war means that France owes money all over the place and, to make matters worse, sometime soon his ministers will urge the King to finance another war. This one will be against England to stop the English preventing their colonists from breaking away and declaring independence. It probably sounds wonderful, this idea of Louis supporting the English rebels, but it will hurt France mortally. We need to do whatever it takes to limit French participation. France could help the rebels by transferring military technologies. But that's for the long term. What we need to work on today is increasing farmer productivity. I have a few ideas in mind if you happen to have your drawing pad and some charcoal in that satchel?'

It was a safe assumption because Breguet always carried such items. He pushed a pad and charcoal across the table. Lambert drew a quick sketch. 'Have you ever seen anything like this?'

Breguet shrugged. 'Of course. It's a scythe. Farmers use it to cut grass and wheat.'

'Right. Now imagine that same scythe, but with wooden extensions on the handle right below the blade. Like this,' And he made some more marks on the pad. What he drew was a bracket made of light wood beginning right after the blade and turning the scythe into the form of a very large sideways table fork in which only the first blade was sharp. The rest of what looked like wooden blades acted as a cradle to catch the cut grass. He said, 'The bracket I've drawn here will hold the freshly cut wheat together after it's been cut. That means that whoever holds the scythe can gather the cut stalks much faster and much more efficiently than they can now.'

'Interesting,' said Breguet. 'Did you imagine this? Or is it something you've seen?'

'I don't have that level of design ingenuity. Unlike you, I may add. No, this is an idea that came to someone now unknown in the American Midwest in the nineteenth century. Next century, in other words.

I don't really understand why it took something so simple so long to be developed. Humans have been harvesting grain with iron sickles for more than three thousand years, and slowly they developed the reaping-hook and then the scythe.

The great thing about this development – call it a cradle scythe – is that the reaper can stand upright. And they can cut twice as much grain in half the time. So you need fewer men to harvest, which means you have more manpower available for other agricultural activities.'

'Something so simple should be easy enough to introduce,' said Breguet. 'But this is France. Developments like this never come from the ground up. They are always imposed from above. We need to show this idea to the right minister.'

'Do you know who that is?'

'I think so – but let me work on it.'

'Before we show the scythe to anyone, take a look at this, too.' He took back Breguet's notebook and started on a new page. 'This is a little more complicated, but it changes agriculture fundamentally.' He started by drawing a harness that could be attached to a horse or an ox. To it, he attached a length of wood and a small hopper. At the bottom of the hopper were some small tubes pointing down and slightly backwards. 'You put the seed in the hopper. There are holes in the bottom of the hopper – say twelve of them.

Each hole has one of those tubes attached to it. It's called a seed drill. By spacing the tubes correctly, you make sure the seed is sown at the right distance and in straight lines. So not only is it easier to sow seed, but it's also easier to weed using a hoe instead of by hand. Seed sowing is faster, weeding is faster and, because the earth doesn't have to be completely turned over to be seeded, there's less soil erosion. There's also less wasted seed.'

'And it's drawn by a horse?'

'Or an ox. Whatever the farmer has.'

'And this is something else that other people – other countries – are using?'

'It's been used in China for hundreds of years. There's been no shortage of contact between Europe and China, and yet somehow it hasn't caught on here. As I recall, the English are going to start using it any time now.'

'Jonathan, I'm going to verify which minister we should be talking to and then I'll take you to him. These two innovations could change the face of French agriculture.'

'And stop people starving,' said Lambert, 'and therefore head off the revolution. Of course, they will free up men who need employment.

It's unemployed men who are most likely to riot. And we could find employment for those men if we could persuade the Minister of Finance to tax the owners of fallow land.'

'I think Monsieur Turgot has too much on his hands already. He'd never get that past the King and the nobles who own the land.'

'A shame. It could just save the King's life.'

CONVERSATION AT TABLES NEARER TO THE DOOR was becoming ever more heated. Lambert watched. How many were genuine plotters and how many were in the pay of the Crown? Would any of those men, later today, tomorrow or at any rate sometime soon, find themselves in a cell from which they would never emerge alive? It seemed likely. He said, 'When I think about it, I'm not sure that going to a minister first is the right thing to do. I realise that that's where we'll end up, but maybe there is a better way of skinning this particular cat.'

'Skinning? Cat?'

'It's just an expression. What I'm thinking is that the best way to ensure that these innovations come to pass would be to get them to market as quickly as possible. And the best way to do that is to control everything around the manufacture, pricing and distribution. It would not be a small investment, and we need to be protected.' He brought his eyes back to his companion. 'What we need is a patent.'

'Hmm. Patents. An English innovation, I think. I've never used one.'

'You should probably start. You deposit details of your inventions with the state to spread industry knowledge. In return, you can receive titles, land, subsidies and all sorts of other things. At least in theory. I have no interest in a title, and I don't want any land. What a patent can do is protect our rights to manufacture the new scythe and seed drill for five years. We won't need longer than that because, if we do it right and do it fast, there'll be competing innovations and whatever advantage we have by being first to market will have disappeared.'

Breguet grinned. 'You propose to pay the King for protection on the idea for five years?'

'Yes. But we'll need money to start manufacturing and distribution. We need start-up funds, an area to manufacture in, and an agreement on the returns they expect.'

Breguet said, 'I can prepare a document with a detailed proposal and a manufacturing plan. I can make an appointment with the appropriate person. I have connections at court I can contact to make the necessary introductions. We have to be careful how we deal with them – they are busy men, and they don't have much tolerance for people who aren't properly prepared.'

'All right, I'll let you take care of that, but listen: we have to ensure they understand our number one goal is to get these tools in the hands of as many farmers as possible as cheaply as possible and as quickly as possible. If they're affordable, they'll be widely used. If not...'

'I understand. I'll send you word when the document is ready, and we can revise it together before it goes to the administration.'

They called the garçon, who arrived with their bill. They paid it and left the café In different directions to pursue their separate goals.

§§§

LAMBERT SMOOTHED BACK HIS DAMP HAIR. He took a deep breath, partly because it was a relief to feel fresh and clean and partly as an attempt to release some of the nervousness from his body.

It didn't help.

Tonight he would spend the evening with the Galimards. His goal was to impress the object of his attention, Amelie, but getting off on the right foot with her parents was crucial. He'd rehearsed the questions he knew they'd ask while bathing and was pretty sure he'd thought of an answer for just about everything they could possibly want to know.

As he smoothed every wrinkle he could out of his best shirt and pants, Lambert wished more than ever for a mirror. He wanted to look his best for Amelie. It was strange, out of everything new and intriguing about this world he'd been thrust backwards into, remarkably enough, Amelie was by far his most fascinating discovery. No way of returning to modern times had arisen as of yet and, in truth, Lambert didn't mind. There was so much to do in this time and space, and he fully intended for Amelie to be a part of it all. After all, love was the same no matter what period of history it was placed.

'Let's do this,' Lambert muttered to himself as he grabbed his coat and headed for the door.

A QUESTION OF TIME

CHAPTER 10

'MONSIEUR LAMBERT,' SAID MADAME GALIMARD. 'Where do you reside?' They were in the family sitting room at the Galimard *pied-a-terre* in Paris, enjoying canapes and finger food. It was a hastily organised party in Lambert's honour however judging from how everything had been presented so far, one could hardly tell. Pétion had made discreet overtures to let the Galmiard Matriarch know of Lambert's interest in her daughter. As an apparently successful businessman, Lambert would not be rejected out of hand, but no prospective mother-in-law was going to look kindly on his present abode, a rented room in the Latin quarter. He could be sure she would never countenance the idea of her daughter living in such a place.

Lambert had anticipated this conversation. He knew it for what it was: an elaborate courtship ritual. He was being observed and questioned as to his suitability even to be allowed to continue to be in the presence of young Amélie Galimard by her ever-protective maman. Fortunately, he had recourse not available to the Galimard matron: he was familiar with the works of Honoré de Balzac and, since Balzac was not yet even born, that was an advantage Madame Galimard could not share. The Galimard family, for all its Parisian pretensions, was rooted in the petty-bourgeois customs and beliefs of la France profonde and anyone who had read Balzac's Human Comedy knew what that meant. What they would admire above all else was financial prudence. And so he said, 'Madame, when I arrived from the colonies, I was determined to make my way in business in a manner that would satisfy my father, should he be able to see me. I had capital, but it was not unlimited, and I did not wish to be profligate with it until I had found a business to invest in and begun to earn a satisfactory level of profit. I was on my own, and my needs were simple. I, therefore, found myself a room in a less than desirable quarter where I have lived until now. As soon as I can find the time, and now that my business is proceeding well, I intend to find a home more suitable to my family background and circumstances – and one in which, in due course, I could invite the right sort of person to share my life.'

It had been the right thing to say. Madame Galimard simpered – there really was no other word for it – and said, 'I am pleased to hear it, Monsieur Lambert. If you wish to be perceived as suitable – I might say eligible – to court my daughter, you must have a proper home.'

Well, thought Lambert, that was certainly to the point and right on target. The people of this era did not mince words. But Madame Galimard could see where Lambert's interests lay and she was establishing the ground rules that must be followed before Lambert could be seen as an appropriate suitor.

'My problem,' said Lambert, 'is lack of time to seek out the appropriate environs. But you, Madame Galimard, are well acquainted with the better quarters of this city. I should be deeply in your debt were you to recommend a suitable place for me to set up an establishment.'

'I have heard that there are satisfactory apartments on Rue St Honoré.'

St Honoré thought Lambert. One of Paris's most expensive neighbourhoods. Knowing this for the test of his financial resources that it was, he said, 'Thank you for your recommendation, Madame Galimard. I shall begin my research at once.'

Pétion broke into the conversation to remark that Lambert's restaurant was acquiring an excellent reputation, and so were Lambert's philanthropic activities with the poor.

'Tell me, Monsieur Lambert,' said Madame Galimard. 'Why do you have this concern for the poor?' Was this genuine interest? Or a suggestion that his concern was misplaced? The expression on her face suggested it was the former. Conscious of Amélie's attention, he said, 'We are all God's representatives here on earth. Our duty is to our fellow man regardless of his station in life. The fortunate should take care of the less fortunate. Did not our Saviour say, 'From those to whom much is given, much will be expected?'' In terms of the modern era, he would have described that as grotesquely over-the-top, but offering a glimpse of a spiritual side, he did not really possess seemed like a good idea.

That thought was born out when Amélie said, 'You are right, Monsieur Lambert, and that remarkable thought does you great credit.'

Not an entitled brat of the bourgeoisie, then. The thought was encouraging if he hoped to have her in his life.

'Quite so,' said the matron as she reached out to the silver tray, took a small canape and popped it into her mouth.

§§§

LAMBERT AND BREGUET MET SEVERAL TIMES during the following week to refine the drawings of the equipment they were proposing and to prepare a detailed description of the benefits it would bring to society. They took great care over their written claim on the idea and set out a proposal that would benefit the King and the people with only a small profit per unit sold left over for them. Breguet was frustrated by the idea of the King receiving the major share of the profits and Lambert had to talk him round.

'The King is in a very difficult position with his personal finances. If we can show him that we are not out for fame or riches, and we can improve his position, we may be able to influence his ministers to listen to some ideas about land reform. '

'Land reform?'

'Land reform. The King doesn't know this, but I do: big famines are coming. They could be avoided if the lands the nobility leave fallow were brought into production. If we could get that land opened up for agriculture, we might be able to increase productivity to the point where we don't need to import grain. I know this is being kept very quiet, but Turgot is already importing grain to stave off shortages and, believe me, the country cannot afford it. Price controls, hoarding and speculators make the grain shortage worse. When Turgot introduced price control, people realised how short the grain supplies were and when that became clear, speculating started.'

'Wouldn't you think that people would put the national interest in front of their own greed?'

'I would if we didn't already have examples like Lavoisier buying a share in the tax revenues. Grain speculators profit from the tribulations of the poor. And so does he. And don't imagine that the common people don't know it.'

'Do you mean... Does he... After the revolution...'

'Lavoisier does not survive.'

Breguet shuddered.

'But please don't tell him that. We need him on our side with the gunpowder, and we can't afford to have him distracted.'

'But if he knew...'

'Please, Abraham. Don't imagine I haven't thought it through. If I could see a way to save Lavoisier from his fate, I'd tell you. In fact, there is a way, but only by preventing the revolution from taking place at all. And that's why we are doing what we are doing with agricultural reform. Isn't it?'

'I suppose...'

'That will have to be enough for now. I don't think you've quite taken on board just how many of the nobility class are going to die if the revolution happens. It isn't just Lavoisier we should set out to save.'

'Well, Turgot is going to have his hands full trying to persuade the nobles to agree to land reform. They don't pay taxes. They don't believe they have anything to worry about.'

'But that's what so interesting about this plan,' said Lambert. 'They can go on enjoying their tax-exempt status as long as they lease their lands to farmers who want to farm it. If the state doesn't interfere, farmers will increase productivity to levels we've never seen in this era. It's in their interest to do so.

Chapter 10

Every time a parcel of fallow land is opened up to agriculture, it immediately gets a one-year exemption on all of its production. That means the farmer gets to keep every sou of his production, but only for that newly opened land, and the noble who owns it continues to enjoy his tax-exempt status as well as getting rent from the land he's leased.'

'What if the nobles resent the plan and try to block it?'

'Under the Lit de Justice, the King has the power to force their hand. What he may not have is the will. Let's hope it doesn't come to that. We have to persuade Turgot and Turgot has to persuade the King.'

'This king has a reputation for changing his mind according to whoever it was who last spoke to him.'

'So we must keep all secret until we have a fait accompli. I think we're done here. There comes a moment when you have to decide you've done the best job you possibly can, and I think we are there. Next comes the patent audience. Shall we wrap this up and wait till then?'

§§§

The maréchaussée recalled Lambert and Breguet from their previous visit and ushered them into the inner courtyard of the Arsenal. 'You are here to see

Monsieur Lavoisier?' Breguet confirmed that that was so, but before they could be taken anywhere, they saw Lavoisier walking across the courtyard towards them.

'Good morning, messieurs. Thank you for coming. I have some business in the courtyard if you would be good enough to accompany me while I attend to it.' His manner was a little gruff, and it was clear that he was distracted. They followed him at a brisk walk, passing straw target dummies towards a man in military uniform standing beside what seemed to be a three-wheeled carriage. It had a large, irregularly shaped metal sphere at one end. Lavoisier said, 'Gentlemen. May I introduce you to Capitaine Nicolas Cugnot, one of the King's royal engineers.'

Breguet and Lambert greeted the captain with a slight touch to the forelock. Lambert always found this way of greeting someone for the first time amusing, but the amusement could not entirely cover the stirring of a distant memory. Cugnot. Cugnot.

Wasn't that... It was. This man was the first in the world ever to demonstrate a self-propelled platform. The first automobile. Sadly, he was also responsible for the first automobile accident.

Cugnot looked nervous, and Lavoisier said, 'Do not be concerned, Captain. These men are here on another matter. They have nothing to do with your platform. As you know, the King's engineer is not prepared to study your latest modifications to your contraption. It is a wonder no one was killed after your last demonstration, though you did manage to damage the Arsenal walls. We will not reopen the funding for your self-propelled cart.'

That was right, thought Lambert. Cugnot had been given the task of building a self-propelled cart to transport cannon more effectively than a horse-drawn carriage could. His invention travelled at about eight kilometres an hour, but there had been difficulties with weight distribution, and he had eventually crashed it into the Arsenal walls, which was why people in today's era said the first automobile accident belonged to him.

A great shame. It was one of those lost opportunities. If it had succeeded, it could have transformed the art of war as well as transportation. The history of Europe and the world could have been very different. But the Cugnot was not to be. It had never become the transportation standard it might have become.

Lavoisier was still talking to the captain. 'We will go on storing your contraption here, but there is no interest in funding your improvements.'

'But Monsieur Lavoisier,' said Cugnot. 'I have designed great changes to the distribution mechanism...'

'Enough! Be grateful that you keep your pension. I recommend you set your thoughts to other pastimes.' He made a gesture of curt dismissal and the captain, visibly shaken, saluted the three men and left. Lavoisier turned back to his guests. 'Follow me, gentlemen.' And he wheeled away from the platform towards a building in the courtyard. 'He is such a disappointment,' he went on. 'The previous King anticipated a breakthrough, but the amount of money he needs to advance this project is not something the current administration will commit to. Apart from which, the King has other pressing matters on his mind.'

Lambert watched Cugnot as he approached the gate in the walls of the Arsenal. Just as the gate was opened for him, a flash of blue light – a blue curtain – flickered over the gate. It was there, and then it was gone, and when it was gone, it left no trace. But had it been there? Lambert was in no doubt. He had seen it.

WHEN THEY ENTERED THE ROOM WHERE the gun cotton was drying, it took time to adjust their eyes to the lack of light. It was clear that Lavoisier had taken great care over safety as there was nothing in the room but the absolute minimum of necessary furniture. Nor were there any torches – what Lavoisier had done was to set up mirrors to bring in light from torches in adjoining rooms and corridors. The room was quite dark, but there was enough light, once their eyes had adjusted fully.

'Well, gentlemen,' said Lavoisier, 'it's been two weeks. Monsieur Lambert, I have followed your instructions to the letter. Please proceed with your demonstration.'

Lambert nodded. 'Monsieur Lavoisier, this material will produce an explosion two to four times more powerful than black powder and with less volume of material.

It is highly explosive and unstable and has to be handled with great care. It can be compacted into differently shaped cases to create charges for military use as well as civil and mining applications. Please pay close attention to the amount of smoke generated.'

He removed the cotton carefully from the drying racks and compacted it into two balls each the size of a tennis ball. He placed them some distance apart on the counter and removed the racks, placing them against the walls. 'I'll need a long candle or stick that can keep a flame.'

Lavoisier had clearly anticipated that request. He produced a long wooden stick and pointed to a torch in the outside corridor. Lambert nodded. 'Please stay right at the outside edges of the room. I don't know the exact concentration of this gun cotton.' Then he walked into the hallway, lit the stick and, shielding the flame carefully, walked back into the room. With great caution, he moved the lit end of the stick close to one of the balls. Before they could touch, there was a great white explosion that caused all three men to jump. There was very little smoke, but the noise was loud. Lavoisier and Breguet smiled nervously. Lambert said, 'I'll light the second ball. Now that you know what to expect, you can pay closer attention to the explosion.'

The second ball was lit and it, too, burned very quickly while generating very little smoke.

Lavoisier said, 'I am very impressed, Monsieur Lambert. Of course, I expected the explosion, but I thought there would be much more smoke than in fact there was. I shall set a date for a demonstration to the Academy of Science, the King's engineers, and representatives of the military. Tell me what you think are the most important points I should highlight to them.'

Lambert said, 'This gun cotton can be manufactured quickly. It would be less expensive to produce than black powder. It can be shaped into charges for a variety of applications. It weighs about one-sixth the weight of black powder, so it's easier to transport. Use it in mining, and you'll get quicker tunnelling because the explosions produce less smoke. For the military, you need less space for storage, and having less smoke in a battle is an obvious tactical advantage. Artillery can be reloaded faster, and the men operating in it will not suffer from smoke blindness on the battlefield or in a naval engagement.'

Lavoisier had been writing urgently. Now he snapped his notebook shut. 'Excellent. That will be more than enough for now.

We must plan to produce large quantities of this cotton. I hope it goes without saying that we need the utmost discretion. You must speak of this to no-one and demonstrate it to no-one.'

Lambert and Breguet nodded. Guncotton was a state secret. Right now, only France had it, and that must remain the case as long as possible. They left the room and began to walk towards the exit. A thought came to Lambert, who had not been able to rid his mind of the blue curtain that had flashed just for a moment when Cugnot left the compound. 'Monsieur Lavoisier. I believe I can improve that three-wheeled carriage of Cugnot's. Would you allow me to work on it with Monsieur Breguet? I'd be happy to do so at my expense and on my own time – there'd be no financial drain for the Academy of Sciences or for the King.'

'You have ideas on how to improve it? You would have the gratitude of a great many people who invested in that contraption. What would you ask in return?'

'Oh... Perhaps an extended audience with some of the King's ministers...'

Breguet said, 'He has ideas he'd like to share with the ministers on the subject of land reform. I've heard them, and they make good sense. They should be heard.'

'Very well. Submit your proposals to my office before you modify the carriage, and if you can make something of it, I'll put you in front of Turgot himself. He'll want to meet you anyway when he hears about the gun cotton.'

At the gates, they exchanged pleasantries and agreed to meet again. The door closed behind them with a dull thud, and they heard the bolts being shot home. But Lambert's attention was distracted by thoughts of the blue curtain.

Chapter 11

Nadeau was filling out the last of his reports when the Director stepped into his office. 'Nadeau. I have a case I need you to look at.'

Nadeau pasted an enquiring look onto his face and raised his head. 'A case?'

The Director handed him a tablet. 'The details are uploaded and ready for your bio print. It's eyes only.'

Nadeau took the tablet from the director. 'I'll get on it right away, Monsieur le Directeur.' Had he overdone the parade ground voice or the underling's enthusiasm? Well, what if he had? The director was not known for his sense of humour. Nadeau's irony would probably go straight over his head. The director left, and Nadeau scanned his print to open the page on the tablet. If it were eyes only, it would have to be handled with discretion. He wondered who had reported it, and what pull they had to get the director to give it that level of secrecy.

Well, there was one way to find out, and that was to read the damn thing.

It was not an edifying story. A dispute had arisen between two families at a famous Paris fashion house. One managing partner had accused another of financial irregularities, and the director had been instructed to assign someone to look into it. The starting point for that investigation would be a visit. Nadeau took out his phone and called for a car. His phone chirped back an estimated time of arrival of five minutes, which was more than enough time for Nadeau to grab his uniform jacket and hat and proceed to the command post's exit. As he ran down the stairs, something flickered across the main door. Something blue. What was it? It looked like a curtain. A curtain of blue light. He knew that should ring a bell. He knew he'd heard about something just like that, and not long ago. But where? From whom?

After a quick moment, the curtain was gone, and the door looked just as it always did. Passing through it, he was greeted by a slow and steady drizzle that had not let up for weeks. The bad weather in France had been a boon for French tour operators who had quickly filled up flights to some of the warmer French colonies in North Africa and the Caribbean.

Nadeau gave a moment's thought to his own vacation which was not far away and thought with pleasure of the opportunity to spend time on the beach of some resort, putting thoughts of his work aside for a while.

The cugnot arrived, the door opened automatically, and Nadeau stepped in and ordered the computer to take him to Place Vendôme, home to the offices of Lambregal. Broadcasting his credentials from the cugnot ensured cooperation from the traffic control lights. Nadeau rarely had to face unnecessary delays in Paris traffic, where other cars yielded automatically to his, and he was whisked quickly to his destination. If only he could enjoy this perk of office in his downtime. A chime in the car counted down the estimated time of arrival, while Nadeau consulted the case file in more detail. It looked like a standard 'He said, She said' story with one partner accusing another of embezzling livres. An old story – as old, probably, as money itself. But this was a nest of vipers that Nadeau was about to step into. A single misstep in dealing with French titans who dominated the industrialised world had ended more than one promising career.

The receptionist was fifty-something and extremely well maintained. Lambregal's reception area was enormous and yet sparsely furnished. One of the ways in which very successful companies advertised their wealth was to take some of the most expensive real estate in the world – and leave it empty. 'Look!' it said. 'See what *we* can do! See how little money matters to *us*!'

Lambregal was a worldwide fashion house with its fingers in many businesses concerned with the various elements that made up the global luxury consumer goods market. Their designers and manufacturing centres churned out the latest in luxury consumer accessories like scarves, footwear, suits, perfumes, bags and watches. Well known throughout the world for cutting edge design, their iconic logo was a staple of French culture throughout the world.

Nadeau presented his credentials and said, 'I'm here to see Monsieur Gendremain.'

The receptionist, who was well aware that Gendremain was not expecting anyone, asked, 'Is Monsieur Gendremain expecting you?'

'I don't have an appointment. I believe he will make time for me. Please let him know that I'm here concerning the issues he has raised.'

The receptionist scanned Nadeau's warrant card into Lambregal's visitor registry and passed it back to him. 'One moment. I will let him know you're here.' She picked up an internal phone and said, 'Monsieur Gendremain. An Inspector Nadeau is here from the... Yes, Monsieur. I'll tell him.' She turned back to Nadeau. 'Take a seat, please, Inspector. Someone will be here shortly to take you to Monsieur Gendremain.'

Nadeau smiled pleasantly but remained on his feet. He spent far too much of his time sitting down. Apart from which whoever was coming to collect him would be standing, and Nadeau was aware of the disadvantage that came when a seated person was greeted by someone standing up. If you are in a meeting and you are the only person sitting while everyone else stands, it's clear to anyone seeing the scene that you are the person in charge. When you're being collected, the opposite is true. He looked at the large Lambregal logo on the granite wall behind the receptionist's desk. He could never afford anything made by this company. Their products were priced way above his pay grade.

Then a bell tinkled from the elevator, and a tall, burly man in a Lambregal suit stood before him. He gestured towards the lift doors. 'Please, Monsieur. Follow me.'

They entered the lift, the man barked at the wall panel for the sixth floor, and a slight hum was the only sign that they were ascending. After a brief ascent, a female robotic voice said, 'Sixth floor,' and the doors opened.

The corridor they entered was carpeted and lightly scented. The man led Nadeau through a left turn to a large and ornate wooden door. Nadeau noted that the man adjusted his jacket and tie before knocking gently and opening the door. Whoever was inside this room outranked the man. But that had been obvious in any case. What Nadeau was prepared for was that whoever was inside this room would believe he also outranked Nadeau. Well, they would have to see how that panned out.

They entered a corner office that used the same vast areas of empty space as the reception floor to indicate that when you came into this room, you were encountering power. There was nothing so vulgar here as a desk. There were tables, sofas, easy chairs, and what appeared to be a place to lie down. To sleep? Wondered Nadeau. Or for therapy?

At one of the tables sat a man, who half-raised a hand to signify that he had seen Nadeau enter. Before leaving the room, the man who had brought him here ushered Nadeau to one of the sofas while Gendremain – if that was who it was – continued his phone conversation. He was using an earpiece, so the fact that he was on the phone was not immediately apparent to Nadeau, but it became clearer when he heard one-sided titbits from the conversation. They seemed to be about inventory levels and the need to make sure that sales projections kept pace with manufacturing schedules. Nadeau tuned out the conversation to take a closer look at the room. You could tell a lot about someone from the things they surrounded themselves with.

In this case, it appeared that Gendremain was a history buff. In one corner of the office was a huge wooden globe of the world that looked almost as old as its subject. Scattered around the office were suits of armour holding weapons from the various eras of French history. There was a bookshelf so large it could more accurately be described as a library, and it was full.

Nadeau's study of his surroundings was interrupted by Gendremain, who had ended his telephone conversation. The man's expression looked friendly enough. 'Inspector Nadeau. I'm sorry to have kept you waiting. I am Nicolas Gendremain, CEO of Lambregal. May I offer you a drink?'

'Thank you, but no. I'm here in a professional capacity.' He took a small recording device from his bag and placed it on the table. 'It's necessary to tell you that everything we discuss will be documented in my report.'

Gendremain opened the top of his globe of the world to reveal a selection of bottles. Nadeau did not think there would be many whose preferences could not be satisfied with the selection on view. 'You won't mind if I have one?' said Gendremain. He poured himself a drink and left the globe open. In case Nadeau changed his mind? Or so that he could have another? He sat opposite Nadeau. 'Where shall we start?'

'You have made certain accusations concerning a director of this company. You reported the disappearance of several million livres of company money.'

'Yes, I have. Monsieur Guy Galimard, the youngest director of this company and head of our horology division, appears to have diverted money to accounts outside our company's control.'

Nadeau made a gesture encouraging Gendremain to continue while at the same time indicating the presence of the recording device. It would not be the first time that a witness had demanded that his testimony be erased. Nor would it be the first time that Nadeau had refused that request. But he sensed himself here in the presence of someone well connected.

Gendremain went on, 'We discovered the embezzlement quite by accident when one of our agents found clocks and watches being sold in the market in a small, third-tier city in China. It would appear that young Galimard has set up parallel manufacturing centres in China using our exact design specifications and quality control to emulate our product in a way that makes it indistinguishable from the real thing.' He paused, for effect or to gather his thoughts. 'Naturally, believing we had discovered a classic case of counterfeiting, we investigated, but our investigation showed that Guy Galimard planned and executed the counterfeiting and has been orchestrating it for a number of years.'

Nadeau nodded. That all seemed fairly straightforward. Provided the supporting evidence was there, it shouldn't be difficult to get a conviction. 'How do you calculate the amount of financial loss?'

'We have projections of the illicit factories' manufacturing cycle. Those factories have now been shut down, by the way, by the Chinese government at our request. Taking those numbers together with typical sales of our watches and clocks, we calculated an approximate amount of lost sales. Our banking partners in Switzerland have also uncovered several accounts controlled by Galimard. The balances in them are close to our projection of loss.'

'And we can have this evidence? So that we can prosecute?'

'Ah, Inspector, it is not quite that simple. Guy Galimard is a direct descendant of one of the founders of this company. A public accusation and enquiry would damage our reputation. We are in a delicate situation.'

Nadeau recalled the casual way in which the Director had dumped this on him. A delicate situation, indeed! You didn't call the police when you wanted someone to deal with a delicate situation.

You called the police when someone needed a good going over. Rubber truncheons may no longer be standard issue, but... He said, 'What do you want from my office?'

'We'd like you to meet Galimard. Show him the evidence. You have the power of the state behind you. Convince him to admit the truth. Document it and have him agree to return the stolen money to the company. In return, we will offer him a generous severance and a pension.'

So, I'm to be your HR department, am I? You're very soft-handed HR Department. I wonder how you would deal with a rank, and file employee caught doing what Galimard has been doing. But he kept all of that to himself. What he said was, 'Why not make that offer to him yourselves? Why involve us?'

'Guy is...' Gendremain was clearly struggling for the right word. 'He is an entitled child. Born to wealth and power. He was being groomed to take over this company someday. Although I have to tell you that another director would have nothing to do with that idea. She too, is from a powerful family and descended from one of our founders.'

'Her name?'

'Mademoiselle Julie Lambert. A direct descendant of Jonathan Lambert, the second of our three original founders.'

When Nadeau stepped back into a drizzly Place Vendôme, his head was spinning. The name Jonathan Lambert had so stunned him that he had been distracted throughout the rest of the interview. He had agreed with Gendremain that he would intervene on the company's behalf and, on his way out of the building, he had made an appointment with Guy Galimard's assistant for the following week. He left his contact information with Gendremain who had promised to send the evidence he had to Nadeau's office so that he could confront Galimard with proof of his embezzlement.

Jonathan Lambert. A coincidence, of course. It had to be. Didn't it?

And then he remembered the curtain of blue light when he left headquarters and recalled where he had heard of such a thing before. It had been across the tunnel that the train had passed through before Lambert had disappeared. Or so the train driver had said. Perhaps Nadeau would need to speak to the driver again to get a clear description of the curtain. Was it like the one he had seen? Had he even seen the one he thought he had seen?

There were an awful lot of questions in the Jonathan Lambert missing person case. Nadeau quite liked questions which, after all, were his stock in trade, but he liked questions that came with answers. There were too many unanswered questions concerning Jonathan Lambert. And now they had invaded this new case.

Nadeau resisted the urge to curse under his breath. It had been some time since he'd thought about Lambert, but he hadn't yet forgotten how that case had proceeded to tie him into knots. However, after the initial annoyance of being unable to solve the case, the agent could hardly deny that it had been rather nice to feel like he was good at his job again. He'd taken the time to work on other things, problem solve (and actually find answers), and had even gained something of a girlfriend. He and Eloise were practically dating now. Still, even the fact that the two of them had first bonded over discussing the Lambert case hardly made Nadeau eager to jump back in. And yet.... He thought back on the intriguing ideas he and Eloise had formed. The past......

Deep in thought, he called a cugnot to take him back to his office. When it arrived, he asked for a non-priority ride. The vehicle would not use his credentials to override traffic control and make other cars yield to him. That would give him time. Time to think.

A QUESTION OF TIME

CHAPTER 12

THE BUSINESS AT THE ROYAL ARSENAL had taken a lot of Lambert's time, but he still had a restaurant to run. Not every idea that was popular in his own era could easily be translated to the 18th-century, but he made some innovations, and one that had great success was to introduce pizza. Perhaps the fact that no-one in 1774 Paris thought the idea of a wood-fired oven was in any way strange helped. He did his best to produce a bread dough similar to those he was used to but concentrated on thin-crust pizzas because those happened to be the ones he had always liked the most. He added cheese and tomato sauce and then created a menu of additional toppings, from which people could choose. He hired people to deliver pizzas and paid the neighbourhood crier to announce the service. No one could telephone through an order, because there weren't any phones, but he hired youngsters to troll with pizza menus everywhere close enough for his staff to deliver, paying a commission when they found a customer for him.

The restaurant boomed. He was making money rapidly, and he set up a profit-sharing scheme so that his staff could benefit from the growth. This was partly about motivating people and partly about buying their loyalty, and it succeeded on both counts.

He ordered glass jars and had a local metalsmith make round lids from tin to fit the jars tightly. Adding wax seals allowed him to store seasonal produce like tomatoes for longer. He boiled the sealed jars to kill any bacteria. He knew that canning as a process was due to arrive about thirty years from now, but he couldn't wait that long. Producing and storing his own sauces and soups meant that he cut his costs but, more importantly, became immune to the volatility of food prices.

Roze, intrigued by the increase in revenues, visited Lambert's restaurant a number of times and went back to his own place to apply the same innovations. On one of these visits, Lambert indicated that he wanted to discuss their business arrangement. 'I'd like to buy out your remaining share in this restaurant.

I'll pay you a fair price and offer you an arrangement that lets you benefit from all of my future innovations in any future restaurants you may open. All I'll ask for will be a percentage of your overall sales.' Lambert, of course, knew that what he was offering was the very first franchise arrangement in the restaurant world, but for Roze, it was something entirely new, and he needed to think about it. Thinking about it didn't take long, because what he realised was that Lambert now had the money to go off and set up his own restaurant. He would be a formidable competitor. And so they agreed, and the money Lambert paid to buy Roze out was enough for the latter to set up a second restaurant of his own.

Lambert wasn't quite finished. He said, 'We need to brand our restaurants so that people can easily identify who they're dealing with and know what kind of service and standard of food to expect. This idea – let's call it a concept – this concept can be expanded to many areas around Paris and one day, perhaps, elsewhere in France.'

'Brand? What is a brand?'

We began as Restaurant Roze. Your name. Let's put the initials RR on everything we possibly can. We put it on our chairs, our door handles, our tables, our menus, our linen clothes – everything. If we build a brand people recognise, we'll have a very strong customer base. Think about it. One of our customers finds himself in a new area of Paris. He wants to eat. He sees maybe six eating places in one street. Five of them he knows nothing about – but in the sixth, everything has RR on it. He's eaten here, or at your place, so he knows what those initials mean. Where do you think he'll choose to eat?'

'I like it.' Replied Roze, extending his hand to Lambert in appreciation. 'Whatever you believe is right for our business, I'd be glad to participate.'

A Question of Time

SOON ENOUGH, THE FERME GENERALE CALLED on Lambert. It did not come as a surprise. And nor did Lambert try to dodge the issue. He knew that avoiding the payment of tax was a standard French game and he also knew that that would still be true more than 200 years from now, but Lambert's position was too precarious to take chances of that sort. His taxes were becoming a burden, but they were a burden he would have to carry.

What was more difficult was to see the effect it had on his workers because the taxmen taxed their bonus payments heavily. But it was what it was.

There was another visit that he should have been expecting because as a historian he knew all about the corrupt practices of the trades guilds, but somehow it still came as a surprise when they hit on him.

It began with the arrival of two men for the early service. They were seated, their orders were taken, and they ate quietly and kept to themselves. The early service was always particularly busy, and so Lambert was almost oblivious to their presence. He had a lot of customers that evening; these men were just two more. It was not to stay that way.

When the two men had eaten, and a waiter had presented their bill, he came looking for Lambert. 'Monsieur Lambert. Those two men at table six. They want to speak to you.'

'Did they say what they want?'

'They are from the Traiteur's Guild.'

The Caterer's Guild. An old guild. Like every other guild of the time, their presence here signalled nothing but trouble. They had no interest in what Lambert was trying to do to improve the standard of restaurant meals in Paris.

None, either, in his work to alleviate the plight of the poor. French guilds were there to protect the interests of their members at the expense of everyone else. They sought to block progress. Most of all, what they wanted was to prevent newcomers from entering the scene. For the Caterer's Guild, the aim was to make sure that only the children and the grandchildren of existing Guild members could operate restaurants in the city.

Lambert paused for just a moment to ask himself why Roze had not mentioned the likelihood that he would receive this visit when they agreed their parting of the ways, for Roze himself must be a member. It was a thought that didn`t last; he'd known about the guilds, and he knew he should have thought of it himself. He approached table 6. `Messìeurs. I am Jonathan Lambert. How can I help you?'

`Monsieur Lambert. It is a pleasure to – finally – make your acquaintance. My name is Jean Adrien Delespine, maître pâtissier and traiteur, and this is my associate Jacques Pages, also a maître traiteur. We are the legal representatives of the Caterer's guild in Paris.'

'A pleasure to meet you both, of course. But I repeat my question. What can I do for you?'

'Monsieur Lambert, we have had complaints about you from our members.'

Lambert took on a mocking expression of surprise. If there was going to be trouble, there was going to be trouble. If these two thought he was going to roll over, they were in for a surprise. 'Complaints? About me?'

'Monsieur Lambert. Your business is operating in our royally protected sphere of economic activity. Your delivery of pastries...'

'Pizzas,' said Lambert. 'They are called pizzas.'

'You can call them whatever you like. They are only one of the many complaints our members have. Our members want to know how someone – anyone – you, Monsieur Lambert, can simply ignore our license. A licence that was granted to us by the King. How you can ignore it and operate a business in direct competition to our members' livelihoods. When you bought your way into an establishment that served simple meals to simple people, it was not a concern of our members. But now... You are taking business away from us.'

The second traiteur, Monsieur Pages, had sat quietly until this moment. Now he said, 'Our clients in this arrondissement have stopped patronising our members.

They are coming here instead.' The force of the sneer in that word 'here' could not be overlooked.

'It will not be tolerated.' His voice had risen to a level that was drawing attention from other diners. Lambert was conflicted; should he try to find a way to work with these people? Or should he do what he really wanted to do and throw them out? He said, 'And what would I need to do to belong to your Guild and be registered?'

Delespine said, 'You would need to apply for status. You would need to retroactively pay the Guild membership which would be about four thousand livres. Of course, there would be fines in addition.'

Pages said, 'He'd have to hire our journeymen and master chefs at current Guild rates.'

'Of course. And they have strict guidelines on how to prepare meals and how to serve them. And you yourself, Monsieur Lambert, would have to serve an apprenticeship under one of our Masters until the membership deemed you eligible to become a master yourself.'

Lambert had heard enough. 'Thank you, gentlemen. Come back one week from today at the same time. My attorney will be here to discuss the matter with you.'

'Attorney? You wish to contest our Royal license?' Pages lept up on his feet and shouting. Lambert thought this must be the first time anyone had ever crossed him.

He said, 'Gentlemen, you are causing a breach of the peace with your shouting. Leave now, or I shall call the Garde.'

Delespine thrust his face into Lambert's. 'You have not heard the last of us, Monsieur Lambert.' They stood, collected their hats and coats, and stalked out. 'Haughty,' thought Lambert. That was the word to describe them, as they left holding onto their dignity. Haughty. He should have been furious, but it was almost impossible to keep a smile from his face. What a pathetic demonstration. Of course, he had the advantage of knowing what was going to happen to the guilds. What he didn't know, though, was who was going to come out best in his own personal battle with them.

The waiter was at his shoulder. 'Monsieur Lambert. They did not pay their bill.'

Well, of course, they hadn't. French merchants had been able to twist the ancient guilds to suit their purposes, and Lambert could think of nothing quite so mendacious as the French merchant class. He was taking on an entrenched and powerful institution. It had powerful friends. He'd need some of his own.

He said, 'Leave it on my desk. I'll pay it.'

Chapter 13

Lambert had spent the week overseeing his buyout of Roze's share of the restaurant, dealing with the taxman and being troubled by the men from the Caterer's Guild. He'd had no time for anything else. The fact that he was fully occupied did not change the urgency of preparations to present his suggestions about agricultural change, including the production of prototype equipment. It was lucky for him that Breguet had been able to take over the business of getting the prototypes made from Lambert's sketches. Now they were looking at the finished tools.

'Amazing,' Lambert said. 'You've done a great job. And the patent presentation?'

Breguet passed some documents across the table.

'I can't tell you how grateful I am to you for taking all this over,' said Lambert. 'And your attention to detail is wonderful. The scythe, the seed drill – they are exactly as they should be.'

'I make timepieces,' said Breguet. 'There's no room in that line of work for anything except precision.'

'Where did you get them made?'

'That was the easy part. Abbott Joseph-François Marie is my patron. He is also head of College Mazarin. I told him what I needed, and he made it available. And I'll tell you something else. These things work. They perform exactly the way you said they would. I took them out to a field in the countryside not far away and tested them.'

'Nobody saw you?'

'I was too careful for that. I tested them under cover of darkness. And I was alone. But I'm telling you: they work perfectly.'

'Assuming we get patents on both,' said Lambert, 'how soon can we start manufacturing them?'

'That depends entirely on how much funding we get. If we have enough for a small workshop with two or three of the right kind of artisans, we can probably make three cradle scythes and one seed drill every day. That's assuming we have no trouble getting the materials delivered.'

'Is that likely to prove difficult?'

'The only thing I can see being a real problem is the tubes for the seed drill. I'm not sure where we are going to get those from in bulk.'

'We could make them ourselves? No need to rely on outside suppliers, surely?'

'Ah, well. The tubes need to be made by master blacksmiths. Or at least by men employed by master blacksmiths. If we try making them ourselves, we'll be in trouble with the Smith's Guild before we know it.'

There it was again. The guilds. Getting in the way, making life difficult, never thinking about making life easier or better for the people of France. All they cared about was making sure that they made money, and no one else did.

'Well, I'm already in a battle with one Guild. I don't have time to fight another.'

'You're taking on one of the guilds? I must hear about this.'

So Lambert told him. He finished the story by saying that he would fight the influence of the Caterer's Guild using whatever means proved necessary.

Breguet said, 'You won't get far with the guilds. The guilds that represent lawyers and the judicial class won't stand for anything that looks like reform.'

'But what people need to understand, and what the King and his ministers need to understand is how much the French economy would benefit if you took away the barriers to trade. Get rid of the guilds, you bring in more merchants, more artisans, more competition and you get much faster innovation.'

Breguet was smiling. He said, 'Jonathan. You do realise that I belong to a Guild? If I did not have my own Guild, I would not have my status in society. As a Guild member, I've been introduced to men of power, prestige and wealth. Men who would not otherwise have noticed me. I'm courting a woman who would be well above my station if I didn't have my Guild membership.'

This was something new. This had never been mentioned before. Lambert realised how little he knew of the private lives of his closest associate. 'You are courting a woman?'

'I am. And if I can gather the necessary funds together, I'll open an atelier. It's my life's ambition. A small shop to build my timepieces in.'

Lambert slapped him on the back. 'My dear fellow. I wish you every success. I hope it goes exactly as you would wish. As it happens,' he went on, 'I, too, am attempting to court a woman. I'm afraid, though, that I have great difficulty in finding the time to set myself up properly to receive her and her family. I can't invite them to a one-room tenement in the Latin Quarter.'

'You would do well to rent a proper apartment and hire someone to look after the details of your life. Otherwise, it will all slip away from you. That was one of my father's constant refrains: live your life while you have it because it leaves you far sooner than you expect.'

'You've never mentioned your father. Does he do what he says you should do?'

'Did, Jonathan. He's dead. Sadly he was thirty-eight when Death took him. I think the point he was trying to make was that you're old before you know it. Or you're dead before you get there, of course. Look after your life, Jonathan. That's what I'm saying. However much time God gives you, it will still be over faster than you would like.'

After a brief pause in the conversation, Lambert leaned back in his chair. 'Let me treat us both to a meal.'

'And a bottle of wine.'

'I very much doubt that we will stop at one bottle. We have a business venture to celebrate and two women in our lives. I'd like to learn a little more about you. But first, let's get these prototypes locked away where no inquisitive eyes can see them.'

Two bottles of wine. Of course, wine bottles were much smaller in the eighteenth century. Three-quarters of a litre, which was what they had grown to in Lambert's own time, was just the right size for two people to enjoy over a meal. How he'd like to make that change now. To get new, larger bottles made and have the vineyards fill them. But no doubt there was a bottle maker's guild, and no doubt it had its own statutes that laid down exactly how a bottle should be made if wine was to go into it and precisely how much wine it should be able to hold. There might come a time to take on such a guild and get changes made. But that time was certainly not now.

§§§

A Question of Time

THERE WERE MANY THINGS THAT LAMBERT, a child of the modern era, found difficult about 18th-century France. One of the smallest was also one of the most irritating: the amount of effort you had to go to arrange to meet someone. You couldn't telephone, couldn't email, couldn't send an SMS. There was no way of knowing if the person you wanted to see would be there, should you choose just to turn up. But he needed to speak to Pétion, and he thought it probably wouldn't wait much longer. So here he was, outside Pétion's office at 10 o'clock on a Tuesday morning. He had no appointment, and little hope that the man he wanted to speak to would be here, but at least there would be some way to get word to him. He knocked on the door. It opened. And there, to his amazement, was the man himself. Pétion. Not a minion, a secretary, someone to take a message. Pétion. The man looked surprised. 'Monsieur Lambert! I was about to go out!' He stepped back inside the building. 'Please. Come in.'

'Monsieur Pétion, I need to see you. Can we arrange a time as soon as possible?'

'Of course, we can. We can arrange now. I mean, now is the time we can meet.'

'But I am interrupting you, clearly. You were going out.'

'That will wait at least an hour. Sit down, please.' He turned to a young man sitting at a desk. 'Jean-Pierre. Please. Coffee for our guest and myself. And for you, too, of course.'

CHAPTER 13

Jean-Pierre hurried out into the street. 'Now, Monsieur Lambert,' said Pétion. 'What is it you want to talk to me about? And while we wait for the coffee, let me offer you a glass of cognac. Or would you prefer wine?'

'A cognac would be splendid.' Lambert looked around him. It was a small study, well-lit and carpeted, with a simple but well-built desk. Off to the side was a large bookcase filled with what he assumed were legal references. Against another wall were two overstuffed small couch chairs, and there was a visitor's chair in front of the desk. Nothing garish or outlandish. Lambert liked it.

Pétion poured two glasses and put the bottle down on the table between them. 'Santé.' He raised his glass in Lambert's direction, and Lambert replied with the same toast. After he had taken a sip, he looked at the bottle, trying to make out the label.

Pétion said, 'it's a small local distillery run by an Irishman, of all things. Richard Hennessy. I met him in a club I belong to. He has much the same sympathies as I have myself.'

'It's a new name to me,' said Lambert, and he found – as he had found several times since he got here – that the lie came easily. The Hennessy brand was huge, and a subsidiary of the enormous Louis Vuitton empire. He continued, 'I came here, Monsieur Pétition because I need legal representation. And choosing who to get it from is not difficult, because you are the only lawyer I know.' Before Pétition could respond, Jean-Pierre returned from his coffee errand and poured both men a cup. 'Thank you,' he added.

Getting back to the discussion Pétition said 'I cannot pretend to be an expert in every aspect of the law, however, what is the nature of your problem?'

'I have fallen foul of the Caterer's Guild. It seems that my business activities are exclusive to them under the terms of their charter.'

A slight smile played across Pétion's face. 'Yes. I see. And what is it that you want of me?'

'I want to challenge the Guild's interpretation of my business. And, ideally, I would like to provoke a deeper reflection on the whole system of guilds.' He said this with studied casualness, though he knew that it was anything but casual. But Pétion kept a straight face.

'Monsieur Lambert. Before you begin an action, have you given enough thought to the alternatives? Surely, one day, the costs of being admitted to the Guild will be recovered, and you will be able to live in harmony with their charter?'

'Yes, Monsieur Pétion. I have given it a great deal of thought. And it is my firm conviction that our society is ready to reconsider the entire Guild structure. Guilds serve only to protect a minority of people. They choke innovation, and they keep creative people down. They enrich their Masters and impoverish their journeymen. They create barriers to trade, they limit the expansion of ideas, and they slow down progress. The English have, to a great extent, drawn their teeth, and that is one reason why that country is forging ahead of ours on every front. We risk being left behind.'

Pétion said nothing. He drank his cognac and refilled both glasses. Then he said, 'Well, Monsieur Lambert, we share similar views, and I have to tell you that voicing those views out loud is dangerous. I myself belong to a small group of people who often debate the merits of a more free society.

I can't tell you their names, but some of them would surprise you. I support your overall cause. Nevertheless, what we have to address first is the immediate concern, which is your challenge to The Caterer's Guild. Tell me what your argument rests on.'

Lambert saw that Jean-Pierre was taking a close interest in the conversation. That must be all right, surely – Pétion would not have mentioned this group of his if there was the slightest danger of Jean-Pierre reporting it to the authorities. Pétion noticed where Lambert's eyes had gone and said, 'Don't worry about Jean-Pierre. You can speak with confidence while he is here.'

'Very well,' said Lambert. 'The Caterer's Guild. As I understand their charter, it protects them in the preparation and distribution of slowly cooked ingredients in a ragout. That is not what I do. I cook food by separately preparing sauces mixed with egg yolks and then pouring the sauces over the cooked meats. And over vegetables, which have been boiled

or baked. The foods I prepare – like my pizza dish –
are not specifically protected by the Caterer's Guild's
charter. You could say that a pizza is technically a
baked pastry; what it is not is a ragout.'

'These arguments are technicalities. What the
court is most likely to look at is the spirit of the
charter and not its specifics.'

'Over the last three months, I have served a daily
meal to the indigent and impoverished people of my
neighbourhood in an attempt to alleviate their
suffering. The Guild's threats could close down my
business and leave these people to return to a life of
slow starvation and misery. Is that not worth
mentioning?'

'It could sway popular opinion,' said Pétion.
'Unfortunately, popular opinion is not the opinion
that matters. The opinion that does matter belongs
to the presiding magistrate assigned to the case. Our
first challenge will be to understand where this
argument will be made and to whom. You are from
the colonies. Perhaps you are not sufficiently aware
of the history of France over the last few centuries.
We have a great deal of duplication, ambiguity and
competition. For perhaps 300 years now, whoever
was on the French throne has hesitated to anger
entrenched and powerful vested interests by
abolishing existing institutions. What they have done
instead is to create parallel institutions that would
slowly take over the functions of the institution they
wanted to see abolished.

Each King accredited new agencies that were intended to replace old agencies without the old agencies having to be abolished. What that means is that there are often several different bodies sharing the same authority to take a particular action or to judge a particular case. The decision we get is likely to have less to do with formal structures and more to do with influence and favour.'

Lambert tried to absorb this. 'What you are saying is that everything depends on which magistrate hears the case, who his friends are, and who my friends are? Nothing to do with the legal rights and wrongs of the matter?'

'That sums it up perfectly. What is important is not which party is right and which party is wrong. It is not what the law says. What is important is how we prepare. We need to identify who can help us and put pressure on the right people at the right time. I believe there are those in my immediate circle who can help. I shall make enquiries. And if you, yourself, have any influence anywhere, this might be a very good moment to call in any favours you are owed.'

Lambert recognised the subtle attempt to find out how far Lambert's business dealings reached. There was Breguet, of course; did he had influential friends who might be prepared to help? Lambert didn't know. And how about Lavoisier? The man was a devout royalist and owned a share in the tax farm, so he might not be a likely candidate to disrupt the current social order.

Pétion broke into his thoughts. 'Monsieur Lambert?'

'I'm sorry, Monsieur Pétion. My mind had wandered.'

'And my retainer? Has your mind perhaps wandered in that direction? Because I will need a retainer of at least 500 livres. I will try to find sources of support in my own social circles that may help defray some of your future costs. Not everyone is as brave as you are planning to be. There are those who would rather remain in the shadows and influence the debate by offering money. I'm sure I can shake a few livres from their purses.'

Lambert shook himself back into the present. 'Of course, I agree to your terms, Monsieur Pétion. I shall have the money delivered here to your office first thing tomorrow morning. Oh, and there's something else... I may want to ask you to establish a simple corporation for Monsieur Breguet and I. We are exploring some business ventures and will need to set up a proper profit-sharing scheme.'

'I'll start work on that immediately. Or, rather...' He looked in the direction of Jean-Pierre who nodded.

'A corporation. I'll start to prepare the paperwork.'

Lambert drained his coffee and his cognac, shook hands with Pétion, nodded in the direction of Jean-Pierre, and left. Breguet must be brought up-to-date with where matters stood.

CHAPTER 14

WHEN HE AND BREGUET ARRIVED AT THE ARSENAL, Lambert was not without some concerns. They were here for the public demonstration of the gun cotton, but this time he had had no part in its preparation. He had left Lavoisier with his notebook full of instructions. If the man had followed them to the letter, all will be well. If he had not, and this new demonstration was a shambles (or, worse, if someone was hurt or even killed), Lambert had no doubt about who would be blamed. It would not be Lavoisier.

Security was tighter this time around – or, at least, there were more soldiers here. Perhaps it was just to make sure that there would be witnesses to the demonstration. Witnesses who would have a vested interest in seeing it go well. And, of course, since Lavoisier was leading, if the demonstration were a success, then everyone would know who should receive the credit.

Breguet, too, seemed to be feeling the strain because he was twirling his pocket watch between his fingers. 'Are you all right?' Lambert asked.

'Nobles always make me nervous. Especially,' and he nodded his head towards the soldiers, 'when they have their dogs with them.'

They were admitted into the courtyard. Some chairs had been set on a raised platform facing one of the outer walls. Target dummies and some larger wooden targets were perched on stakes along the walls. There were several different muskets on tables, and measured markers on the ground indicated the distance to a target. It all looked very controlled and scientific. Lavoisier's personal touch was all over it. The most casual observer would see that the man had an eye for detail and left nothing to chance. He saw them approaching and broke off from an animated discussion with some nobles and military men to approach them. 'Good day, gentlemen. The weather is cooperating. It should be a fine demonstration.'

Breguet said, 'You have a good turnout, Monsieur Lavoisier.'

'Indeed. I was able to get some notable people to attend. Come with me, and I'll introduce you both.' He led the two men back to the small cluster of nobles near the reviewing stand. 'May I introduce you gentlemen to Monsieur Philippe de Noailles, Marshal of France, and Monsieur Philippe Trudaine, His Highness's royal engineer. Messieurs, I have the pleasure to introduce Jonathan Lambert and Abraham Breguet. '

The dismissive way the two nobles touched their tricorn hats was barely polite. Lambert realised that he had until now had no great exposure to the nobility apart from Lavoisier. French aristocrats rigidly maintained the strict strata of social class distinctions. Breguet and Lambert were beneath their attention.

'Lambert and Breguet helped me with this breakthrough,' said Lavoisier. 'They were in my company when I first made the discovery.'

Lambert could see the irritation on Breguet's face and held the man's elbow to silence him. 'Thank you, Monsieur Lavoisier. It is kind of you to say so, but this part of the discovery was all yours. '

Lavoisier took out a pocket watch and consulted the time. 'Gentlemen, it is almost time.' He gestured to an area of seats. 'Please, take your positions. Lambert, Breguet, please make your way to that area over there and wait for me after the demonstration.' He pointed to an area where some of the Arsenal's staff had gathered before turning and joining the nobles on the podium.

As they made their way to the appointed place, Breguet said, 'He gave you no credit for the discovery.'

'And I need none. We need Lavoisier's support. By letting him take credit for this discovery, we assure ourselves a grateful patron. The stakes are higher than my ego. Tell me, Breguet, why did those nobles look irritated when Lavoisier looked at his watch?'

'It is considered rude to look at a watch in the presence of high society,' said Breguet. 'Essentially, you are signalling that they no longer hold your attention.'

'I see. What would be helpful is a watch that can be consulted without being looked at. Perhaps with raised indicators so that you can tell the time by touching it.'

'An interesting concept,' said Breguet, seeming to pause to take a mental note...

They stopped in the general area that Lavoisier had instructed, and turned to watch the unfolding demonstration.

Lavoisier began the demonstration by describing gun cotton and comparing it with the black powder that was all these people knew from experience. He explained the objective of getting a larger and more powerful explosion with the same amount of gun cotton while generating less smoke. When he raised his hand, assistants brought out two tubes, one of which contained black powder and the other a similar amount of gun cotton. The men placed each of the tubes on a table of exactly the same size at a safe distance from the reviewing stand, before lighting the fuse to the black powder tube. They then ran, rather than walked, to a place of safety as the fuse burned. There was a sharp explosion, and the table was concealed under a large amount of smoke. The assistants came back and turned the top of the table to show the size of the mark that the explosion had left.

Lambert could see that the audience was not impressed. What they had seen was no more than they had expected to see. They were chatting amongst themselves, their attention wandering. Lavoisier said, 'We will now demonstrate the guncotton using the same volume of material.'

The assistants returned, lit the fuse and fled the scene once more. The explosion that followed was 2 to 3 times more powerful than the one from the black powder tube. It was so powerful that the table was partially destroyed. The excitement of the crowd on the reviewing stand was obvious, and Lavoisier had to shout to be heard above them. 'Notice that there is very little smoke. We can increase the size and force of the blast with the same amount of material and less smoke.'

Both tables were now removed and two new tables produced. Lavoisier's assistants laid out standard-issue muskets on the tables while two other assistants set up wooden target dummies near the outside wall. Two Grenadiers walked up to the tables, carefully loaded and prepared their muskets and waited for the signal from Lavoisier. Lavoisier said, 'We will now demonstrate the difference in the firing of muskets. Please note the amount of smoke that each musket produces and the effect on the target.'

The Grenadiers raised their weapons and were given the order to fire. There were two sharp cracks that would have been familiar to those serving in the military, but one musket produced far less smoke than the other. Both targets had moved slightly when struck by the lead balls, but one of them – the one hit by the musket that produced less smoke – had lost a large chunk of wood from the force of the impact. The Grenadiers put down the muskets, moved to the targets and brought them closer to the reviewing stand.

'You will observe,' said Lavoisier, 'that the target of the musket using gun cotton suffered a much larger impact than the other. It is obvious even to the untrained eye that this new material will improve battlefield strategy and communication.'

A series of smaller-scale demonstrations followed what they had already seen. Large stones and timber logs were brought out and quickly broken up with charges of gun cotton. It was clear that this material would improve civil engineering and mining as much as it helped the military.

When the demonstration was over, Lavoisier returned to the podium and thanked the guests. The applause was genuine. Lambert watched Lavoisier beaming and basking in the adulation.

The reaction of both the Marshal and the engineer suggested that the demonstration had been a resounding success. Guncotton would come quickly to France. Lavoisier and the two men were talking as the crowd thinned. Lambert spotted something under a tarpaulin tucked away in the corner of the grounds and gestured to Breguet that they should take a look at it.

He flipped back a corner of the tarpaulin and instantly recognised the vehicle. 'Abraham, look! It's Cugnot's device! I know how crude it looks now, but it will evolve to change the course of world history. It will unlock opportunities that people today cannot imagine. This device will free ordinary people from the limitations of where they are. It will create mobility on a scale you cannot imagine.'

Breguet looked at the carriage. 'I would never use a simple double piston and gear like that. It's inefficient. Multiple gears are much better. In many ways, it's just like a timepiece.'

Lambert felt a touch of excitement as he listened to what Breguet had to say. An idea was forming in his mind. 'Could you improve the gear ratio?'

'I should certainly hope so. We have to consider the added weight, of course. And three wheels – I ask you! It's highly impractical. The weight will be distributed more evenly and efficiently if the carriage rests on four wheels. I don't know how you'd steer it, though.'

Lambert said, 'What I'm thinking is that we replace these wheels with wheels that can sit on metal rails. Imagine this carriage being able to move back and forth between two fixed points on a set of metal rails instead of a dirt road.' Although there was no one near to hear him, he dropped his voice almost to a whisper. 'I was travelling on a train immediately before I wound up here. This device – or one very like it – will eventually be used to pull a long line of cars on wheels. Because there is much less friction between the wheels and the rails, a single-engine like this could pull many carts, and each cart could carry far more goods than you can move today by horse and cart.'

How much should he tell Breguet? That, before the train, people either lived in the city and worked in the city or lived in the country and worked on a farm?

That, once you had a rail system, suburbs grew around it and people could live on the outskirts of the city and still be able to get to work without any problem? Rail changed the way goods were produced and distributed, and it also changed the way armies moved. It speeded up communication and the flow of information. 'Abraham. You and I need to prepare a presentation involving this carriage. We need to produce some drawings and build a case to present to Lavoisier. He has to understand that this device can change the world, and if France can set the stage, there will be stability here.'

The two men were so sunk in the study of the carriage, with Breguet thinking about the gears and Lambert about the coming of the railway that it took them some moments to realise that someone had joined them. Turning quickly, they were surprised by the silent presence of Cugnot.

Where had he come from? How long had he been there? Most important of all, what had he heard? The pair feigned a warm greeting. 'Captain Cugnot,' said Breguet. 'It's good of you to join us. We were just discussing this marvellous carriage of yours.'

'Oh? You must be the only ones who think it's marvellous. I think it's doomed.'

Perhaps he hadn't heard enough to worry them. Lambert said, 'What was your inspiration when you built it?'

'By training, I am a military engineer. I served as liaison in the Austrian army in the recent war against Prussia.'

Lambert knew all about that war. It was taught to all French Canadian children as the seven year's war and a war between the French and the English but, in fact, it had been possibly the first truly global war. Every European power of the time was involved. It spanned five continents, changed the balance of power in Europe, and it had resulted in the loss of Nouvelle France and the eastern half of Louisiana. It was a sore spot for French Canadians because it heralded British rule in the former French colonies of North America. That war's outcome had affected Lambert directly.

Cugnot said, 'I developed a new musket for the cavalry units. Shorter than traditional muskets, allowing them to fire while mounted. That brought me to the attention of Major General de Gribeauval, who gave me time and flexibility to work on this project. What he wanted was a device that could transport guns more efficiently than a horse-drawn cart.'

'By guns,' said Lambert, 'you mean heavy artillery?'

'Of course. But when the war ended, I lost his attention, and I left the army. I went to Belgium for a few years and wrote two books about modern warfare and fortifications. That brought me into the orbit of the Duc de Choiseul, who financed this project and allowed me to demonstrate it here. With disastrous results, unfortunately.'

Lambert and Breguet nodded. The costs of such a project would be heavy. Cugnot would have needed financial support from a noble.

'Captain,' said Lambert. 'We believe we can make some improvements to your design. And in the way, the carriage could be used, for that matter.'

Breguet said, 'I think the cylinders are unmanageably large. I would replace them with atmospheric cylinders to condense the steam drawn in and create a partial vacuum. That way, you use atmospheric pressure to push the piston into the cylinder. We could get much more power from a smaller design. Also, the gear ratios need to be improved. If we do that, we can deliver the power produced by the pistons much more efficiently.'

Lambert said, 'We also think that you need to distribute the weight of the carriage across four wheels and not three. And those wheels need to roll on a set of rails. That way, you are not subject to the condition of the ground you happen to be moving over.'

Breguet said, 'Lavoisier is on his way here.'

They turned to meet the newcomer. He glanced at Cugnot. 'Captain, you were impressed by the guncotton demonstration?'

'I thought it was a resounding success. It will most definitely transform tactics and communications.'

'That is precisely what I have been discussing with the Marshal and the King's engineer. They have agreed to finance large scale production. We are to meet soon to discuss the logistics.' He turned to Lambert. 'Monsieur Lambert, you have my gratitude for your involvement in this innovation. If there is anything I can do to help you in the future, please don't hesitate to come to me.'

Lambert said, 'Thank you, Monsieur Lavoisier. In fact, I am under legal difficulties at the moment with the Caterer's Guild. Perhaps I could presume on your connections at court to help me navigate the issue?'

'The Caterer's Guild? In relation to your business?'

'Yes, Monsieur. They believe that my concept of food preparation and delivery is encroaching on their protected economic activity. They have asked me to cease business or join their Guild. Joining them is out of the question because the expense involved would be far greater than any economic benefit, to say nothing of the time I'd have to devote to ensuring we meet their labour classifications.'

'Yes. I see. I'll look into the matter for you with friends. I'll be in touch when it's time for us to meet. And now, I have to take my leave of you all. Please make your own way out.'

'Before we do, Monsieur Lavoisier, may I impose on you for one more moment?' Lambert gestured towards the carriage under the tarpaulin. 'As you arrived, we were discussing modifications to this design that could make for a very interesting concept for the King's artillery. We'd like to present you with a detailed plan. I believe we can produce something even more important to France than the gun cotton.'

Lavoisier stared at him in silence for some time. Then he said, 'Lambert. The last time you suggested an idea, it was very fortunate for me that I gave you time to present it. Have your presentation ready for the next time we meet. We can tackle it at the same time as we address your legal problems.'

With that, they raised their hats in salute. Lavoisier turned towards one of the Arsenal's buildings, and the three men headed back into the city.

CHAPTER 15

LEADING UP TO THE PRESENTATION THAT HE HAD been working on all week with Cugnot and Breguet, Lambert could focus his mind on little else. They had hired an apprentice draughtsman to finalise the rough drawings of the locomotive. That was the word that Lambert kept using to refer to the carriage, and it had stuck.

Breguet had drawn his proposed changes to the pistons and gear mechanism, and he and the draughtsman had refined the design together. While the concept was still very much theoretical when they looked over the specifications and debated them, they were satisfied that it would be possible to turn theory into reality. As for Lambert, he had guided the project's direction and drawn a schematic for the rails, showing how one locomotive could pull several cars carrying goods and people so long as the power to weight ratio was high.

They had discussed the railway and how to plan its construction. Lambert had insisted that for the demonstration they build a small railway between two points on the outskirts of Paris. At the same time, though, they planned a route from Versailles to the Tuileries. A project of this size would go nowhere unless it had the King's support and the state's resources. Planning a route to Versailles would make it that much more likely that they would get Royal assent. Nothing could be lost, and everything might be gained by pandering to the King's self-interest.

And what else? The patents had been approved for the cradle scythe and the seed drill. Production had begun on both item, and they would have plenty of them to sell for the 1775 spring planting season. Both he and Breguet stood to make a nice amount of money.

A sudden whiff of particularly bad body odour brought his attention back to the present. People were bustling back and forth hawking food and fuel in the form of sticks and other small combustibles. Beggars targeting men and women of means thronged the streets. Streets that reeked of refuse, urine and animal dung. Lambert would never quite get used to the lack of modern hygiene, but this era was immensely exciting.

Possibilities for great change and innovation were almost without end. And perhaps that was why the thought of settling down with Amélie and never going to what he still thought of as 'home' was not such a pain as it might have been.

As he walked away from his newly rented apartment, he took no notice of two men on the other side of the street, leaning against the wall and pretending to talk to each other. One rested his hand on the pommel of a sword whose hilt peeked from under his great cloak. The other, wearing a nondescript uniform, scribbled in a small notebook. They glanced at the address of the apartment building before moving away in the opposite direction to Lambert.

§§§

LAVOISIER'S VALET TOOK LAMBERT'S HAT, COAT AND CANE. 'Monsieur Lavoisier asks that you wait for him in the study. Please follow me.' He turned and climbed a flight of stairs, Lambert following.

The study was a small room, richly appointed with wooden panelled walls and a large desk. There were two seats opposite the desk and two small couches and a small table to the side.

A large bookcase against one wall was host to a collection of leather-bound books and some items of scientific curiosity. Lavoisier was, first and foremost, a scientist. He was known as the father of modern chemistry, and Lambert had understood how important it would be to appeal to his sense of curiosity.

The valet lit a lamp. It gave out a horrible smell and as much oily smoke as light. Lambert recognised it as whale oil. What made it even worse was the thought of how the oil was procured. Lives risked just so that people could see in the evening. He was reminded of a history lesson from his youth.

Then Lavoisier burst into the room, crying out protestations of welcome and asking what Lambert would like to drink. Lambert took a seat on one of the couches. 'I will have whatever you have.'

Lavoisier told the valet to bring a bottle of red wine and two glasses. 'So, Lambert. I have looked into your situation. The Caterer's Guild is old and prestigious, and it is under the protection of powerful patrons. Foodservice touches all social classes in Paris.'

'I understand that,' said Lambert. 'What I am hoping is that we can use this opportunity to argue the case for the abolition of guilds.'

Lavoisier paused before replying. 'I won't deny that some of my progressive acquaintances share your idealistic ideas. But I fear they would be difficult to put into practice in the present climate.'

'I was hoping to appeal to Minister Turgot's progressive ideals. I understand that this would not be the only controversial idea he has taken on?'

Lavoisier looked thoughtful. 'I'm negotiating with Minister Turgot right now to reform the lease arrangements concerning gunpowder manufacture. He is considering my ideas on streamlining gun cotton manufacture. Your innovation has moved the discussion in the right direction.'

'I'm happy the King's Minister finds good use for the cotton. Do you think he would be able to intervene on my behalf? I have hired a lawyer to represent me.'

'Have they determined who the magistrate is to be?'

'My lawyer tells me that the court has not yet been determined. Apparently, there is some confusion over who should hear the case against me.'

'Well, it will be difficult. We should not hide from how difficult it will be. But I will do my best to help you. I will try to move Turgot's agenda to intervene on your behalf. And on behalf of everyone whose dreams have been crushed by the guilds.'

Lambert nodded his thanks. The flame of the lamp was no brighter, and the smoke was as obnoxious as it had been. The valet returned with a tray carrying two glasses and a bottle of red wine. He put it down on a table and began to pour the wine. Lambert said, 'Monsieur Lavoisier. Do you have a small laboratory? Or at any rate, a room in your house that we could retire to? I have an idea I'd like to share with you.'

'I certainly do have a small laboratory. It's by no means as well equipped as those at the Arsenal, but it can serve most scientific curiosities. What did you have in mind?'

What was asphalt known as at this time? Lambert could not remember. But what, after all, is asphalt? It's a mixture of polymer-modified bitumen and stone. No stone would be required for today's purpose. What he needed was bitumen. And he knew that bitumen was used for sketching. He said, 'I'll need an amount of bitumen. The sort artists use to draw with.'

Lavoisier said, 'François, bring my drawing kit to the laboratory.' He stood up, drained his glass and motioned to Lambert to follow him.

The laboratory was on the third floor. It was an intimate room, full of personal objects so that entering it made Lambert feel like an intruder. This was one of Lavoisier's most personal spaces. The way he carried himself as they entered told Lambert how proud of it he was.

There was a workbench in the centre cluttered with instruments, beakers and other scientific paraphernalia. Lambert pointed to a big copper retort of the kind used for distillation. 'I'll need that. And a flame. We are going to distil.'

The valet arrived with the drawing kit which he placed on the workbench and opened to reveal its contents. Lavoisier said, 'François, a bath of cold water, please.'

Clearly, Lavoisier was comfortable with the idea of distillation. And Lambert was grateful because he had forgotten that to distil something you needed a bath of cold water to help the process along. It would be wise to remember that he was a historian by training. It was Lavoisier who was the scientist. He took some of the bitumen from the kit and asked Lavoisier to heat it in the copper pot. 'We need it slightly soft and sticky. We need to heat it just long enough to get the viscosity right.'

They watched the bitumen slowly become a gooey substance. The valet coughed to capture Lavoisier's attention. 'Of course!' said Lavoisier. 'Return to your duties, François. But stay nearby, in case we need your services again.'

When he judged it ready, Lambert asked Lavoisier to transfer the gooey substance to the copper retort which they placed straight back onto the flame. Lavoisier, the trained scientist, expertly directed the retort's spigot to pass through the cold water bath and placed a beaker at the end to capture the distilled liquid. This was by no means the first distillation the man had carried out.

Lambert said, 'Bitumen has certain qualities that can be distilled to economically produce a liquid that you can burn and yet it is stable. Give it about thirty minutes, and we should have enough liquid for this demonstration. Why don't we go back to your study and enjoy another glass of wine while we wait for enough liquid to be distilled?'

When they were back in the study, Lavoisier asked the question that Lambert had feared but had known must come. 'Is this, then, another recipe from your time in the colonies?'

'Yes. My uncle used this process instead of whale oil. We couldn't afford that, and there was plenty of bitumen near our farm.' Not for the first time, he regretted the need to lie. But telling the truth was out of the question. What they were doing in Lavoisier's little laboratory was the first-ever production of kerosene, which really should not be available for some years yet. Before Lambert began rewriting history, kerosene was discovered in the nineteenth century by a Canadian geologist. It was cheaper than whale oil, cheaper even than candles, and it burned brighter and cleaner.

But with those thoughts of changing history came another thought – was he doing the right thing? Time travel was much discussed in his own era, and the general consensus was that it had never happened because, if it had, the results would be visible. There was also agreement that anyone who did travel into the past should take great care not to change whatever she or he found there. And that was exactly what Lambert was doing.

His intentions were good. He wanted to avert the French Revolution, make life better for the masses of the poor and save huge numbers from the guillotine and the wars that followed the rise of Napoleon. Those were praiseworthy objectives, surely? And yes, Lambert was aware that recent opinion in his own time was that it would be wrong to interfere. History was history. Mankind has choices. Things developed as they did. And something else nagged at him: could he really be sure that what he would be leaving behind if he did manage to change history would be better than what had evolved without his intervention? Lambert was a historian. He knew about the sufferings of the English poor that resulted from enclosures. He also knew that the end result of enclosure – admittedly it had been more than a century later before it became clear – was a great rise in prosperity for the entire population. If he had been propelled back into 18th-century England instead of France, would he have been right to try to ameliorate the conditions of labourers thrown off the land by enclosure? In the long run, possibly not.

Everything he had done here in this time had been step-by-step. One thing followed another. He needed to survive, so he got a job in a restaurant preparing vegetables. He needed to do better for himself, so he showed the restaurant owner how the business could be improved. That led to him buying the business and, in effect, franchising it. But what about the guncotton? Why had he done that? Was it simply because, as a French-Canadian, he wanted to damage the interests both of the English and of the people to Canada's south who were now their colonial subjects but would soon free themselves on the way to becoming the most powerful nation on earth? And he found that that was not a question he was keen to answer.

Well, it was what it was, and he was where he was, and he had taken the steps he had taken, and that was that. He could hardly now tell Lavoisier that he was not prepared to offer any more assistance. And nor could he tell the man to forget about the distillation taking place upstairs and about what the result was likely to be.

To take his mind off these matters that worried him, he looked around Lavoisier's study.

A massive upholstered chair was wedged tightly between the desk and a side table on which were scattered manuscripts and scientific paraphernalia. He said, 'Monsieur Lavoisier, I believe you may have difficulty navigating your desk and your various side tables. Your chair seems a little large for such a small space.'

'Yes. I admit it; it can be difficult to manoeuvre when I am writing.'

'Why not get another chair with a round seat? Cut the chair at the base. Attach a spindle where the base connects to the seat and insert castors so that the top part can spin?'

Lavoisier cupped his chin in his hand. 'You mean so that I can turn easily in the chair without having to move the base?'

'Yes. And if you put castors also on the chair's feet, you can move easily between your desk and the other tables.'

Really, what did he think he was doing? All the concerns he had just had about changing history, and here he was recommending the introduction of the swivel chair which had gone on to become a mainstay in offices around the world, but not before Thomas Jefferson had invented it.

'You continue to surprise, Monsieur Lambert.'

'I wonder whether we might discuss the concept I mentioned at the Arsenal when we looked at Captain Cugnot's contraption?'

Lavoisier made a gesture that said, 'Go ahead,' but his face wore an expression of doubt. Lambert began to describe the conversation he had had with Breguet about improving the gear ratio and changing three wheels to four. He went on to describe modifying the wheels by making them smaller and putting lips on the inside and outside.

Lavoisier said, 'The wheels would be damaged as soon as you start enrolling it on the road.'

'Have you a piece of paper and some charcoal?' Lavoisier rummaged in his desk and found what he had been asked for. Lambert drew a small wheel with the inside and outside lips he had described. He then drew a stretch of track. He described making it from iron bars about two metres long which would be attached to a wooden tie of the sort that was already in use in mines so that the ore could be easily taken out. 'It would work best if we gave it a stable base of crushed stone so that rain does not wash the track away. You see? It becomes a transport device, with no need for horses. Attach light cars to the main carriage, and you increase the number of people – or the number of goods – or the amount of heavy field artillery – that you can move across great distances.'

He risked a quick glance at Lavoisier. Did he look convinced? Sceptical? It was difficult to be sure. He said, 'I have discussed the beginnings of this concept with Cugnot and Breguet, and they feel that the modifications are easily achievable. We've discussed how to increase the power of the engine. With an alternative to wood as a fuel, I believe we could get a carriage that would match the speed of a horse at a full trot. Eventually, even at full gallop. And, unlike a horse, it would not become tired.'

Lavoisier sat like a man in a dream. 'The cost! Have you considered what it would cost to build something like this?'

'It would be considerable. But just imagine rails like these connecting every major city in France, with multiple carriages and cars hauling people and material all over the country. Think of the toll revenues. The ticket revenues. The cost of construction would easily be met.'

'Perhaps. I suppose it would bring down the cost of transport. Regional goods would become more affordable.'

'Yes, and the project would employ a huge number of people. People who need employment. People whose children can be saved from starvation by a regular income from their labours.' He turned the drawing over and drew a crude map of France, showing how tracks could connect all the major cities. 'Imagine being able to get food quickly from one part of France to another. Or soldiers. Or communications.' The choice of examples was not random – if they were to have any chance of getting this proposal accepted, those were the three things that had to be delivered.

And Lavoisier was sold. 'I will task Cugnot with expanding on this idea. And I'll speak to the King's engineer, Monsieur De Montigny, and get his support. Once we have the necessary funding, I will ask them to build a rail on the grand boulevard just outside the Arsenal.'

A smell had become increasingly noticeable from the hallway. Lambert recognised it for what it was and told Lavoisier that there should be enough liquid now for the demonstration. 'Please ask François to bring us a small lamp. Dry of fuel, and with a new wick.'

When they reached the laboratory, and the valet brought the lamp, Lambert extinguished the flame under the retort and set it to one side. He opened the lamp, poured the clear liquid into the base, dipped a fresh wick into it and made sure it was well soaked. He threaded the wick into the lantern and wiped his fingers with a cloth. Then he lit the wick. A bright yellow flame burned steadily. He covered the lamp with the glass cylinder and stepped back. He extinguished the lamp that was burning whale oil. The room was noticeably brighter than it had been. 'See,' he said, 'how much less smoke this produces than the whale oil.'

'Monsieur Lambert, I am yet again surprised by the ingenuity of your family.'

'Monsieur Lavoisier, I give you this knowledge to do with as you see fit. I make no claim and expect no reward. What I ask in return is your best efforts to protect me against the Guild. Please do everything in your power to help me. My restaurant business will be destroyed if I am made to bend to their will.'

Lavoisier reached out his hand, and Lambert shook it. Lavoisier said, 'I will do everything I can to help you. This fuel you have demonstrated and the system of transport has so much potential for France. I will make sure that the people I discuss these innovations with know who brought them to us. What do you suppose we should call this oil?'

'Kerosene. My uncle called it kerosene.'

CHAPTER 16

CHRISTMAS IN EIGHTEENTH-CENTURY PARIS may not have been able to rival Montreal for decorations, lights (of course, there were none of the kind Lambert was thinking of), open-air skating rinks or street entertainment, but it was festive for all that. The markets were booming, and people seemed generally happier. Although it was by no means as cold as Eastern Canada could be, it was well into the Little Ice Age. Cold weather acted on the streets as an antiseptic. Snow and ice-covered the smell of refuse, and other people's body odour was not as strong as it would be when summer came.

Lambert was walking to his restaurant, having just caught up with the news of the day at a reading room.

He had read with trepidation about attacks on Fort William and Mary in New Hampshire. This rebellion by the colony had crossed the line into overt insurrection. Patriots had faced gunfire to storm the colony's provincial arsenal, a fort in the British Empire's American defence system manned by soldiers who reported to a Royal Governor appointed directly by the British Crown. Could they be called patriots when the country they were patriotic for did not yet exist? Lambert thought they could. American patriots for an America as yet unformed but to which its people were already loyal In a way they never would be to a 'motherland' on the other side of the Atlantic that was out of touch with their needs but expected to call the shots.

This was the opening salvo of the American Revolution, and it reminded Lambert of the urgency of what he needed to do. The French King would be welcome to help the fledgeling cause of freedom on the American continent (though how anyone so autocratic as a French King could have the audacity to support freedom was beyond Lambert) but must not become mired in an adventure that would bankrupt the French state.

THE MOMENT HE ARRIVED AT THE GALIMARDS, Lambert found that his only wish was to whisk Amelie away, outside of the house so that they could be alone. But, the presence of both Monsieur and Madame Galimard in the parlour with Amelie made this quite impossible. Once formal greetings were taken care of, he allowed his gaze to settle on Amelie who blushed with pleasure when he kissed her hand.

'I'm very interested to hear about your recent....discoveries, shall we call them?' Monsieur Galimard plunged in.

Lambert chose to take this in stride, figuring that talking about his accomplishments with Amelie's father could only prove beneficial.

'Yes, monsieur, I feel that is an apt way to describe my work,' he said, setting aside his gloves and taking a seat, accepting the cup of coffee offered to him by an attending servant.

'Where do you get these ideas for your innovations?'

Lambert would have been a fool not to anticipate this question from Monsieur Galimard, and if it didn't come from him, it would certainly be asked by someone else.

He crossed his legs, leaning back in a posture he hoped portrayed leisure. 'Just as in business, I feel that a certain knack is required in order to be successful as an innovator—a certain...' he waved his hand, searching for the right words. 'God-given talent, you might say. I seem to have been blessed with that knack.'

Lambert took a drink from his coffee cup, considering how to seal this explanation most convincingly. 'That, coupled with my voracious love for learning, I've done extensive reading and research which provide the necessary knowledge to make my visions reality.'

He scanned the faces in the room, doing his best to estimate how his words had been taken. Madame Galimard's expression was relatively nondescript,

Monsueir Galimard looked mildly impressed, and Amelie, perfectly love-struck. Lambert unabashedly kept his eyes fixed on her for a few moments, enjoying her enthusiasm. After all, she was the one he most wished to impress, important though the others may be.

'I believe a rented room still serves as your living quarters, is that correct?' Madame Galimard piped up then.

The topic of his apartment being raised once again reinforced the value of holding conversations with Amelie's parents. In a time where dating involved the parents in almost every step, it was a great way to gauge how he could ensure that he came across as worthy enough for the woman he desired. Learning about his work was important to the father and, it would seem, material well-being in accordance with propriety was the chief concern of the mother. Though he would have preferred to discuss his innovations, Lambert knew he must bend to the Galimards whenever possible at this stage.

'That's correct, and the invitation to join me in my search still stands.'

Madame Galimard's upper lip curved up in a kind of sneer. 'I'm sure you don't intend to remain there for long...How goes your research into the St Honoré neighbourhood? You must look forward to improving your situation?'

In truth, Lambert had grown rather comfortable at the boarding house, but, of course, if he were to marry, he'd need to secure somewhere more prestigious.

'It has served me well thus far. For the time being, it will do while I search for another location,' Lambert explained. 'You see, I only chose it initially so that I would have somewhere to lay my head and not feel rushed into selecting a place merely out of necessity. I do want to choose carefully. I'm sure you understand.'

He was finally rewarded by a look of approval from Amelie's mother at this statement. 'Yes, I do. There are a great many places around town. Still, it is important to choose carefully. And to pay the most reasonable price without sacrificing suitability if you know what I mean.'

Lambert made a great show of shaking his head, grinning as if Madame Galimard had just solved his every problem.

'You've quite read my mind, Madame. Perhaps when I've located a living situation that is more....suitable for my needs, I could prevail upon you to offer your valuable opinion on the place?' Lambert's pretence of needing feminine input was purely a step in the direction of his own interests. He had played the card of the naïf male bachelor. He had no doubt that Madame Galimard was as aware as he was that they were, in fact, conducting a courtship ritual. Courtship not of her, but of her daughter

Amélie. It was a formality that both were happy to observe.

'I would be happy to render my services,' Madame Galimard readily replied, her appreciative expression making it clear that the flattery had worked.

'Well, unfortunately, my own work calls for my attention,' Monsieur Galimard said, standing, reaching over to shake Lambert's hand. 'I hope we'll be seeing more of you soon, Monsieur.'

'As do I,' Lambert responded. As he settled back down, Lambert mentally checked gaining Amelie's father's approval off of his list. Now, all he needed to do was secure a place that her mother would find acceptable. The restaurant was doing well, so he'd have the money. He figured this task wouldn't be particularly difficult.

'Monsieur Lambert...' Madame Galimard said, angling herself toward him, obviously eager to ask her next question.

However, Lambert was saved by the bell when a servant rushed into the room, exclaiming that her mistress' attention was needed immediately.

'Good heavens,' Madame Galimard murmured. 'Sometimes, I wonder why I bother hiring servants at all. Will you excuse me?'

'Of course,' Lambert said, rising out of respect, resuming his seat once she'd disappeared. He turned his attention then to Amelie, who was looking rather pleased that they were alone. So, it seemed they'd both been wishing for the same thing.

CHAPTER 16

Lambert felt sure that Amelie could keep a secret, so he decided to test this out by offering her a few whispered words of confidence. 'I must say,' he said, his voice lowering as he leaned toward her. 'Judging by the kind of tribulation the house staff causes your mother, the idea of obtaining a larger apartment does not appeal to me very much at all.'

Amelie laughed, covering her mouth with a gloved hand, glancing around to see if she'd been heard. 'Monsieur, I can see why you would feel that way. However, a man like you would sooner or later wish for a place all his own.... One where he can rest after a long day, stretch his legs in front of the fireplace and relax.... Wouldn't he?'

'Well, when you put it that way,' Lambert said. Grateful not to have to conceal his wish to flirt any longer, he continued. 'However, I feel that I would be inclined to agree with anything you say. That sweet voice of yours, I must say, has the ability to cast quite a spell on a man.'

Colour crept once more across Amelie's cheeks as she fiddled with the lace on her gown. 'On any man? Or a specific man.....?' She glanced up rather sheepishly in order to catch Lambert's reaction.

Now was his chance. Lambert knew that he might be jumping the gun a little, considering formal blessing hadn't been given to him in regards to pursuing Amelie, but he decided to take the risk and send a direct gesture to the object of his attention herself.

He grinned, leaning toward her. 'Perhaps if we could get some fresh air, some time to ourselves, you might find out.'

Amelie was on her feet in a moment, proceeding Lambert to the doorway. They had barely stepped into the hall when Madame Galimard's voice could be heard.

'Amelie! Where are you going?'

Lambert looked to Amelie in surprise, shocked that Madame Galimard had been able to hear their footsteps from such a distance.

Amelie rolled her eyes, a wry smile coming to her mouth. 'I'm only going to show Monsieur Lambert the garden, Mother,' Amelie called back. 'We won't be gone long, but we're both in need of some fresh air.'

When there was no answer for the space of a few seconds, Amelie rushed for the door, followed by Lambert.

Once outside, they laughed, both equally surprised and pleased their getaway had been successful.

One of the elegant Galimard carriages was already stationed in front of the entryway, prepared at any moment to accommodate a member of the family.

'Your parents won't mind, will they?' It wasn't as if there was time to turn back now, but Lambert decided to check anyway.

CHAPTER 16

Amelie laughed, throwing her head back before her eyes glinted with mischief. 'If they have any problem with it, you'll just have to follow my lead when I tell them that it was all my idea. I absolutely insisted.'

Lambert was thrilled by her easy teasing and approval of his wish to be alone with her.

The couple clambered into the carriage before the driver whisked them off. Lambert didn't know where they were headed, and he didn't even care. No more thinking about parents or propriety or innovations or apartments for the time being. At the moment, he would focus entirely on Amelie.

A SMALL CROWD IN THE RESTAURANT'S WAITING AREA reminded him how business was booming, and his income with it. The second restaurant opened by Mathurin de Roze was gaining traction, though he had drawn some very strange looks when he used that word in a conversation. He waited for the Host to finish explaining to an irritated man that the empty tables were not free because they were reserved and that if the man wanted to ensure prompt seating in future, he would be wise to reserve a table himself. When the conversation was done, and the man turned away, Lambert asked how the day was going.

'Lots of missing vegetables,' said the Host. 'The vendors sent word that there was another backlog.'

It was winter. Disruptions in vegetable delivery were to be expected. You couldn't expect fresh tomatoes, for example, to reach Paris in December unscathed without occasional disruption. The canning process Lambert had introduced ensured that his establishment was spared the worst of the shortages.

Having near fresh produce in his dishes was a constant marvel to his patrons who were not accustomed to eating certain foods in the middle of a cold European winter. Lambert said, 'We'll have to make do with what's in the stores. I'll talk to the kitchen manager.' He went to the back office, removed his coat and hat and handed it to the Host, who said, 'Some letters came for you, Monsieur. They are on your desk.'

Lambert went to the kitchen and authorised opening some of the preserved goods. Then he sat at his desk and opened the letters. Most were formal invitations to salons, book readings, store openings and other social events. Christmas was clearly a busy time for the party circuit. Most of these invitations would be turned down because Lambert's interests lay elsewhere. He chose to spend as much time as he could with Amélie and her mother. He had been invited to Christmas dinner at the Galimard house and had ordered a new set of clothes for the occasion. He'd bought baubles for her mother and – taking a deep breath – a ring for Amélie that was clearly intended as an engagement gift.

CHAPTER 16

He would ask Madame Galimard formally for her daughter's hand, but he did not expect to be refused.

Inevitably, his thoughts turned towards his own mother. She would be at home in Montreal, probably facing brutally cold weather. She would have been so happy if she could have known of his forthcoming engagement, but all she knew of him – all she could know of him – was that he had disappeared in mysterious circumstances. Another loss to add to the death of his father. He wiped a tear from his eye. Was he really wise to be setting roots here so deeply? Just suppose he *could* find his way back to his own time. Now that he had Amélie – or, at least, he thought he had – would he be prepared to leave this time?

If there was a time for sad thoughts, this was not it. Taking paper and quill from his desk, he began his replies to the ever-mounting pile of correspondence.

St Honoré was, as Lambert had known it would be, a great deal more expensive than his rented room in the fifth arrondissement. It was a mark of the extent of his feelings for Amélie that he did not feel like simply walking away. The rent was more than he had wanted to pay and it seemed fairly clear that Madame Galimard had been surprised that he had not haggled. Haggling was the way of it with almost any exchange of goods and services. In fact, Lambert suspected that the building manager – a man of indeterminate but probably advanced age who had almost certainly expected a prolonged struggle – had been so surprised when Lambert accepted his first price that it had awakened doubts about Lambert in the man's mind. Well, that was as may be. Number 91 Saint Honoré was close to his restaurant, close to Lavoisier's home, and in a good area of Paris. It also had space for entertaining and a room for a domestic servant.

'Your views, Monsieur Lambert?' Asked Madame Galimard.

'I believe it will do perfectly,' said Lambert.

'You will need to hire at least one and possibly two full-time domestics. The apartments are rather large.

I don't believe you would be able to manage with part-time help.' She coughed politely. 'Men are not the best people to recruit domestics.'

'I very much hope, Madame, that I will be able to rely on your assistance in the selection process.'

She nodded as if to say that she had expected nothing less. And now Lambert paused for just a moment. This process he was engaged in – this courtship of the woman's daughter. What did it mean? He would not, surely, seek to marry a woman and then desert her when the opportunity arose to get back to the 21st-century? Would he? No, he assured himself, he would not. And that meant... Yes. It did, didn't it? It meant that he had accepted that he wasn't going back to his own time. That whatever the process had been that brought him here, it had been one-way. There was no returning.

He put this thought to the back of his mind, to be considered later when he was on his own. For now, there was the apartment, the domestics – and furniture. The place had to be furnished. And this was not his own era. There would be no driving to a huge warehouse on the outskirts of town and picking out mass-produced items to be delivered.

He'd already been through this with the restaurant a few months earlier when he had explored a possible remodelling, only to have to scale back on the idea when the quotes began to arrive. Furniture here at this time was crafted by artisans, and their guilds made sure of scarcity and very high standard of production that forced prices up. But there was an idea here that he could cash in on. He said, 'Do you think, Madame, that your daughter might be interested in giving me advice on furnishing my new apartment?'

Was that a smirk on the Galimard face? Lambert rather thought it was. Of course, she was as aware as he of the nature of the intricate dance they were performing. And she was on his side. Provisionally. She wanted him to succeed in his courtship. Provisionally. Provisional that is, on his actually having the financial resources he appeared to have. If he were as soundly based financially as he seemed to be, he would be an excellent capture for her daughter. And if he did not, that would become very clear when he had bills to pay or even when he had price estimates to accept. Lambert had no doubt that Amélie's mother would be sure to tell her daughter to recommend that he purchase one or two items of real expense.

He was being tested. This was eighteenth-century romance as performed by the French bourgeoisie. Love had nothing to do with it. What would decide whether he succeeded or failed would be the amount of money he could come up with and whether it met the Galimard expectation? She said, 'I'm sure she would love to take on such a project, Monsieur Lambert. I will make her aware of the opportunity. She would need to be at your apartment several times while it was being outfitted. I trust you would not find that distracting?'

Lambert smiled in return. 'I'm sure, Madame Galimard, that we will have our minds entirely on the task at hand.'

Madame Galimard performed a small curtsy and bade him farewell before setting off in the direction of her own apartment.

§§§

THE COMPANY'S HOME PAGE proclaimed its dominance in the world of luxury goods. One of the signposts was to the company's historical roots, and that was what Nadeau clicked. The company had been founded in 1775 by three people.

Abraham-Louis Breguet. Jonathan Lambert. Amélie Galimard. It had begun life as a manufacturer of agricultural implements, a timepiece business, and a distributor of gloves and perfumes. A strange mixture thought Nadeau. What combination of circumstances had caused one company to deal with all three of those things?

A companywide reorientation had phased out the agricultural implement manufacturer, allowing the company to focus on consumer and luxury goods for the high society of France. And then...

'Oh, Holy Mary, Mother of God.' Nadeau thought for a moment he would lose control of himself. He was not a religious man, and those words remembered from his grandmother at times of high stress simply slipped from his lips. They were followed by something more usual when Nadeau had discovered something he really would have preferred not to know: 'Merde!' For he was looking at a face from more than 200 years ago – and he knew the man! On his screen was a graphic designer's rendition, a painting that had been digitised and touched up before being put online.

The face was the spitting image of one in a Canadian passport that sat in his office in a box under his desk. It was Jonathan Lambert. The Jonathan Lambert who had been one of the founders of Lambregal in 1775 and the Jonathan Lambert who had disappeared from a TGV on a twenty-first-century journey from Brussels to Paris were one and the same.

It was impossible.

It could not be.

But it was.

§§§

Lambert was still not sure how it had come about that he and Amélie had been allowed to go to inspect fabrics unchaperoned. Did it mean that he was regarded as safe? Or was it something different – was he a good catch, and would Amélie be encouraged by her mother to do whatever was necessary to bag him? It struck him then that you could know everything there was to know (and, of course, he accepted that he did not know everything there was to know) about kings and queens and social institutions and wars and treaties, and still be ignorant of the mores of the day. How people lived, what they did, and how they treated each other. In any case, here they were, and Amélie was beaming as she fingered a piece of cloth. 'You must have this.'

It was a cold day. They both wore thick overcoats, and Amélie had given Lambert a pair of gloves from her family's store. They were lined in fur, heavily scented, extremely practical and he was very grateful. But the material? He said, 'Do you not think it a bit feminine for my apartment? I am a bachelor.'

'At present, you are. But you will not always be a bachelor, Monsieur Lambert.' That look in her eyes – was she teasing him?

Or was it something else? A message? Even a challenge? 'And when you are married,' she went on, 'your wife will appreciate the touch of lilies.' Lambert looked again at the rich creme fabric and the blue and white pattern of fleur de lys typical of the era.

Lambert turned to the vendor. 'How much is it?'

'This is an Overkampf design.' He flipped the cloth casually to show the quality of the print. 'It has been manufactured in the style of the Englishman, John Kay. It's very exclusive.'

Yes, yes, thought Lambert, but what I asked, and what you have not answered, is how much it's going to cost me. He did not know the name Overkampf, though it was clear that Amélie had recognised it; however, he had certainly heard of John Kay. The inventor of the flying shuttle, an innovation that allowed greater weaving of fabrics. And perhaps that would always be the difference between Amélie and him – that she would recognise the names of designers and artists and know those that carried prestige, while he would be more interested in the how and the why.

The vendor said, 'What quantity do you think you'll need?'

'Oh. Enough to upholster about a dozen chairs and half a dozen couches of about the size for two people.'

Amélie smiled. It was that most attractive of all

smiles – the one made by the eyes and not by the mouth. 'And your bed canopy?' she asked.

Why did he need a bed canopy? He'd never had a bed canopy in his life. But, clearly, he would have to have one now. 'Yes,' he said, 'of course. Enough for a bed canopy, too.'

He could see calculations going on behind the vendor's eyes. Then the man said, 'That is a lot of fabric. I will consult with the Overkampf production team and send you a formal quotation.'

Lambert handed him a card. He'd only had them for a week and was still getting used to using them. His life since his early teenage years had involved exchanging contact information electronically, but now he needed cards. 'Thank you. We will await your quote.' We? Don't make your assumptions too easily, Lambert. But Amélie did not seem to have responded in any negative way to the use of the word.

How did one manage these things in 18th-century France? If he'd been at home – but he was at home.

Wasn't he? At home was not what he had meant to think. If he had been back in the time in which he originated, he would have known what to do when he was drawn to a woman, and the woman gave signals that she was drawn to him. He would have taken her hand. He would have kissed her. They would both have known that she could signal either that he had overstepped the mark, that it was too soon, or that she simply wasn't that interested. And they would also both have known that she could kiss him back. And, if that's what she wanted, that she could demonstrate an interest in taking things further. But how did you manage these things in this time into which he had been transported? He didn't know. He was going to have to take it step-by-step.

They walked out into the street. There was a large puddle, and he thought it had more to do with horses than melted snow, and so he took her hand to guide her around it. She gave his hand a gentle squeeze. No, he hadn't imagined it – that was a squeeze. As they moved on, he did not release her hand but instead held it tight by his side so that they were close together. He said, 'Amélie. I am attracted to you as I have never been attracted to anyone in my life before. I need to know. Am I wasting my time?'

She turned to look up at him as they walked. 'No, Jonathan. You are not wasting your time.'

If he had been back in his own time, this would be the moment for their first kiss. Well…He stopped walking, turned her towards him, stepped even closer… And he kissed her. If it were the wrong thing to do, he would find out very quickly.

It was not the wrong thing to do. She was kissing him back. Inexpertly, as though this was something she had never done before, but with enthusiasm. In fact, with passion. She said, 'Is there somewhere you must be? Or do you have time for us to go to your apartment together? So that we can make plans for the furniture you need.' She dropped her eyes with a becoming show of modesty. She took one of his buttons in her fingers and played with it. She said, 'And we can talk about what should go where.'

As they set off towards Lambert's new apartment, he felt an exhilaration greater than anything he had ever known. The only thing in his mind was Amélie. Which was, of course, as it should be – but if he had been less absorbed in the woman he loved, he might have noticed the man who stepped out from the alley across the street, scribbled into a notebook, closed the notebook and walked off in the opposite direction.

CHRISTMAS WAS OVER, AND LAMBERT WAS ENGAGED to Amélie. Breguet was also engaged – in his case, to Mademoiselle Cecile L'Huillier, daughter to a Valet de Chambre of the Marquis de Breuil. Socially it seemed to be an even match for Breguet and Lambert was happy to see his friend in love. The Galimard women immediately began preparations for a spring wedding. Lambert, seized with energy, had his own preparations for the new year to make.

He and Breguet fleshed out the next stage of their plans. They paid for a stall at the traditional January exhibition for farmers held at the Halles aux Blés, just up the road from the Louvre. It was an occasion when farmers prepared for the new season. They met other farmers and considered their crop priorities. They also looked for new lands to buy or rent to expand their holdings, and new methods and equipment that might be available to improve their work. That was where Lambert and Breguet hoped to impress.

WHEN HE AND BREGUET ENTERED THE HALL, Lambert had one of those 'good grief' moments he had become accustomed to when comparing how something was in the eighteenth century with what it would become. This hall was new. Lambert knew that it would, in time, become the Bourse de Commerce, a museum showcasing the history of Parisian market forces, but right now it was the clearinghouse for wheat and other cereals – some of the most important commodities in France. And something else that Lambert noticed was that the dome by which everyone in his time knew the hall was missing. Had he known it was a later addition? He knew it now.

Breguet said, 'I asked our apprentice to have the scythes and drills delivered last night. He should be around here somewhere.' And, leaving Lambert to take care of the stand, he strolled off through throngs of milling people.

It had been Lambert's idea to organise a demonstration of the new equipment at this market. He wanted to make sure that the target audience was convinced enough to order equipment in advance so that he could estimate what kind of capital investment would be needed for full-scale manufacture.

Using crowdfunding techniques from the time he was familiar with and Breguet was not, he had overridden Breguet's pleas for larger unit profit margins and planned to sell the first iterations of the tools for close to cost. He would take deposits from the farmers, and that money would finance the first delivery of tools. The cash flow would snowball to support second and future waves of anticipated orders.

Breguet returned, dragging their apprentice and a few hands hired for the day. They carried large cases and bags. 'Found him,' said Breguet. He pointed to the empty tables and told the men to open the bags and cases and start setting out the tools. Lambert opened his satchel and laid out his order books, as well as sketches of the tools drawn by a local artist. The sketches showed the advantages of the scythe and how it would improve harvesting. They illustrated the user's movements and presented simple figures on the number of acres that could be harvested by three men in a single day and how this compared with the traditional scythe. Simple visual marketing, but Lambert knew it was a practice no-one in this era had seen.

The seed drill was a little more complex and required a live demonstration. Farmers were traditionalists and always would be. The right way to sow seeds was the way seeds had been sown by their great grandparents. To persuade them that there might be a better way would not be easy. He could talk about preventing soil erosion, which had been a problem as long as humans had farmed. He could talk about making the job less labour-intensive, thereby saving them money. Whatever he tried, the scythe was likely to be an easier sell.

Breguet said, 'We are ready, Jonathan.'

The hired hands had laid out the demonstration implements on the tables, and they were already receiving curious looks. Breguet said, 'How do you want to do this?'

'I'll do the explaining, and you take the orders. If anyone wants to take one of these demonstration units with them today, tell them will be selling them at the end, and there'll be a small premium on the price.'

IT WASN'T LONG BEFORE A SMALL CROWD HAD GATHERED. Lambert was used to addressing an auditorium full of students, and he didn't find it hard to speak to these people in public.

As he began, they gathered in a semi-circle in front of the table.

He started by describing traditional methods of cutting cereals and told them that the sickle had been used since the stone age when men attached flint edges to bone or wood. Was he being too much the academic? Difficult to tell, though his audience did have a professional interest in what he was saying. He went on to describe changes to the sickle in the Bronze Age and the Iron Age and the way that smooth blades were popular in some parts of Europe and toothed blades in others. Then he described the arrival of the scythe in Europe five or six hundred years earlier. What he was doing was preparing his audience for the idea that farming methods and farming equipment were not fixed in time forever. They did evolve. Should evolve. Innovation in the scythe should be a foregone conclusion. And so he led into the end of his lecture by telling them that they were a lucky generation of farmers because they were to witness the latest agricultural revolution.

And they would be not just witnesses, but practitioners. And they would benefit because this simple innovation of a cradle added to a scythe would save hours of work by collecting the grass, hay or grains in an orderly fashion.

The farmers stood in silence, looking at the cradle scythes on the table. Lambert knew that the surface stolidity hid racing minds. How would they have reacted if instead of the scythe he'd been able to tell them about the threshing machine or the combine harvester? Well, he knew the answer to that – they'd have assumed he was an idiot and no sales at all would have been made today. Of anything. And what would be the point? He could spend his whole life in this era implementing agricultural reforms and be richly rewarded for it, but that was not the goal. It would not of itself stop the regime's mistakes and head off the impending troubles. The Revolution had not broken out only because there wasn't enough bread to go around. Agriculture was merely one facet of a complicated mix.

CHAPTER 16

Breguet had watched Lambert's presentation with interest and a certain amusement. Now he stepped forward with his order book. Lambert listened to him telling the crowd that they had only limited production planned before the next harvest. The message was clear: place your order now or risk missing the boat. Breguet was as much the born salesman as Lambert was the born lecturer.

And it was working. Buyers were handing over cash in return for a place in the queue. There were, of course, those who were undecided; Lambert had expected that and now handed out the calling cards that he had printed with the address of their atelier.

And now it was the turn of the seed drill. Lambert took the lead once more, this time with a short lecture on the history of sowing and how a seed drill would change both the scope and the speed of the planting season. There were a lot of questions at the end, but Lambert was pleased to see the orders coming in for the drills, too. He knew what these men were putting down their money for. It was an expression that he had long been familiar with, but Breguet would never have heard it: Sell the sizzle, not the steak. Yes, what they were ordering and he and Breguet were promising to deliver were scythes and seed drills – but what the farmers were really buying was an end to drudgery and the chance to make more money.

The day was a success. Lambert had entertained and instructed with his lectures, and then Breguet had gone for the kill by creating a sense of urgency and scarcity. Their order books were filled. A handful of lucky farmers stayed right to the end to be able to leave with their new purchases and so there weren't even any demonstration units to take back with them. Lambert said, 'Let's go to my restaurant. We can celebrate the day and prepare for the next manufacturing run.'

As they drew closer, they smelled smoke and heard the commotion a crowd makes. The smell was the smell of fire. They started to walk faster. When buildings had so much wood in them, and when they were as close together as buildings were here, the fire could spread. The restaurant could be in danger.

But when they turned into the street, they realised that the restaurant was not in danger of being set alight by another building. It was the restaurant itself that was on fire. Lambert began to run, with Breguet close behind him. Men and women were frantically ferrying buckets of water into the restaurant. Off to one side, Lambert could see some of his own employees and they were lying prone on makeshift cots put together from tables and chairs, being treated for injuries.

'An explosion?' said Lambert to Breguet.

Breguet snarled. 'A human explosion, if so. There's nothing accidental about this.'

One of Lambert's waiters came up to him. 'Monsieur Lambert. Some men came to your restaurant. They made an argument with your host.

CHAPTER 16

He refused to evacuate the patrons and the employees, so they attacked him. They set fire to some of the furniture. They had brought with them what they needed to make it burn quickly. See, there,' and he pointed to some well-dressed people who were being helped. 'Everyone was able to get out, and no one died, but some of the guests were distressed by the smoke.'

Breguet said, 'It's the Guild. They want to shut you down.'

Lambert said, 'Take the receipts and the order books and the purse to your apartment. Lock everything away in the strongest box you have. I will deal with this, and then I'll call for you.'

'But wouldn't you like me to...'

'What I'd like you to do is to make sure that everything you have there stays safe. We need to protect our production line because there's no way to be sure that they won't attack somewhere else in my affairs.

Don't tell anyone what a good day we've had. Protect the books. I've lost the whole of my revenue stream for the foreseeable future. We must protect the production run, or I'll be ruined.'

Breguet nodded and was gone.

LAMBERT STRODE TOWARDS THE DOORWAY, fury visible in every move. The fire had been contained, but the restaurant was in a dreadful mess. The main entrance would need to be completely redone; the doors would have to be replaced, the hosting station with his precious reservation book was gone. The waiting area and several tables near the entrance had been damaged by the fire.

'Monsieur Lambert, monsieur Lambert!' It was one of his waiters, further into the restaurant and surrounded by several Maréchaussée, the oldest police force in France, and an officer-provost of the watch. Lambert strode up to the group. 'What happened, Albert?'

The officer stepped forward and waved Albert away. 'Monsieur Lambert, you are the proprietor of this establishment?'

'Yes, I am. Can someone please tell me exactly what happened here?' Impatience threatened to overcome him.

The officer said, 'It looks as though there was a disagreement between your host and a group of patrons and a disturbance resulted.'

'Have you caught the men responsible?'

'We arrived late in the proceedings,' said the officer, 'but we have interviewed eyewitnesses, and we have a good idea who they were. Now we need you to come with us.' And he signalled to the men standing next to him, who moved closer to Lambert as though they were taking him into custody. It was an invasion of his personal space, and it told him that this conversation was over. There was no point in refusing to cooperate. He nodded to the men surrounding him as if to signal that he would not resist. The officer said, 'Take him to the Châtelet.'

Lambert knew the place he meant – it was the Grand Châtelet, an important building in Paris at that time. But what he didn't know was which part of the Châtelet he was being taken to, because it contained the offices that administered the city's courts, the police headquarters, and a prison. When you were taken to the Châtelet, which section they took you to was clearly of great importance.

He'd seen the building several times on his earlier commutes to and from the fifth arrondissement, but he had come to prefer to avoid the route because of the smell. The Châtelet was near the slaughterhouse district and not far from where the great sewers poured their effluent into the Seine between Pont Notre-Dame and the Pont-au-Change.

Was he under arrest? He had no idea, but he knew he had no option but to go with the men who marched him without ceremony out of the restaurant and onto the street. Crowds were now gathered there in large numbers. It seemed they made the Maréchaussée nervous, because they chose to march him down to the Quai de l'Ecole by way of the front of Perrault's Colonnade, the eastern face of the Louvre Palace. He did not fail to see the symbolism. Here was one of the city's monuments to power and it instilled in him a fear of what might be waiting for him in one of Paris's most notorious buildings.

The party marched past the Colonnade and towards the Châtelet. Hemmed in as he was by Maréchaussée, Lambert was unaware that they were being followed by several small groups of men and women who watched their every move. But followed, they were.

CHAPTER 17

WHEN LAMBERT HAD ASKED HIMSELF which of the three functions of the Châtelet was to be concerned with him, he had assured himself that it would not – could not – be the prison. He had been wrong. He wasn't – yet – in a cell, but the bare, windowless, stone-walled room he was in was not much more reassuring. There was a table, two chairs, and two large lanterns that hung from a hook in the ceiling and spewed dark and acrid smoke. There was very little in the form of ventilation, and Lambert for the first time in his life experienced claustrophobia. Iron rings embedded in the walls did not improve the way he felt. There were sounds, faint but there, and he could only identify them as screams.

Unaware himself of the increasing groups of people following them, Lambert had nevertheless noticed that the Maréchaussée were nervous about something and when they had delivered him here their relief was palpable. They processed him quickly, didn't ask him to surrender any of his personal possessions, and did not at any point lay a hand on him. Lambert did what they told him as to where to walk and where to sit, and he answered the administrator's questions about his identity and profession. He stayed true to the story that had worked so far, that he was from the former French colony of Québec. Then he was led down a dark hallway to this room where he sat patiently and waited to see what would happen.

After about an hour, when the door opened, he realised that it had never been locked. That seemed like a good sign, but who knew? Two men entered the room. One of them was clearly a noble, a man of medium height aged somewhere in his forties and wearing a dark shirt, a dark coat and a white foulard. His face was powdered, and so was his wig.

The man with him was several years younger and wearing what looked like an all-weather greatcoat with the collar popped up, and a tricorn hat bearing the white cockade. The hilt of a sword was just visible under the opening of his greatcoat. He said, 'Monsieur Lenoir, this is Jonathan Lambert. 'Lambert noticed that the honorific 'Monsieur' had been omitted from his own name. 'He owns the Roze restaurant where this evening's disturbance occurred.'

They both studied Lambert. Lambert, unsure what the protocol might be, remained silent.

'Lambert, I am Jean Charles Pierre Lenoir, Lieutenant General in charge of His Highness's police force in Paris. It seems you have caused quite a commotion today.'

Lambert said, 'I had nothing to do with the attack on my establishment.'

The younger man said, 'Lambert when the Lieutenant-General wishes to hear what you have to say, he will ask you to speak. Until then, I suggest you remain silent.'

'Leave him be, Inspector,' said Lenoir. 'The man is provincial and uninformed about our ways. Lambert, it seems you have been operating your establishment without a charter from the Guild that regulates your craft. And I, as the arbitrator in matters of the trades in Paris, have a moral obligation to regulate such affairs. I have received an official complaint from the Caterer's Guild that they attempted to mediate with you on one occasion and that again today their representatives tried to discuss the matter with a member of your staff when this unfortunate incident escalated out of control. It is lucky for you that no-one lost their life, although I understand that you have an employee you may not be able to walk again. Another charge that will fall on the municipality. And on you, Lambert.'

The Inspector handed Lenoir a document which Lenoir sat down to read. 'It seems that this matter has been scheduled for decision in the courts and yet you have continued to operate. What do you say to these charges?'

Lambert paused as he looked at the two to make sure that he was now allowed to speak. 'Yes, the matter is before the courts soon. My lawyer is Monsieur Jérôme Pétion de Villeneuve.'

Lenoir turned to the Inspector. 'Make a note of that name. We will need to see this lawyer.'

Lambert did not know yet just how serious his position was, but he did know something about this man who was questioning him. The Lieutenant-General of police had many roles in Paris in the late 1700s, of which the regulation of trade and maintaining public order were only two. He also had an unwritten role as the King's master spy in domestic issues. A stock saying in Paris at that time was that, when two people talked to each other, a third listened. The Paris police force was the largest in Europe. There was one police officer for every five hundred and forty-five residents and each one had his own network of watchers and informants.

Lenoir said, 'Lambert, your crime has not yet been recorded, and no charges have as yet been brought against you. We have to verify and corroborate statements from many witnesses about this... This incident. A public disturbance was created that could have been avoided if you were operating under your Guild's charter. Causing a public disturbance carries serious consequences.'

There was a knock at the door. When the Inspector opened it, a young uniformed Maréchaussée whispered to him. Lenoir scowled, and the Inspector stepped out of the room leaving Lambert alone with the Lieutenant General.

'You see, Lambert, the King's first duty is to his people's welfare and ensuring public order is perhaps the most important part of that. We cannot have people setting up in business without adhering to the regulations enshrined in our charters.'

'No,' said Lambert. 'And, of course, the monopolies of the guilds must be protected because it is the guilds that fund the police.'

There was a moment's silence as Lenoir interpreted what Lambert had just said. Then he said, 'Lambert, given the nature of the charges that may be brought against you, making accusations that could well be interpreted as seeking to overturn the normal functioning of the state is a very foolish thing to do. Of course, as a native-born Frenchman, I expect to have to make allowances for a *colon*, but you would be unwise to try my patience with any further remarks along those lines.'

At that point, the door reopened, and the Inspector came back into the room. 'Monsieur Lenoir, I have to report that there appears to be a gathering of people outside the Châtelet.'

'Yes? What do they want?'

'Monsieur, one of their leaders, is a homeless man well known to my people. He has requested the release of Lambert.'

Lenoir's expression was a picture of astonishment. It took him a few moments before he was able to speak. Then he said, 'How many of the vermin are there?'

'Monsieur, it is too dark to be sure, but there appear to be several hundred.'

'Several hundred? Are they armed? Are they agitated?'

'No, Monsieur. They are calm. They have made the request for the release of Lambert respectfully pending the outcome of our investigation.'

The two men stared at Lambert. Lenoir said, 'I am impressed, Lambert. You not only have a lawyer, but you also have supporters too. Facing the possible charges that you do, fomenting an insurrection is the worst thing you could have done.'

'I? I have not...'

Lenoir waved a dismissive hand in his direction. 'What you have and have not done will be for the courts to decide and not for you. Inspector, wait till first light and then send a messenger to the Bastille and the Arsenal asking for more men.

I want these miscreants given fair warning and then dispersed under the watchful eye of artillerymen. But right now, take Lambert and lock him up on suspicion of mounting an insurrection. We'll deal first with this mob of his, and then we'll deal with him.' He stood up. 'You have much to learn of our ways, Lambert. One hopes your future does not contain a rope, but it is never possible to say how these things will turn out.'

The two men left the room. Shortly afterwards, two uniformed Maréchaussée entered, hauled

Lambert up by his armpits, and pushed him out of the room and down the hall towards a staircase leading down into the basement.

NADEAU HAD SEEN THE BLUE CURTAIN AGAIN THIS MORNING when he arrived for his last day at work before his holiday. And now it was almost time to go home. Or so he wished. The reality was that he couldn't even think about leaving his desk for at least another ninety minutes, Christmas holidays or not. He decided to use the time to upload to his tablets all the material he had on the Lambert case. He'd be able to look at them while he was away if he happened to feel bored and to think about the case without the Director appearing before his desk to instruct him to take care of something else.

His holiday was scheduled to begin later that evening on a direct flight to Cap Francais, a resort town in the north of Haiti. The Empire had many Caribbean islands Nadeau could have chosen from, but he always felt at home in Haiti, the Pearl of the Antilles as French travel agents called it – the French language there was pure and unadulterated by the Spanish, American and British tongues you were likely to hear elsewhere. It helped, of course, that the Emperor's family still had their winter estates in Haiti. That made sure that the infrastructure was well developed and that only Paris had a more advanced cultural life.

Louis XXVII had invested on a large scale in the French province of the Caribbean, and it had paid off.

There was a never-ending stream of tourist revenue from the Free French provinces of upper and Lower Canada as well as the British, the Spanish and the indigenous peoples of North America. Diversifying away from agriculture had been good for the Caribbean economies. Louis XXV, the grandfather of the present emperor, had had a bold vision, leaving the growing of cash crops to the British, the Spanish and the North American indigenous peoples while the French-built urban centres of entertainment, culture and banking.

The Caribbean province had world-class ports that had mostly been financed by the Second Estate, and mega yachts went back and forth seeking the next pleasure.

Nadeau's tablet chirped that his upload was complete. He looked into the Lambert box once more and took pictures of a few personal effects, not sure what would be useful and what would not if he was ever to complete the puzzle that was Jonathan Lambert. Nadeau did not like cold cases. In his experience, they could come back to bite you. He had decided that while he was on holiday, he would look more closely into the connection – whatever it might turn out to be – with the company Lambregal. Not only did he intend to accomplish these two tasks on his vacation, but he intended to enjoy every minute with Eloise under the Haitian sun. He'd never taken a woman on vacation with him before, so inviting her was a big step for the 'eternal bachelor' type. He was still a bit in shock about how their relationship had continued to develop. She was interested in his work, had an intelligent head on her shoulders, was beautiful, and conversation (that he, surprisingly, never wanted to end) came as easily as breathing.

He found himself hardly able to grasp the fact that he literally could not wait to take this trip with her, something that had never sounded the slightest bit appealing with another woman—too committed-sounding. Eloise was different.

Julie Lambert had given him some time a few weeks earlier and told him some of the history that could help his investigation. Her ancestor, just like the disappeared man who so resembled him, was also called Jonathan Lambert. Two hundred and forty-two years ago, Lambert had started the company with his partner at the time, a man called Breguet, and Amélie Galimard, his wife. All three family names were still present in the day-to-day running of the company, though the most strongly represented branches were the Breguet and Lambert names.

Was his research into Jonathan Lambert obsessive? Well, perhaps. But he wanted to know how the man had disappeared. He wanted to know what connected the 18th-century Jonathan Lambert and the twenty-first century Jonathan Lambert. They looked just like each other. Nadeau smiled as he recalled a conversation he had once overheard between an actor and a society hostess. Although she didn't realise it at first, the hostess had been to the theatre to see a play in which the actor was appearing. 'I didn't see you,' she said. 'What part were you playing?'

When the actor told her, she almost spat out the next words, and it was clear that she thought he had been cheating. 'Oh,' she said. 'But that must have been so easy. You look just like him.'

All right, society hostesses were easy to make fun of. But Jonathan Lambert of today and Jonathan Lambert of so long ago really did look just like each other.

He hadn't got very far when he tried to demonstrate that to Julie Lambert. When he showed her the picture from Lambert's passport, she froze. She stopped cooperating, cut the interview short and wouldn't let Nadeau persuade her even to speculate as to what might have happened. There was a secret of some kind there. Nadeau was sure of that. But he also knew his limitations. If he became aware of a secret involving some ordinary Parisian, he could bring pressure to get answers. Police officers at his level did not bring pressure on someone from a family like Julie Lambert's. Not without being reassigned to traffic duty somewhere in the Camargue. But he really did want to know.

And then he had a thought which, as soon as it occurred to him, he knew he should have had a lot earlier. He opened again the box containing Lambert's property.

CHAPTER 17

He took evidence bags from his pocket and inserted into separate bags a comb, a toothbrush and a handkerchief. He sealed the bags with the heat seal on his phone, marking his authorisation and credentials and summoned an interoffice bot to his desk. When it appeared, he opened its hopper and put the three bags into it. He said, 'On my authority, a complete DNA workup on any workable material in any of these three bags.'

The bot scurried out of his office, presumably on its way to the Imperial Forensic labs. Nadeau thought, 'Maybe I need from young Julie just one more piece of the puzzle.' Then he tucked his tablets into his satchel and cleared his desk. He'd been longing for this holiday. And now it was here.

As he walked through the entrance to the Paris Louis XXIII Airport a few hours later, Nadeau passed once again through that strange blue curtain. That was something else from this damn case that he'd like to get to the bottom of. What was it? Where did it come from? Why was it there? And how did it come to be that no-one else ever seemed to see it?

A Question of Time

CHAPTER 18

FOR THE FIRST TIME IN HIS LIFE, LAMBERT UNDERSTOOD what the expression 'pitch black' really meant. Because, here in this cell, the darkness was total. It really was as black as pitch. He'd heard people say when the light had been poor, 'You couldn't see a thing,' and it was of course never completely true – you could always see something, even if only in outline. But here – nothing. Not even the hint of a glimmer of a trace of something that might not have been utterly, totally, unchangeable blackness. As if to prove it to himself, he held his hands close in front of his face. He couldn't see them.

He sat on the floor because there was nowhere else to sit unless you counted the chamber pot. The cell was not large – in fact, it was small – and he had found that pot, a low, lipped metal thing when he had run his hands around the cell. He had found nothing else. The floor was a little damp, but there was nowhere else to sit, and he wasn't going to stand when he had no idea how long he would be here. The floor was a little damp, too, if it came to that.

What was needed now was to stay calm. Clearly, his position had deteriorated since he had entered the Châtelet. There was probably good cause for panic. But if Lambert knew anything, he knew that panicking never helped. It only made things worse.

Lenoir was detaining him not just on the faintly ludicrous grounds that he had been responsible for other people's attack on his restaurant. Lenoir was detaining him now on suspicion of mounting an insurrection. Probably also on suspicion of sedition. Both of those were capital crimes in this era.

He'd have to have a trial, of course, but Lenoir had already made it clear that anything Lambert had to say in his own defence would be of negligible consequence. And the fact was that, at this time in French history, his fate could be sealed at the whim of the King if the wrong person presented him with a distorted version of the facts. This present Louis was notorious for taking the word of the last courtier to speak to him. Lambert's only hope was that his lawyer, or possibly Breguet, could find a way to help him.

The screams of which he had been vaguely aware while being questioned were much louder now. He was, without doubt, a lot closer to whoever was making that noise. When he listened, he thought that they were probably not caused by pain being inflicted at that moment. What he was hearing was closer to abandoned hope than to immediate hurt.

He moved closer to the door frame. When he put his fingertips to the ground, he realised that there was space between the bottom of the door and the floor. In a way, that made things worse because no light shone beneath the door.

It was not just his cell that was totally dark; the whole area that housed the cell – the corridor or whatever it was was utterly without light. But in a way, it also improved things because a small amount of air was circulating under the door. You couldn't call it fresh air. Not this far below ground, you couldn't. You couldn't call it sweet. But you could call it life-supporting, because if the door had fitted completely snug against its frame would he, in a windowless cell, exhaust all the air and die of asphyxiation?

Because that was where the air was, and possibly because that was where help would come from if it ever came, Lambert settled close to the door. He could hear a shuffling and movement close by. Well, the assumption had had to be that there would be other cells down here and clearly there were, and clearly at least one of them held another prisoner just as this one held him.

A voice spoke. Not loudly, but clearly enough. The French it spoke was thickly accented. 'Hey. You. What are you in for? What have you done?'

All of Lambert's senses warned him to take care. His questioner might not be a prisoner at all. He might be someone planted here to get Lambert to incriminate himself. Proceed with care. 'I haven't done anything. Monsieur Lenoir will see that soon enough. I expect I'll be home in time for breakfast.'

Was that a laugh? Here, in this awful place, did someone find humour? The man said, 'I wish you good fortune with that. I have been here so long, I've forgotten what brought me in in the first place.' Another scream echoed down the corridor. 'But at least,' said the man, 'I haven't been reduced to madness like that poor beggar. Although I sometimes wonder whether he is not better off than me, because he has simply given up. I am Edward Calvin, at your service. One time second leftenant in the Third Regiment of Foot.'

'So,' said Lambert. 'You are English?' He realised as soon as the words were out that he had spoken in English. If this man was not who he claimed to be, but someone sent to spy on Lambert, then Lambert might just have signed his own death warrant. Growing up in Canada in the 1980s he had been exposed to a great deal of the English language, both in the provincial school system and in the mass media.

English was not his first language, but he had mastered it at a young age. But he was supposed to have grown up in the 1750s, not the 1980s, and he would have had no exposure to English then unless he had spent time in the English colonies further south, in which case he might very well be executed as a spy. In any case, if this man Calvin was a plant,

Lambert had just blown an enormous hole in his cover story.

There was a moment of silence. There was a cough. Calvin said, 'It is wonderful to speak my own language after all these years. I am most grateful.'

They talked for hours. There were occasional interruptions when the jailer checked on his prisoners, but they always had fair warning of that because the jailer carried a lamp and there would be a faint flickering light as well as the sound of boots on a hard floor. When that happened, Lambert would switch immediately to French and Calvin would follow him.

Calvin, it appeared, had been a junior officer in a regiment that saw action in the latter days of the Seven Years' War. They had taken part in many battles, the most notable being the capture of Belle Île, a fortified island off the coast of Brittany. Calvin had participated in the amphibious assault and spent the better part of two years on the island.

Lambert said, 'So how did you end up here?'

'I fell in love with a French woman. And I'd do it again, for all the grief it brought me. We set up home here in Paris. We bought food in bulk and sold it on the street. My wife was a wonderful woman. She knew exactly how to develop relationships with people. They'd tell her about their children and their lives, and she would always remember. But the Grocer's Guild was watching us.'

That word 'Guild' again. Another institution that took care of itself by crippling its competitors.

'We were arrested for operating without a charter. I was sentenced to 5 years. My wife was pardoned. The last I heard, she married a French soldier. Luckily, we had no children.'

Was that regret Lambert was listening to? He thought it was. But here was a man who had learned acceptance of his lot. Lambert didn't want people to be saying that about him. He said, 'What year was that?'

'I was sentenced in May 1765. The first Monday after Trinity Sunday.'

Lambert breathed in sharply. Calvin had been in this hole for the best part of ten years. Was that how it was going to be for him? If this man could be forgotten for five years, what hope was there?

The conversation was brought to an end by the sound of locks being worked. Whatever door it was that was being opened, it was not the one the jailer had used. Footsteps approached his door, and it was unlocked. It opened to reveal two Maréchaussée, one of whom held a flaming torch that cast a bright light on Lambert's face. His eyes struggled to adjust from the darkness.

'Get up,' said one of the men. 'You have a visitor.'

CHAPTER 18

LAMBERT FOUND HIMSELF IN THE SAME ROOM that he had been interrogated in the evening before. The two whale oil lamps were still lit and spewed a dark and choking smoke.

He was not restrained in any way, and he still had all of his personal items. He glanced at his Breguet. It was 10:15 a.m. Whoever this visitor was, he wasn't here. And then there were footsteps in the corridor outside. Lambert had learned by now what metal armour sounded like when worn by moving men. He knew that was what he was listening to. Then the doors swung open, and Lambert saw a richly dressed noble with a heavily armed soldier on each side of him. These were not the lightly armed Maréchaussée who ran the Châtelet. This was a more serious force altogether. Whoever this noble was, he was well guarded.

The noble stepped into the room. 'Monsieur Lambert?'

'Yes, Monsieur.' Lambert bowed his head. Better safe than sorry. You never knew how a noble was going to react. They seemed able to detect social slights where none had been intended.

'Excellent.' The noble signal to his two men who pushed aside the single Maréchaussée who had been guarding the door and closed the door themselves, leaving Lambert and the noble, whoever he was, alone.

The noble pulled a crude wooden chair away from the table so that he could sit opposite Lambert. 'This mob outside the Châtelet. What is your intention concerning it?'

'Monsieur. I know nothing of any mob. The inspector told Monsieur Lenoir about it last night.' Lambert made sure that he had eye contact with the aristocrat opposite him, and that he held it. 'I seem to be caught up in developments over which I have no control.'

'Well, I assure you, this mob is here for your liberation, and they refuse to move unless their demands are met. They are peaceable so far, but... You understand the difficult position the Provost finds himself in?'

'Monsieur, I did not call for them to come. Nor did I expect to be arrested. The Caterer's Guild burned down my establishment. If I had assumed anything, it would have been that it would be the men they had sent who would be here under arrest, and not me, a completely innocent party. All I want is the return of my freedom and the ability to pursue my interests unmolested. The Guild harmed a member of my staff, and I wish to see to his welfare.'

The noble had said nothing in reply, and Lambert was unable to divine from his face what might be going through his mind. He said, with what might have struck Lambert as breathtaking irrelevance, 'I understand you are from Québec?'

'I am Monsieur. I could not see myself living under the Rose instead of the Lis.' He crossed his fingers and quickly uncrossed them when he realised that he didn't know how old that gesture was as self-protection when telling an untruth.

'You are, then, in your heart, a supporter of France?'

'I left Québec last year because I refused to become a British subject. I believe that says everything there is to say about where my loyalties lie.'

'The Act of Québec.'

'Exactly so, Monsieur. The act gave us two choices. We could stay, in which case we would live under British rule as British citizens. Or we could retain our loyalty to the French Crown, in which case we would have to leave. That was the choice I made.'

'Well, many others made the same choice and have returned to France, and I commend them for it. As I commend you. But what about your family? The aunt and uncle who raised you? Did they swear an oath and remain in Québec?'

Lambert felt a cold shiver run up his spine. Who was this man? And how did he know of the story that Lambert had fabricated as a cover story for Lavoisier? He said, 'I see you know something of my past, Monsieur. May I inquire who you are?'

The noble shifted on his seat and paused before replying. He said, 'I am Jacques Turgot, Monsieur Lambert. Baron de l'Aulne. I am here to help you.'

It wasn't often that Lambert was stunned into silence, but that was certainly what happened now. He was sitting opposite one of the most powerful men of the time.

The King's Finance Minister. A friend of Antoine Lavoisier. Turgot was the man who had appointed Lavoisier to the gunpowder commission. They were both involved in the tax collection farm. Socially, they swam in the same waters, and now Lambert understood how Turgot came to know so much about his supposed background. Lavoisier was behind this visit.

'Monsieur Turgot,' he said, 'I am honoured by your presence, but why does a simple merchant and restaurateur merit your attention?'

'I think we both know that simple merchant and restaurateur does not describe you. We have observed you, Monsieur Lambert, ever since your first social introduction at Madame Bolduc's salon last season where you struck up a relationship with the lawyer, Pétion.'

He had been observed. Or perhaps Pétion and Lavoisier both reported to Turgot's network of spies. He had known, of course, in his capacity as a historian, how thoroughly spying had penetrated French society as a means of control but knowing was one thing, and coming face-to-face was another. He would need to tread with care.

Chapter 18

Turgot said, 'You came from nothing to someone of worth. You circulate in the salons. Your altruistic benevolence towards the peasants has won you support among them. But that must always raise the question: is it, in fact, altruistic benevolence that motivates you? Or a long term plan of sedition?' He raised his eyebrows. He was asking a question.

'Monsieur Turgot. If it seems that I have mobilised support among the poor for my release, I promise you that nothing could be further from the truth. I am a man who desires peace. I am a supporter of the King. My only disagreement is with the Caterer's Guild – in fact, with the whole system of guilds which, in my opinion, stifles the entrepreneur and discourages innovation.'

He knew he was taking a risk. He knew that Turgot had at some point in his career become an opponent of the guilds, but he did not know when. He knew the man was a reformer who encouraged free trade, but he did not know whether the time was right for the approach he was making. Nevertheless, in for a penny...

He said, 'There is a man in the cells below here. A British man. An honourably discharged veteran.

He chose to make his home here in Paris with his French wife. He could not find work, so he and his wife developed a small business reselling groceries to an ever-growing list of clients. Their business flourished. The Grocer's Guild took exception.'

Turgot was paying close attention. He leaned forward, hands clasped, listening intently.

Lambert went on, 'He was charged and convicted and sentenced to five years imprisonment simply for trying to survive honestly. If he had been able to make a successful career as a grocer, he would have paid his taxes and been a productive member of society. Instead of which he lost his business, he lost his wife, he lost his freedom, and he has been forgotten. He was sentenced to five years, but he's been here for ten and has no indication that he will ever be released.'

Turgot leaned back in his chair. 'Monsieur Lambert, your concern for others does you credit. I agree with you; we must address the issue of the guilds. We have, however, a more pressing matter which is the hundreds of men, women and children outside these doors facing a regiment of musketeers and artillery. That is the matter that, right now, has the attention of my colleagues at court and of the King.'

'If you would like me to, I can address the crowd.'

'I think the Provost would appreciate a reduction in tensions.' Turgot wrapped his knuckle loudly against the table, and the door swung open. Turgot said to the two soldiers standing there, 'Inform the Provost that we want an audience with the mob. And please see to our security.'

One of the soldiers left, leaving the second with them. Turgot said, 'Whatever you do, Lambert, do not try to incite the crowd. Our actions today will be watched closely. I have influence, but it is not unlimited. The Provost and I are rivals, and if I am successful today in resolving this impasse, the Court will value him that little bit less.'

It was not until this moment that Lambert had realised that Provost and Lieutenant General were one. Lenoir was the Provost; the Provost was Lenoir. And he was furious. The two heavily armed soldiers had escorted Lambert and Turgot to an antechamber from which a door leading to a small balcony that overlooked the courtyard where soldiers stood on one side and peasants on the other. 'What are you doing, Turgot? How dare you take a decision like this?' Lenoir gestured contemptuously towards Lambert.

'A few carefully constructed accusations, and this man will spark a confrontation.'

'Lieutenant General, calm yourself.' Turgot's use of Lenoir's rank reminded all present that Turgot was the ranking noble here. He turned to the Inspector of the Maréchaussée. 'Inspector, you have one task that you must carry out immediately. Send word to the commander of our forces below. Under no circumstances – NO circumstances, Inspector – are his men to fire on the people. If any soldier fires without a direct order approved by me, he will be tried and executed without delay. And you may inform them that Monsieur Lambert here will be addressing the crowd very soon.'

The Inspector clicked his heels, nodded, said 'Oui, Monsieur le Ministre,' and scurried away.

Turgot turned to Lambert. 'Before you speak to them, let us make sure we communicate our message correctly, shall we?' Lambert nodded, and the two men pulled away from the others in the room for a private conversation.

LAMBERT STOOD ON THE BALCONY, drawing his speech to a close. 'Please be in no doubt. I have been treated with the utmost respect by the King's men. My safety is assured, and I will be returning home soon in good order.' He held up his hands and waved to the crowd in a cheerful, calm and reassuring way. Then he re-entered the antechamber.

Turgot had arranged everything with the greatest care. Lambert had been given a change of clothes – a crisp dress uniform with no indication of rank that probably belonged to a Châtelet staff member. At Turgot's insistence, he had stood on the balcony alone as visual confirmation that he was not under duress. The speech he had delivered was short and calming. He had been careful to mention the King in favourable terms, and the people seemed not to question his flattering remarks either about Lenoir or about the Maréchaussée.

Turgot waited in the antechamber, smiling, but Lambert trembled. He had been able, while on the balcony, to mask his nerves, but now that the tension had gone so had his control. 'I never want to do anything like that again,' he said.

'That is a pity,' said Turgot 'because you are very good at it. Never underestimate the power of oratory. It can do wonders for your career.'

They were interrupted by Lenoir who looked furious at the success of Turgot's operation. He pointed at Lambert. 'What do we do with him now? He may have got rid of his troublemakers for the time being, but there is still the matter of operating with impunity outside of a legal charter.'

Turgot said, 'My dear Lenoir, you simply must learn to hide your agenda. In the name of His Majesty Louis, King of France and Navarre, I am taking charge of this man. We are to make for Versailles. But not until you have provided him with a meal, a bath and clean clothes. His Majesty is waiting; I suggest you do not damage your own case by unnecessary delay.'

When Turgot had invoked the King's titles, most of the Maréchaussée had removed their tricorne hats in respect for the Crown. Even the mention of the King brought immediate obedience from the soldiers. It was almost as if a spell had been cast. One of Turgot's bodyguards barked, 'You heard Monsieur! Get to it! Draw a bath and inform the kitchen to prepare a meal. '

In contrast to other units of the Royal household, the Garde du Corps was exclusively aristocratic. Even the rank and file were drawn from families with appropriate social backgrounds. They were noted for their courtly manners. The Maréchaussée reacted instantly to the parade ground voice.

Lambert said, 'Prepare a meal and baths for two men if you please.' He turned to the Provost. 'Monsieur Lenoir, you have in your charge a man named Edward Calvin. He has served his sentence and then served it again.' He looked towards Turgot for support. Turgot nodded and turned to his bodyguards, snapping his fingers. 'Bring the Englishman from the cells and see that he is properly fed, bathed and clothed for an audience at the Palace. And then bring me parchment and a quill, for I have some correspondence to see to.'

CHAPTER 19

THE RIDE IN TURGOT'S LANDAU WAS COMFORTABLE enough in spite of the roughly paved road out of the city. A four-wheeled carriage with room for four people on two facing seats with an elevated front seat for the coachman, the Landau was distinguished by two folding hoods, one at each end, which met at the top to form a box-like enclosure with side windows. It was a lightweight vehicle, and this one was drawn by four black horses. Lambert admired the richly appointed interior with its gold embroidery and comfortable cushions. In summer, the windows could be lowered to turn it into an open carriage, but now in the dead of winter, he was grateful that the roof was tightly closed.

A Landau was an expensive conveyance and could be owned and operated only by a noble. The reaction of passing pedestrians suggested that it was admired in the same way as a rare luxury motorcar might be in the modern era.

The three men travelled quietly. Turgot was reading dispatches under the light of a lantern and Calvin, the Englishman whose fortunes had been so suddenly transformed, silently gawked at the countryside rolling by. Lambert noticed that Turgot's lantern was bright and did not spit out the usual black smoke produced by whale oil. Turgot noticed him looking. 'I believe kerosene is what your uncle calls it?' Lambert nodded, not daring to take the conversation any further. What the King's Minister knew of him was remarkable. Lavoisier had briefed him thoroughly.

Calvin said, 'I don't understand why you gentlemen require my presence at the Palace. I am more grateful than I can possibly tell you for what you have done for me, but all I want now is to be on my way, to return to my family if anything is left of them. Or to my company if any of my comrades are still serving.'

Turgot said, 'Monsieur Calvin, you will need to bear witness to what has happened to your person over the last decade. Once you have done that, I will personally see to your safe passage home along with a purse that will let you establish yourself properly when you are back with your countrymen.'

Calvin grinned nervously. 'I certainly hope I can find good company back in England. I've been gone so long. Things change.'

Lambert said, 'Edward if we get past this next adventure, there's a place for you in my staff. I seem to have picked up some rivals at the very least and enemies at the worst. I could use someone to help me defend myself.'

'I would consider that, Monsieur Lambert.'

'Jonathan, please.' The three men fell silent again, each thinking their own thoughts. What Lambert was thinking was that he knew very few men in this era by their first name. Etiquette demanded formality in how one person addressed another, and an invitation to be on a first-name basis marked development in the relationship.

His thoughts drifted to his other friend, Breguet. He was relieved that Turgot had given him the chance to send Breguet a brief dispatch before they left the Châtelet. He had asked Breguet to secure the contracts and deposits somewhere safe and join him at his earliest convenience at the Palace.

The coach turned, and Lambert looked out to see a grand boulevard instantly recognisable even in this era. 'Avenue de Paris,' said Turgot. 'It is still fascinating every time I see it. We will soon be at Place d'Armes.'

Lambert said, 'When will we be required to explain our situation?'

'First, I will arrange rooms for you gentlemen, and then we will wait for the arrival of Monsieur Lavoisier. I will confer with my staff, and we will meet to discuss the next strategies. You must be fully prepared. Please don't be alarmed if you don't see me for some days after our arrival. I have matters of state to attend to. This little disturbance of yours has caused a backlog in the supplicant schedule.'

'Do you mean we'll be here for days?'

Turgot laughed. 'Monsieur Lambert. Once we pass into the orbit of the King, I no longer control your destiny. You will serve at the pleasure of King Louis XVI. If he commands you to wait, wait is what you will do.'

The coach pulled up to the gates, turned north and entered the stables of the administrative offices of the Grand Écurie. Lambert marvelled at the sights and sounds of Versailles. It was said that more than ten thousand people lived and worked in the buildings around the Palace. He marvelled at the opportunities he would have to change the destiny of France. And, eventually, the destiny of the world. In the weeks ahead, he would need to draw upon his memory of his historical studies. He would have to recall and write down every little thing that he could remember to ensure that he could strike quickly when an opportunity occurred. The Revolution had to be stopped, and time was running out.

Turgot had spoken no more than the truth when he said that Lambert would see the King when the King was ready to see Lambert and that all Lambert could do would be to wait until that moment arrived. Lambert was impatient – of course, he was. He had a restaurant to rebuild and put back in order. He had a court case against the Caterers' Guild to fight. He had a nascent agricultural equipment business to nurse towards success.

CHAPTER 19

He had hanging over him the threat that the Provost would seek to advance his personal war with Turgot by bringing a case against Lambert, possibly with the aim of having Lambert executed for sedition. And then there was the matter closest to his heart – the matter of Amélie.

He discussed these worries with Calvin but, although Calvin expressed heartfelt sympathies, he could not hide his own relief at having been released from imprisonment that he had feared would only end with his death. As far as he was concerned, he wouldn't care if they waited a year to be seen. Lambert discussed them next with Breguet when his partner came to see him. Breguet at least reassured him that the farm tools business was making good progress in Breguet's hands and that he was also devoting time to ensuring that renovation and refurbishing of the restaurant proceeded as Lambert would have wished. He said, 'You have a good staff. They are well trained, they understand what is required of them and – most important of all – their loyalty to you is such that they will not allow themselves to fail. I suggest, though, that you authorise me to appoint your Host as a sort of deputy in your absence. He has followed you in everything you've done.

When I say anything or suggest anything he says, 'Monsieur Lambert does it like this,' or 'Monsieur Lambert prefers it to be that way.' I believe the restaurant will be ready to reopen within the next seven days. I also believe that, if you are not present, your Host will manage things as well as if you were.'

'Good idea,' said Lambert. 'Go ahead.'

On the subject of court cases, prosecution and Amélie, however, Breguet could not help. He said, 'I have seen Madame Galimard and your betrothed a number of times. In fact, Amélie and Cecile have become good friends, and so, even when I have not seen Amélie myself, I get news of her.'

'And how is she?'

Breguet shook his head. 'She is concerned, my dear fellow. How could she not be? She knows that your restaurant was attacked and burned. She knows that you were arrested. She knows that, even now, there are those – and they include the Caterers' Guild but are not restricted to them – who wish you ill. If she could visit you here – but can that be made possible?'

Lambert could think of nothing he wanted more. 'It's safer for her to stay away from here... out of this mess.'

Breguet nodded, his expression readily voicing his regret. 'Unfortunately, I must agree. I will keep you informed about any developments. I have a feeling that Turgot will be paying you a visit.'

Lambert's brow furrowed. 'That would be a good thing, right?'

'It could be,' Breguet responded, carefully. 'If he brings good news, it will be. We'll simply have to wait and see.'

This was not what Lambert wanted to hear, but there was little he could do about it. 'Thanks. Give everyone my best, will you?'

'Of course. Don't worry, Johnathan, everything is going to work out.'

These words meant to comfort did little in the way of convincing the incarcerated man, but Lambert simply thanked him again and watched him go, being left alone once again. All he could do was wait in agony while his fate was decided. Lambert dropped down onto his bed, exhaling. This was not how he'd pictured his plans panning out. Try as he might to think of a way out, he couldn't think of anything that he could do to help speed up this process. This appeared to be one time when even his knowledge of the future would be of no help.

The waiting turned out to be even worse than Lambert had anticipated. He grew both bored and anxious as he sat idle, thinking non-stop. He thought about his restaurants, the inventions he still hadn't had the chance to introduce to society, and about Amelie. At night his mind was filled with nightmares, ones where he never married Amelie, and he was forced to watch the Revolution destroy the past world he'd become quite fond of while he remained incarcerated. The recurring dream made the week he spent waiting in his room in Versailles feel more like a year.

Finally, Turgot arrived to see him.

'Welcome!' Lambert exclaimed when the other man arrived in his room. He knew that his enthusiasm at seeing Turgot was more than obvious, but trying to conceal it would be to no avail. He was ready to get this nonsense sorted out and was unabashedly thrilled to finally have another visitor from the outside.

'Please, have a seat.'

'Thank you,' Turgot responded.

Lambert jumped right in, remaining standing. 'This mix-up with the Guild is quite outrageous. Breguet has assured me that the restaurants will likely be able to reopen soon and that my staff will be able to manage without me for a time, but it would be my preference that I be there to resume my duties. I'm sure you understand.'

'Of course,' Turgot said. 'Your business matters are for you and Monsieur Breguet to deal with. You and he have skills in that direction with which I cannot hope to compete. But as for your other concerns, allow me to put your mind at rest. The Provost has received what amounts to a dressing down over his zealousness in persecuting you in the interests of a Guild and not of the kingdom. A judge has been appointed, and he will hear your case, but he has already been instructed as to the conclusion he must hand down at the end of it. He will find that your business is sufficiently different from those conducted by members of the Caterers' Guild that you cannot be considered to be depriving them of business that is rightfully theirs.'

Lambert heard this with mixed feelings. Of course, he was aware that what passed for justice in 18th-century France was very far from anything he could approve of.

What Turgot was telling him was that the fix was in and the case brought by the Caterers' Guild would be decided not on the facts and not on the law but according to instructions coming right from the top. In fact, either from the King or someone very close to him. This way of administering justice was part of the whole complex of things that Lambert felt had to be changed if revolution and the huge number of deaths it would bring with it were to be avoided.

On the other hand, he was going to win his case. He could not avoid a rueful smile. He said, 'And the insurrection I was accused of mounting?'

'You will hear no more of that. His courtiers have heard the King expounding on your success in single-handedly defusing a situation that the Provost was in danger of allowing to get out of hand. They have heard it several times. No-one is in the slightest doubt about the opprobrium that would fall on anyone foolish enough to accuse you of anything as a result of that incident.'

'Ah, yes. The mob. Monsieur Turgot... about those people...'

'Yes? What of them?'

Care was needed here. Lambert had as yet no close working relationship with Turgot, but Lambert knew, as Turgot could not just how much depended on this moment.

Preventing a meeting between Turgot's neck and the guillotine's blade, for one thing – but he could hardly say that; Turgot would think him mad. 'Monsieur. Even I can see that grain supplies are not enough to feed the number of mouths the kingdom has to feed. And yet, in the countryside, idle men are milling about looking for work while fields that could produce all the grain needed by the nation, stands empty and unproductive. Would it not make sense to open up the lands *en chaume* so that these workers can produce more food?'

'Those lands belong to the nobility. Men with no need to add to their leisurely lives the trouble of managing farms.' It sounded like a rejection – but Lambert could see that Turgot was thinking about what he had said. He said ' Monsieur Turgot, if the King could be persuaded to force their hands with a simple solution, you might be able to press the matter. For we know that the Devil makes work for idle hands and the King cannot wish to see the Devil intrude on his domain.'

'So your suggestion is...what?'

CHAPTER 19

Lambert took a deep breath. 'That the king informs the nobility they will be taxed on undeveloped land.'

Silence. Turgot was staring at Lambert, but what was going on behind that impassive face was impossible to tell. Then he said, 'Monsieur Lambert. The nobility does not pay tax. They are exempt. That is the one certain way to tell that someone belongs to the nobility.'

'Quite, Monsieur. And their exempt status can continue. All they have to do...'

'...is open up land to development. Yes. I see.'

'But subject, Monsieur, to two conditions. The first is that the land must be leased to the peasants for a minimum of five years.'

'And the second?'

'The peasants get to keep everything they earn for the first two years. Everything, Monsieur.'

'Everything? No tax? Nothing to the Church? Nothing to the nobles who own the land? Mon Dieu. The nobles would resist. It would be impossible to get such a tax registered in the Parliament.'

Lambert had considered this. He closed in for the kill. 'Then the King could invoke the Lit de Justice.'

Turgot was staring at him again. 'For a colonial, you know a lot about our ancient legal customs.'

He stroked his chin while considering the use of the Lit de Justice. The king needed only speak a few preliminary words, followed by the formula 'my chancellor will tell you the rest', whereupon the chancellor seated at his feet would read aloud the rest of the royal declaration, such as the declaration of a new tax, or declarations of war or peace. The lit de justice equally served to cow recalcitrant parlements, imposing the sovereignty of the king.

'And about our problems. Now that you put this idea before me, I am surprised that such a simple plan has not already been presented by one of my advisers. Jobs to keep the masses out of mischief. More food – which the country needs. And all the nobles have to do to continue their tax-exempt status is to cooperate. Hmm.'

'Once you have the needed security of the food supply, Monsieur, your administration can focus on building the infrastructure needed to distribute food to the towns and cities.'

A rye smile from Turgot. ' 'Your automated horse on rails?'

'The train, yes. It is not unimaginable that France will produce extra grain and other surpluses, and these will need to find their way to where they are most needed in order to alleviate the suffering...'

Turgot nodded. We will spend some time together, you and I, to discuss these matters in detail. In the meantime, let us discuss another matter. I understand that you are engaged to be married to Mademoiselle Galimard?'

'That is so, Monsieur.'

'And I expect that, in the way of young people everywhere, you would like to expedite that marriage?'

'I should love to, Monsieur. But since my arrest, I don't even know whether her mother will still allow the marriage to take place.'

'Ah, Lambert, the fussy ways of the French bourgeoisie! She should be proud of the upstanding man who is willing to marry into her family. Let me tell you what I'm prepared to do. I would like you to spend the next twenty-four hours contemplating whether marriage to Mademoiselle Galimard is still what you want to do. Your name and reputation are now such that I have to tell you that you could do better. You could almost certainly marry into a higher level of society. Not, to be sure, into the Second Estate, but certainly, you would be able to attract a young lady of higher social standing.'

He paused to look closely into Lambert's face. 'And someone likely to bring to the marriage a dowry of some size.' He held up a hand. 'No, Lambert, I see you are about to reply immediately, and that is precisely what I do not want you to do. I'll ask you to take a day to think about it. I shall return here at the same time tomorrow, and you will tell me your decision.'

'And if I still wish to marry Amélie?'

Turgot smiled, and it was only at that moment that Lambert realised he had never seen the man smile before. 'Then, my dear fellow, I shall make it my business to see that you and the young lady are united in the eyes of both the church and the law with no delay.' He tapped Lambert on the chest. 'Whatever her mother might have to say on the subject.'

CHAPTER 20

LAMBERT SPENT A RESTLESS NIGHT. Turgot's remarks had awakened doubts in his mind. Lambert was a child of his time as everyone is, and the twenty-first century is a time when men have learned to think about what is to their own advantage. Turgot had made it clear that this was at least as true in the eighteenth century, and possibly more so. Lambert, he said, might be able to find a better match than Amélie. Better meaning richer and better connected.

Lambert had a restaurant business to rebuild and an agricultural implements business that had barely begun. What would help build both of those businesses? Why, money, of course – money and contacts. Exactly the things that a more socially upmarket bride might bring with her.

He would not have been human if he had not, at the very least, been tempted. But that was not the only thing that played on his mind. There was that other thought – one that had been with him many times since he had fallen in love with Amélie. To marry now meant accepting that he would be for the rest of his life a child of the eighteenth century. That he would never go home. In fact, that the eighteenth century would *be* home from now on.

And that was a consideration neither simple nor straightforward. Life as a 21st-century Canadian academic and life as an 18th-century French restaurateur were unlike each other in every conceivable way. He would be giving up a world in which he was protected by the rule of law for one in which, as he had already discovered, he was at the mercy of others who were richer, more powerful, better connected – and quite without scruple. He would be giving up a world in which he could very reasonably expect a lifespan of eighty years or more for one in which dying at forty-five was regarded as having lived a good life. A world that, as he knew, but those around him did not, was soon, if he did not mend its ways, going to be consumed in a terrifying social conflagration – in which, if he did not tread with great care, he might also end his life.

And being seen as a Turgot protégé made that more and not less likely. A world that lacked the standards of hygiene and health that he had learned to take for granted.

It was a lot to give up.

He was still awake at three that morning when he saw in his mind's eye a scene of great tenderness. It was from that day when Amélie had first accompanied him from the cloth merchant to his new apartment. When she had suggested they should discuss 'what goes where' and he had understood that she had not been talking about the arrangement of his new furniture. That day when, at the very moment when they were about to join together for the first time, she had looked into his eyes and said, 'You do love me, Jonathan? You will not think less of me when I have given myself to you? You would not desert me? I do not believe I could live with the shame.'

He had known the answers to those questions then. He knew them now. He did love her. When she had given herself to him, he had thought not less of her but more, for such a yielding in the days of hypocritical moral positions and no contraception was an immense risk for the woman. He would not desert her.

And so, when Turgot made his appointed visit, and asked, 'Have you decided?' He answered, 'I have. Amélie and I will be married. And as soon as possible. Monsieur Turgot, if I could ask you for an additional favour? Could I have a fresh journal book and quill? I believe I need to put to paper my feelings before this monumental decision. A journal would help me focus my thoughts.'

Turgot bowed his head. Then he called his page to his side and gave him instructions.

Two hours later, Turgot's carriage drew up at the foot of the staircase that led to Lambert's apartment. Amélie and her mother stepped down. Amélie's face was a picture of excitement barely restrained. Her mother's face was one of suppressed fear.

When Turgot appeared and told Madame Galimard that he proposed that the marriage should take place at the chapel on his own estate, Lambert thought he would be unable to keep his mirth hidden. On the face of his future mother-in-law to was visible a range of conflicting emotions. She was affronted that the marriage should not take place in her hometown of Grasse so that her neighbours could be impressed into silence.

She was overwhelmed that her daughter should be married in a place of such high standing. She was annoyed that the decision that the marriage should proceed was to be made by Turgot and not by her. She was stunned by the company her potential son-in-law was keeping, and the opportunities it opened up for her whole family. How could she make use of these new connections to sell gloves and perfume to more aristocratic people at higher prices?

At least, however, she had the sense to keep her reservations and her ambitions to herself.

THE WEEKS FOLLOWING THE PROPOSAL were a flurry of activity as preparations for the big day were made. Lambert, unused to what went into planning a wedding even during this own era, was more than happy to leave most of the hustle and bustle to his fiancé and Madame Galimard. Amelie was a-glow though Lambert saw less and less of her, so busy was she with the planning and himself with the work at the restaurant.

When Amelie, a week and a half before their wedding day asked Lambert to take the night off from work and come to the Galmiard's for dinner, he could hardly refuse.

However, the moment he stepped into the house and sensed Madame Galmiard's frantic energy, he decided he'd dodged a bullet by being able to stay mostly out of the family's way as of late.

Upon arriving for dinner, Lambert made his way past Madame Galmaird who was switching back and forth between compiling some sort of list at the desk in the parlour and issuing hurried orders to any unfortunate servant who passed by her. She offered Lambert only a brief hello, going on to murmur something about how much she was putting into this whole affair when her wishes on the event were not even going to be observed.

'Such a shame,' she kept repeating.

Instead of interrupting her muttered objections, Lambert continued on his way through the house to locate Amelie. She found him first, meeting him half-way down the front hall.

'You're finally here,' Amelie said, rushing up to take Lambert's arm, her face beaming. 'It feels as if I haven't seen you in ages.'

'And whose fault is that?' Lambert teased. 'I'm not the one making all of these elaborate wedding plans. Couldn't we just do something simple so that I may actually see my intended every once in a while?'

Amelie laughed. Lambert loved the sound which tinkled like crystal, as bright and cheery as Amelie herself. 'It's really not all that elaborate, my darling. It's just that any wedding is important and I want it to be something special.'

Lambert slipped an arm around his fiancé's shoulders, leaning close. 'You're already something special.'

Amelie chuckled. 'As are you.'

Lambert glanced in the direction of the parlour where Madame Galmaird could still be heard as she ordered yet another servant to do her bidding in a loud voice. 'I feel as if your mother is having a difficult time of it all,' he remarked.

Amelie shrugged absently. 'Mother is just being mother. No matter what the situation, she always has a qualm or two about something.' She leaned in a bit closer then, her eyelids lowering, seductively. 'But, we can't let that bother us, can we?'

Some things never changed over time and evidently that included the expected behaviour of mothers-in-law. 'Seeing as you say she'd have something to complain about no matter what, I am inclined to agree with you.'

Amelie's face was content as she smiled up at him.

Though Lambert's future bride appeared more than happy to remain right where they were, stealing a few precious and relatively quiet moments together, he had other plans.

Chapter 20

'I have an idea,' Lambert said.

'What?'

He pushed back from her so that he could see her face. 'Let's go to the house, get away from all of this commotion.'

Amelie's expression made it clear that she believed he'd taken leave of his senses. 'Are you mad? How can we do that?'

'Easy. We'll go in my carriage.'

Though Lambert was sure that he'd be assisting in the introduction of more advanced personal transportation very soon, he'd purchased a carriage of his own a month earlier out of necessity.

'I mean how can we simply leave....?' Amelie's brows were arched quizzically and most adorably, only strengthening Lambert's resolve to make his plan successful.

'It's not as if your mother needs us here in her way.' Lambert sidled closer, drawing Amelie in as he spoke directly into her ear. 'Besides, I'd like a little time alone with my future wife.'

Amelie fought a smile but was unsuccessful. 'I believe you relish the breaking of rules.'

Considering he was visiting from a different time period and attempting to change the course of history in more way than one, Lambert was in no place to deny this fact.

Perhaps someday he could share his time-travel experience with Amelie. But, not now. Now he wanted to fully enjoy the historical world he'd learned to embrace in real life and not just through textbooks and research.

'The house is ours. Tell me how that makes us rule-breakers.'

Amelie's countenance lit up with the realisation. 'I suppose you're right!' she laughed.

'Let's go,' Lambert said, ushering her quickly down the hallway and out the front door before Madame Galimard could notice a thing. By the time they'd hopped into his carriage and taken off toward their future home, Amelie was giggling like a school-girl experiencing the exhilaration of acting against decorum for the first time.

Lambert drove the carriage a little too fast down the road, arriving at the house in record time. The couple nearly tumbled from the carriage, running to the front door with child-like excitement.

Amelie reached for the doorknob, but Lambert stopped her, pulling her in for a kiss. She was beaming by the time they broke apart.

'We're going to make such a life together, Amelie. You have no idea what's in store for you. For us.'

'I can't wait to find out,' Amelie said, her face radiant. 'Let's go in.'

Chapter 20

The house wasn't as large as the Galimard's by any stretch. Nevertheless, Lambert was proud of it as it was his success in the restaurant business that had made this possible. The property was respectable for certain and plenty large enough for the two of them plus a few more when it came time to grow their family.

Amelie wandered in before Lambert. He could practically see the thoughts going through her head about the role she'd soon hold as mistress of this household.

Lambert was having thoughts of his own on the matter. As he followed Amelie from room to room, he pondered all of the inventions he could bring to their new home. Indoor plumbing, modern lighting.....perhaps even an electric stove. Amelie's chef would be the envy of the town with that kind of equipment at her disposal. Their house would be a wonder, and far and away the most modern house anyone had ever seen. At that moment, anything felt possible to Lambert.

§§§

Lambert recounted the wine bottles in front of him for the third time, thinking that it had never taken him so long to review the stock.

'Lambert!'

He turned around to find Breguet standing behind him in the doorway of the dining room, an almost appalled expression on his face.

'Oh, hello Louis,' Lambert responded, going back to his wine inventory list.

Breguet positioned himself on the other side of the counter, resting his arms to lean over the edge and survey Lambert. 'Don't you have somewhere to be?'

Lambert continued to count bottles. 'Why do you ask?'

'No reason,' Breguet said, his tone sarcastic. 'I suppose it would just be nosy of me to wonder why you are here doing inventory that is not due for another week when you have a wedding to attend. *Your* wedding nonetheless.'

Lambert sat back, looking unseeingly down at the list in front of him. 'I just thought it would be good to be productive.' The words were unconvincing even to his own ears. One look at Breguet confirmed that he wasn't fooling him either. 'I think that being nervous on one's wedding day is normal.'

Breguet raised his hands in surrender. 'You don't have to justify it to me. But, believe me, you have secured a prize for a wife.'

Lambert smiled. 'I know.' He exhaled, laughing, sheepishly. 'It doesn't really make it any easier to swallow though. I have to admit that before Amelie, I didn't consider much in the way of marriage.'

'That's saying quite a lot then. You two will be just fine.' Breguet glanced at the clock on the wall, his brows rising. 'I don't mean to disrupt your chosen method of coping with this dramatic life-change, but if you don't head to the church, you're going to miss your own wedding.'

Lambert truly observed the time and had to agree. Hastily putting aside his list and apron he stood to his feet and smoothed out his shirt and pants.... His wedding outfit. It was time to take the biggest step he'd taken yet.

Being transported back in time was certainly an adventure. Still, Lambert was convinced there would be none that would quite match that of matrimony.

A Question of Time

Chapter 21

Lambert had given up wracking his brain about all of the materials necessary to 'invent' a refrigerator long ago. At this point in the waiting, nothing could distract him. He'd started out at the restaurant. When it became clear that he was all thumbs and couldn't seem to focus on any one thing for a solitary second, his host and manager insisted he go home.

Out of habit, Lambert had fallen into working in his inventor's lair. When it turned out he still couldn't focus, he turned to refrigerators.

'How long can it possibly take for a baby to be born anyhow?' He muttered to himself, walking from one end of the living room to the other once again. Reminding himself that all of the medical technology doctors had access to in modern times hadn't been invented yet only made him more agitated.

'Jonathan, you fool,' he said, his voice growing louder now. 'You should have worked on medical breakthroughs rather than wasting your time on toasters and swivel chairs and....' Lambert stopped short when he noticed one of the servants standing in the doorway, looking both uncertain and uncomfortable.

'Monsieur?'

Lambert cleared his throat, giving his dishevelled coat a yank. 'Yes?'

'The midwife says that it'll be anytime now.'

'How is Amelie doing?'

'Uhhhh....' The servant stammered.

'Oh, nevermind,' Lambert snapped, more forcefully than he'd intended. He took a deep breath, working hard to compose himself. 'I mean, thank you for letting me know. I'm sure they'll update me as soon as possible.'

The servant nodded before ducking out of the room.

Lambert exhaled, dropping down into a chair. He saw little point in remaining at the house as he wasn't even allowed to see Amelie. Pacing back and forth downstairs was torture. However, there was really no way to alleviate his anxiety at this point so, unless he wished to wreak havoc on the restaurant, it seemed best for him to stay put, agonising though it may be.

He let his head fall back on the chair, staring up at the ceiling while the elaborate pendulum clock Breguet gave him as a wedding gift ticked incessantly in the background.

Minutes crawled by as slowly as hours, but at last the midwife who'd arrived with the doctor appeared in the doorway.

Lambert shot to his feet.

'Monsieur Lambert,' she said, smiling.

'Yes. Is it over? Is she.... He.... Is it a boy or a....?' Lambert's own inability to complete an intelligible sentence frustrated him to no end, leaving it up to the nurse to put him out of his misery and anticipate his questions.

'The baby has been born. He's in perfect health.'

'He....' Lambert breathed, relief that the baby had finally arrived hitting him in a huge wave. He shook himself inwardly. 'And Amelie?'

'She's fine too. You can go in and see them now.'

Lambert stumbled toward the door, hardly able to believe it was over, his mind whirling as he tried to take it all in. Never had he felt this way before—no discovery or invention even came close. He was barely aware of the Midwife's offer of congratulations as he made his way up the staircase toward the matrimonial bedchamber.

The moment his knock was answered with a call to enter, Lambert charged into the room. When Amelie saw him, her face broke immediately into a smile, outweighing the traces of exhaustion around her eyes.

'Amelie,' he said. 'Are you alright?' It was still hard for him to believe that she'd fared so well.

Amelie's laugh still rang like tinkling crystal in spite of the gruelling task she'd just accomplished. 'Of course, Jonathan. Come and meet your son.'

Even seeing his wife's smile hadn't completely alleviated Lambert's concern for her well-being though taking in her smiling face as she lovingly ran her fingers along the baby's face helped him begin to relax.

Nonetheless, his main reflexion, while observing his son was that the introduction of modern-day medicinal practices definitely needed to be a priority. If anything had gone wrong that an advanced medical practice could have helped, he never would have forgiven himself. As he wasn't a doctor himself, this would be the biggest task he'd sought to tackle, but he felt more than ready to face the next challenge head-on. The entire experience had certainly set him on fire, determining the course of his future efforts.

Lambert settled down on the bed next to his wife and child, consciously trying to relax for now. All was well with Amelie and the baby.

'You're the future, son,' Lambert said, scarcely able to take his eyes off of his newborn child.

Amelie's face was glowing. 'Yes, he is. Look at him, Jonathan. Isn't he everything you could ever wish for in a son?'

CHAPTER 21

Lambert leaned in to plant a kiss on his wife's forehead. 'Much more, my love.' Sitting back, he watched his small family in awe at where his journey had led him.

He'd achieved a great deal in an atmosphere that was completely foreign to him. It was an experience he'd had to, quite literally, travel through history in order to find. He might never know who'd sent the blue veil, but what he did know what that he'd forever be grateful that he'd ended up in this time and space.

One thing was for certain: he wouldn't have changed any of it for the world.

A Question of Time

CHAPTER 22

NADEAU RETURNED FROM HIS HOLIDAY refreshed and rejuvenated. He had not, as he had hoped, spent any time on the Jonathan Lambert cold case because the distractions in Haiti with Eloise had been too much to avoid. If he'd thought himself attracted to her before the trip, he didn't know what to call himself now.... Infatuated? Obsessed? Either description fit and his attraction to her was only growing.

And now he was back at his desk, and Haiti seemed so far away, and waiting for him was a DNA report from the Imperial Forensics Laboratory. He opened it with his fingerprint and prepared to compare the DNA from Jonathan Lambert who had vanished from the TGV with the DNA of Julie Lambert.

Everyone's DNA was on file. Under the previous Emperor, France had introduced DNA controls for all its citizens. The aim was to classify the three estates and make sure that no-one infringed upon the privileges guaranteed to the nobility by the French Constitution. DNA controls made it easier for citizens to deal with the day to day delivery of state services including managing the life permits that governed each citizen's tax tiers, access to travel, marriage permits and consumption of goods and services. DNA and basic biometric ID ensured that the Second Estate remained as pure as possible and that no undesirable elements charmed their way into the hearts – and the pants – of an aristocrat. Citizens earned rewards and tax treatment based on how they performed in the service of the Emperor and his Noble class. It was a remarkable feat of social engineering and Nadeau, as an Imperial investigator, had access to the DNA database.

He spoke into his microphone. 'Cross-reference DNA in evidence bag number 151217 – 02 with Citizen Julie Lambert, Director of Lambregal.' It was a matter of seconds, and then the result was in front of him.

Nadeau was looking at something that he simply did not believe. He ran the cross-reference again, and the same result appeared on the screen. He closed his tablet, took his satchel and uniform coat, and called a cugnot to meet him at the entrance to the building.

As he walked, Nadeau fished his phone from his pocket. Never in his life had he rushed to update anyone about a case development, but this, he had to tell Eloise right away. The phone rang twice before she answered.

"Hello?"

"Hey, Eloise. You won't believe what I'm about to tell you."

"I had a good day, thanks for asking," Eloise said, her voice teasing.

"Seriously, Eloise. I'm called a cugnot in just a minute, I'm heading out, so I only have a second."

"What on earth happened?"

"I think I've figured it out. Lambert was real. No doubt about it now."

"What? How do you know?"

"I've got hard, proven evidence and I'm going over to see one of his relatives right now," Nadeau said, his own excitement continuing to mount.

"Oh, babe!" Eloise exclaimed. "Gosh, that's thrilling! It means you'll finally solve the case!"

"That's the hope," Nadeau said as he spotted the cugnot waiting for him. "I'd love to talk to you the whole way, but I gotta get off the phone, so I can close the case. Wish me luck. I think this is it."

NADEAU STRODE INTO THE LAMBREGAL RECEPTION AREA with the air of a man who was not about to be put off. He flashed his badge at the receptionist. 'I have no appointment, and I am here to see Madame Lambert.'

The receptionist pressed a key and spoke quietly into the mouthpiece. 'Agent Nadeau, Madame. No...

No... But I believe he means business, Madame. Very well, Madame.' He turned to Nadeau. 'Someone will be down for you very soon.'

"Very soon" turned out to mean the usual wait, but at last the burly man turned up and escorted Nadeau to the sixth floor where he was shown into Julie Lambert's office. His reception there was cold. 'How can I help you?' she asked without preamble.

'Madame Lambert, a little while ago I spoke to you about the file on a missing person. A man who closely resembled your ancestor. A man who shared his name.'

'You did, Monsieur. I have not forgotten.'

'My research got me nowhere. Wherever I turned, I faced a brick wall. I believed that you did have something to tell me but that you did not wish to assist in any way.' He noted her blank expression. An agent as seasoned as Nadeau is well aware when someone is refusing to let her thoughts appear on her face. He pressed on. 'And so I took my investigation in a new direction. I carried out a comparison – a cross-check – between the DNA of the Jonathan Lambert, who was missing from the TGV and the DNA of a Lambregal Lambert. In fact, Madame, with your DNA.'

The blank expression was gone. He was looking at fury. 'How dare you invade my privacy? Do you understand what I can do to your career, you impudent fool?'

'Madame, I have full authorisation to conclude this investigation. A man from a country whose citizens are under the protection of the Emperor has gone missing from a high-speed train on the way to our empire's capital from the province of Belgium. Our jurisdiction is clear.'

She was not deflated, because women of that class in France do not deflate, but she knew she was on a course she could not sustain. 'So what is it you want to tell me?'

'DNA does not lie. *The* Jonathan Lambert, who disappeared in 2017, is your ancestor and the founder of this company. That is irrefutable. He disappeared a year ago, he would be approximately the same age as you, and yet you are descended from him and separated by several generations. I believe that you could tell me something about that, should you choose to do so.' He raised his eyebrows and fell silent.

It seemed at first that silence would also be Julie Lambert's recourse, for she stared at Nadeau without saying a word. But then her shoulders collapsed just a little. She applied her palm print to a section of her desk, and part of the wall behind her opened to reveal a small alcove in which an old paper book stood on a pedestal under a dim yellow spotlight. Gloves and tweezers were in a compartment next to the manuscript, together with a magnifying glass.

Julie Lambert walked to the alcove and motioned Nadeau to join her. 'I am placing my family's trust in your hands. This book is a family secret, and it must remain so.'

The book's cover carried a simple title which, translated into English, would read, *The prophecies and personal journal of Jonathan Lambert*.

Beneath that, and embossed in gold leaf, was the date 1775. Julie Lambert put on the white gloves. She handed Nadeau the magnifying glass, took the tweezers and opened the book to the first page. She stood back. When Nadeau had read the first two sentences, he returned to his seat and sat down heavily. There was more to read – a lot more – but first, he had to come to terms with those opening words.

"I write this from a comfortable apartment in Château Versailles, where I am a guest of King Louis XVI. It has been quite a year since that fateful ride on the TGV from Brussels..."

§§§

AFTERWORD

THE PROCESS OF WRITING A NOVEL such as 'A Question of Time' is a strange experience; it takes on a life of its own. You start with an initial spark, that eureka moment where you think, 'This is an interesting idea.' And you build from there. All writers experience this moment when the initial idea takes shape. Lucky writers can put the idea to a very rough sketch in their heads, and build upon it while handling the mundane actions of the day. Actions such as standing in line at a grocery checkout counter, while driving somewhere, or for me, that best of time, at the dusk of the day, lying in bed drifting off to sleep. Only the very fortunate can keep it all together without writing it all down on notepads and papers strewn about the house.

I have always been a fan of L. Sprague de Camp's story 'Lest Darkness Fall' - A story of a relatively modern man, from 1938, who inexplicably finds himself transported back in time to 535 AD (or for those of you who prefer CE) in the Eastern Roman Empire. Many stories have sprung from De Camp's initial foray into this form of alternative history writing. Notable writers who were influenced include Harry Turtledove, who writes many offshoots of alternative history. Examples include ideas such as the Byzantine Empire survived the Fall of Rome or where, in the middle of World War Two, the earth is invaded by a hostile alien species.

Other writers influenced by De Camp include Frederik Pohl who wrote 'The Deadly Mission of Phineas Snodgrass', a thought-provoking story of a man that travels back to 1 BC and teaches modern medicine, causing a population explosion. It ends with the fantastically overpopulated alternate timeline sending someone back to assassinate the title character, allowing darkness to fall for thankful billions.

A similar story style to De Camp is 'Outlander' written by Diana Gabaldon and now adapted for television by Ronald D. Moore. A story of Claire Randall, a married World War II nurse who, in 1945, finds herself transported back to 1743 Scotland, where she encounters the dashing Highland warrior Jamie Fraser and becomes embroiled in the Jacobite risings of Scotland.

It was this most recent story that convinced me that a similar tale could be told with a focus on the 'Ancien Regime' era of France. Watching the series on Television with my wife, I was enthralled at how Claire Randall dealt with the historical change, stunned at how her circumstances had changed and accepting the fact that she had just reverted to an era 200 years in the past.

My mind stayed on the concept and eventually focused in on an era of history that always held my fascination. I'm a pretty big fan of a podcast hosted by an American Historian named Mike Duncan. I've listened to his podcasts for years, starting with the 'History of Rome' podcast and eventually following him to his 'Revolutions' podcast. It was this podcast that gave me the idea for the backdrop of my novel.

Using a little bit of 'poetic licence,' my protagonist would suffer an event that would propel him to the first day of the reign of Louis XVI, the last reigning absolute monarch of France. It's important to note that there were other monarchs of France after Louis XVI, but no preceding monarchs ruled with the absolute authority as Louis had.

So I settled on a date, now I needed to settle on a character. Living in Montreal, Canada, most of my life, my first choice naturally settled on a French Canadian. I fleshed out a character outline, gave him a name and a little bit of background. Jonathan Lambert was 'born.'

How could Lambert find his way in the outskirts of the small village of Villiers in the parish of Pontoise? I needed to explain this in a somewhat believable fashion. I've been to France a few times in my life and had the opportunity to take a TGV twice. If you ever have an opportunity to take a Train à Grande Vitesse, do it. It's a surreal experience. Looking at a map of France, I saw how the TGV ran through the parish of Pontoise, and this gave me the idea.

Lambert would be returning to Paris from a conference in Brussels.

More backstory needed to be fleshed out but suffice to say, Lambert needed to be on the outskirts of Paris, far enough from Paris to ease him into the past, react with the locals yet close enough to walk to the outskirts of Paris where he would begin his adventure in 1774. So Pontoise it was.

I spent days researching old maps of Paris, finding a treasure trove of maps that had been digitised and settled on a map of Paris from 1775 by Alexis-Hubert Jaillot, a French cartographer under the employ of Louis XIV. This would be my reference point for most of the landmarks in the novel.

Lambert needing money posed another challenge for me. What was the currency of the day? How did the currency appear? What was the value of money? What could it purchase, and how did it break down to the smallest divisible unit? Everything described in the novel is accurate in history, verified by several independent sources.

Small details like the custom of bringing your own cutlery into an eating establishment kept popping up on my creative radar, and I was determined to flavour the background of the novel painting an accurate picture and lend authenticity to the era.

The route Lambert took into Paris, along with the gate of St Denis still exists today. However, most of the major landmarks have changed, most notably the Fountain of the Innocents.

AFTERWORD

The novel brings light to the three estates in France at the time. I felt that I needed to highlight the grinding poverty of the masses. The proper balance had to be established early on because I tended to drag on and on about the poor. This wasn't a novel about the poverty of the epoch, so a lot of the early descriptions of the state of poverty ended up being cut. If you would like to read a deep analysis of this era, a historian by the name of Oliver Bernier wrote a fascinating book called 'Pleasure and Privilege' that really paints an accurate picture of pre-revolutionary France. You can find his book here;
http://bit.ly/2IOWGWH

The moment that Lambert decided that he was stuck in his lot and that he needed to protect himself from the coming turmoil of the French revolution cemented the general story arc. Lambert wasn't going to attempt altering history to save the French people, he needed to save his own skin and survive. Being a historian gave him the knowledge of what was coming and the motivation to change things.

My first story Arc did not have a parallel story of an Agent from the Central Directorate of the Judicial Police in it, and the story got really interesting when I added Nadeau to the storyline. The Central Directorate of the Judicial Police, abbreviated DCPJ, is the French national judicial police responsible for investigating and fighting serious crime. It really is a part of the National Police service of France. I was very happy with the premise that someone in the modern era would be looking for Lambert and trying to solve the mystery of his disappearance. Plus it allowed me to show how the incremental changes in the past that Lambert was involved in affected Nadeau in the present.

Every character in the modern era or the 'Nadeau Timeline' is purely fictional and not based on anyone in real life. The characters in the past, however, were ripped right out of history, beginning with De Roze, Lambert's first meaningful interaction with someone of historical interest. A colourful character, De Roze is often credited with starting the first full-service restaurant in history.

Now I know historians might chafe at this suggestion because people have been eating out for thousands of years, so let me clear up the definition. I'm describing a modern restaurant, not a hall where people were served whatever was up on offer. An 18th-century widely-circulated gossip column dished on Mathurin Roze de Chantoiseau, calling him the 'creator' of restaurants. It was this idea that sprang Lambert's first job to survive.

Anyone that knows me knows I like watches. Automatic self-winding mechanical watches are my favourite. My watch passion had taught me about the Breguet brand, and as I was fleshing out the story arc, I thought back to Breguet and did a little research. Breguet founded his first atelier in 1775. This was particularly convenient so the Breguet on

Lambert's wrist was born and Abraham-Louis Breguet became a part of the story. Suddenly I need to research everything I could find about Breguet.

Where his first atelier was situated (59 Quai de L'horloge or Quai des Morfondus, situated across from Place Dauphine) who he was born to and who he married. This research was facilitated by a correspondence I struck up with Emmanuel Breguet, current Vice President and head of Patrimony and Strategic Development at Breguet. Emmanuel was very helpful in fleshing out some details of his ancestor Abraham-Louis Breguet, and I will be eternally grateful for his input. The timing of Breguet in actual history fit right into my story arc, so in it went.

Like most historical characters in the novel, I didn't know exactly what I would need, so I went pretty deep with Breguet. He was going to play a pivotal role, and I wanted to make sure I knew him well. To my surprise, I found vast amounts of information about him, his family, his business, and how he survived the revolution. Breguet really did study mathematics at College Mazarin before he became a famous clockmaker (and later watchmaker), and so did Antoine-Laurent Lavoisier.

Lavoisier was a legend, a French noble and chemist who had a very large influence on both the history of chemistry and biology.

The fact that he studied at the same college that Breguet did give me the idea that perhaps they knew each other and this opened the opportunity for an introduction to Lambert. More ideas flowed like the proposal of Smokeless gunpowder and the introduction of Kerosene, innovations that were set to explode on the scene (no pun intended) in a few years anyway.

Jérôme Pétion de Villeneuve, Lambert's legal representative, was actually a lawyer in history, although very little is known of his early career which gave me a little bit of leeway with the story. Pétion later became the Mayor of Paris from 1791 to 1792, right smack at the start of the French Revolution.

My initial story arc did not have a love interest, so Amelie Galimard was added after it was pointed out to me by one of my beta readers. 'Is Lambert a Monk?'

The Parfumerie Galimard, founded in 1747, is one of the first French Houses of Perfumes. Jean de Galimard, Lord of Seranon, a member of the « Glove makers and Perfumers» guild, supplied the court of Louis XV « the well-beloved » with olive oil, pomades, and perfumes of which he invented the first formulas.

I don't know if he died and left a widow and daughter; however, the Galimards in the novel are inspired by the existence of the Perfumery Galimard, today the third oldest perfume maker in the world.

Other smaller part characters named in the novel also existed. The two guild representatives really existed. I found their names on old guild rosters around this same era. If these two guild members were militant guild supporters at the time, I could not say as there is very little information about them in the records.

Nicolas-Joseph Cugnot was a French inventor who built the first working self-propelled land-based mechanical vehicle or the world's first automobile. He really did cause an accident at the arsenal in his demonstration, and the vehicle actually exists at the Musée des Arts et Métiers in Paris. I liked this tie into the story because I wanted to hint at the introduction of rail as a solution to the problem of the movement of goods in the Ancien Regime.

Jean Charles Pierre Lenoir was a French lawyer who headed the Paris police force taking up his post in Limoges.

Lenoir was appointed lieutenant-general of police through the influence of Antoine de Sartine, who had been promoted from this post to become Minister of the Navy. Lenoir took office on 30 August 1774. He objected when Turgot as controller general announced that the extremely liberal grain policies of the 1760s were to be restored without consulting Lenoir. In the spring of 1775, the disorders called the Flour War spread through the heart of France. Lenoir fell into disgrace and was dismissed by Turgot in May 1775 when the riots in Paris spread out of control. In the novel, I attempted to recreate the intense rivalry of these two men and their mutual dislike of each other.

AFTERWORD

Edward Calvin, a second lieutenant in the third regiment of the foot, is a totally fictitious character. He never existed in a historical context, but the third regiment of the foot really did take part in the capture of Belle-Ile, a fortified island off the coast of Brittany. I felt Lambert needed a reminder of the dangerous situation he found himself in, and what better story than a man, wrongfully imprisoned and forgotten for a decade by the agents of the Guild system. He doesn't play a major role in the novel, but I set him up as an important character if ever the novel becomes widely popular and requires a sequel.

Anne Robert Jacques Turgot, the king's first minister, comes very late in the story, although his name is often mentioned in the background. In my opinion, he was a brilliant man who could have changed the course of human history if his reforms were allowed to take root and mature. But Turgot's worst enemy was the poor harvest of 1774, which led to a slight rise in the price of bread in the winter and early spring of 1774–1775. In April, disturbances arose at Dijon, and early in May there occurred those extraordinary bread-riots known as the flour wars, which may be looked upon as a first sample of the French Revolution, so carefully were they organised. Turgot showed great firmness and decision in repressing the riots and was loyally supported by the king throughout. I like to think that Turgot suspected that Lambert was 'special' and he alluded to his suspicion when in the carriage ride to Versailles.

Speaking of rides, this ride has been great, and I am kind of sad to see the book come to a close, but as an old saying goes, 'All good things must come to an end.' I hope that you the reader have been properly entertained and feel that you might have learned something in the process. I certainly did.

I have a rough outline of a sequel that may or may not ever see the light of day. It will all depend on how 'A Question of Time' is received, and how much encouragement I get to carry on with the story. Writing can be a lonely business at times. The only validation comes after everything is said and done. This validation mechanism will become apparent when you arrive at the very end of this work, You will have the opportunity to rate the book and tell all your friends about it on your social media feeds. I will be eternally grateful for any sort of feedback from you, *the reader.*

Will I produce a sequel? To borrow a moniker that I may or may not use, 'Time will tell.'

AFTERWORD

More books from Steven Lazaroff

HISTORY'S GREATEST DECEPTIONS AND CONFIDENCE SCAMS; Even though the first formally recorded 'confidence trick' was uniquely American in its origins, throughout history, there have always been fraudsters ready to part people from their money with smooth-talking and tall tales. From the ancient Egyptians to the modern era, take a romp throughout 4000 years of human history and discover the tricks and schemes that were perfected by colourful characters throughout the ages.
http://bit.ly/2Uxb6g2

WHERE ARE THEY? AND WHY HAVEN'T WE FOUND THEM YET?; Does Alien life exist out there? The purpose of this book is not to take one side or the other in that argument. It is to explore the present state of knowledge and to say where humanity now stands on the question of whether or not we are alone in the universe. Because there isn't the slightest doubt: that is a question that has occupied humans since they became human, and it's a question that shows no sign of going away.

And if there are intelligent beings elsewhere in the universe - where are they?

http://bit.ly/2UwSxbW

Printed in Great Britain
by Amazon

56225839R00194